Betsy and Joe

Maud Hart Lovelace

Illustrated by Vera Neville

📚 HarperTrophy®
An Imprint of HarperCollinsPublishers

Harper Trophy® is a registered trademark of
HarperCollins Publishers Inc.

LC Number 48-8096
ISBN 0-06-440546-X (pbk.)
First published by Thomas Y. Crowell Company in 1948.
First Harper Trophy edition, 1995
❖
Visit us on the World Wide Web!
www.harperchildrens.com

To DELOS

Contents

Foreword

When I was first asked to speak about Maud Hart Lovelace I had to reread all ten of my Betsy-Tacy books. I would like to make this sound like a hardship, but most of you know better. There are three authors whose body of work I have reread more than once over my adult life: Charles Dickens, Jane Austen, and Maud Hart Lovelace. It was, as always, a pleasure and delight.

And the truth is that I have been preparing for this speech, in a variety of ways, for thirty years, and especially for the last ten. That was the decade in which I began to examine most closely what it meant to be a feminist in America, as I am, and why I felt so strongly that the women's movement and what I believe it stands for has changed my life.

Many of those issues have been explored in my column in *The New York Times*, and over and over again I have tried to reinforce a simple message that I believe has been distorted, muddled, misunderstood, and just plain lied about in recent years by those who want women to go, not forward, but backward.

And that is that feminism is about choices. It is about women choosing for themselves which life roles they wish to pursue. It is about deciding who does and gets and merits and earns and succeeds in what by smarts, capabilities, and heart—not by gender. It is about honoring individuals because of their humanity, not their physiology.

And that is why my theme today is: Betsy Ray, Feminist Icon.

Could there be better books, and could there be a better girl, adolescent, young woman, to teach us all those things about choices than the Betsy-Tacy books and Betsy herself, along with her widely disparate circle of Tacy and Tib, Julia and Margaret, Mrs. Ray and Anna the hired girl, Mrs. Poppy and Miss Mix, Carney and Winona, Miss Bangeter and Miss Clarke? All these different women, who go so many different ways, with false starts and stops, with disappointments and limitations, and yet a sense that they can find a place for themselves in the world.

Do you realize that not once, in any book, does any individual, male or female, suggest to Betsy that she cannot, as she so hopes to do, become a writer? Can anyone possibly appreciate the impact that made on a child like me, wanting it too but seeing all around me on the bookshelves the names of men and seeing all around me in my house the domesticated ways of women?

In the early books, of course, this is not what we see. We see prototypes, really, as surely as Snow White and Rose Red, or Cinderella and her stepsisters. We see three little girls who begin as types: the shy and earnest one; the no-nonsense and literal one; and the ringleader, the storyteller, the adventurer, the center—Elizabeth Warrington Ray. Then the adventures and, more important, the traditions begin—the picnics on the Big Hill, the forays to little Syria, the shopping trips at Christmastime, and Betsy's sheets of foolscap piling up in her Uncle Keith's old trunk.

The books are simply stories of small town life and enduring friendship among little girls, and so it is easy to overlook their importance as teaching tools. But consider the alternatives to children in the early grades. The images of girls tend, overwhelmingly, to be of fairy princesses spinning straw into gold or sleeping until they are awakened by a prince.

Even the best ones usually show us caricatures instead of characters. Recently, for example, I wrote an introduction for a fiftieth anniversary edition of *Madeline* (Viking, 1989). It is one of my favorite picture books for children, has been since I myself was a child, mostly because of one line which sums up the rest of it: "To the tiger in the zoo Madeline just said 'Pooh, pooh.'"

Madeline, unlike the straw-spinning princesses, has attitude. She is nobody's fool.

But attitude, truth to tell, is a surface, two-dimensional characteristic, attractive as it may be. The stories of Betsy, Tacy, and Tib transcend attitude just as the simplistic drawings of the early books give way to the more realistic (albeit, to my mind, slightly oversweet) pictures. They are ultimately books about character, and especially about the character of one girl whose greatest sin, throughout the books, is to undervalue herself.

For those are the mistakes Betsy finds she cannot forgive, when she sells herself short, when she is not all she can be. As opposed to the shy, retiring, and respectful girl who became so valued in girl's fiction, Betsy does best when she serves herself, when she is true to herself. In this she most resembles two other fictional heroines who, not surprisingly, also long to be writers and take their work very seriously indeed. One is Anne Shirley of the *Anne of Green Gables* books, and the other is Jo March of *Little Women*.

But the key difference, I think, is a critical one. Both Anne and Jo are implicitly made to pay in those books for the fact that they do not conform to feminine norms. Anne begins life as an orphan and never is permitted to forget that she must work for a living—in fact, you might call her the Joe Willard of girls, although she is far less prickly and far more easy to like than Joe Willard. Jo March of *Little Women* habitually reminds herself how unattractive she is and settles down, in one of the most unconvincing matches in fiction, with the older, most unromantic Professor Bhaer. It is her beautiful sister Amy who gets the real guy, the rich and romantic Laurie.

Betsy, by contrast, never had to pay for the sin of being herself; in fact, she only finds herself under a cloud when she is less than herself. At base, she is a charmed soul from beginning to end because she can laugh at herself and take herself seriously at the same time, because she is serious but never a prig, and interested in boys but never a flirt. Can anyone forget the moment when, returning from the sophomore dance at Schiller Hall with that absolute poop Phil Brandish trying to worm his fist into her pocket, she turns to him with desperation and blurts out, "You might as well know. I don't hold hands."

In fact it's probably in that book, *Betsy in Spite of Herself*, that we see Betsy most the way I think we were always meant to see her, as a girl who will do what is right for her, not necessarily what the world wants her to do. But first, like most of us, she has to do what is wrong for her to find out what is right. She decides to nab Phil just for the fun of it, and to that end she adds the letter E to the end of her perfectly good name, sprays herself with Jockey Club perfume, and uses green stationery to write notes instead of her poetry or stories. It's inevitable—when the real Betsy sneaks out, in the form of a song parody she and Tacy invented before the Phil/Betsy affair began, they break up. But instead of a sore heart, Betsy is left with Shakespeare: "This above all: to thine own self be true."

Betsy already knows, as do we, that that self varies widely from girl to girl, that there is no little box that will fit them all. In *Heaven to Betsy*, she says, in the passage that made the future so clear and yet so mysterious for me:

> She had been almost appalled, when she started going around with Carney and Bonnie, to discover how fixed and definite their ideas of marriage were. They both had cedar hope chests and took pleasure in embroidering their initials on towels to lay away. Each one had picked out a silver pattern and they were planning to give each other spoons in these patterns for Christmases and birthdays. When Betsy and Tacy and Tib talked about their future they planned to be writers, dancers, circus acrobats.

Betsy never looks down on those aspirations of Carney and Bonnie's. But she never looks away from her own aspirations. She follows a sensible progression from writing, to dreaming of being a writer, to actually saying she is going to be one, to sending her stories (when she is a mere senior in high school) to various women's magazines. She makes the mistake so many of us make—like Jo in *Little Women*, she learns early on that writing about debutantes in Park Avenue penthouses is doomed to failure if you've neither debuted nor visited Park Avenue—but her gumption carries her through.

And there are, interestingly, no naysayers among her

family members. While the Rays have three daughters, early on two of them are already committed to having careers outside the home, Julia as an opera singer, Betsy as a writer. Betsy's parents are totally committed to this idea for them both, sending Julia to the Twin Cities and even to Europe to further her training as a singer, and arguing vociferously that Betsy's work is as good as any that appears in popular magazines.

The idea of something that is yours to do became narrower and narrower as my mother grew up. As Betty Friedan wrote in *The Feminine Mystique* (Dell, 1963), by the time my mother was ready to enter what Julia always called The Great World, it had narrowed to one role and one role alone, that of wife and mother.

I don't know when exactly I knew that that was never going to be enough for me. But I know where I got the idea that more was possible. It wasn't from career women or role models—when I was a girl, there really weren't any.

I learned it from books, and none more than from the stories about Betsy, Tacy, and Tib. Because the most important thing about Betsy Ray is that she has a profound sense of confidence and her own worth.

Of course, if this had been wrapped in a sanctimonious, plaster saint package, Betsy would have been—perish the thought—Elsie Dinsmore, the perfect, boring little girl of popular fiction who Betsy herself once mocks. And, if there had been no boys in the books, I, for one, wouldn't have read them.

But we did read them, many of us, for so many reasons: because Maud Hart Lovelace had a real gift for adapting the prose to the appropriate age level, and the themes, too; because we fell in love, not only with Betsy but with Tacy and Tib and all the others, and wanted to know from year to year what was happening to them; because of Magic Wavers and Sunday night sandwiches and smoky coffee brewed out of doors and all the other little ordinary things that, in some fashion, became our ordinary things.

And because they were just like us.

But we know there are many us's, with many different goals and aspirations. For many years those goals and aspirations were truncated by one simple fact: our sex. Everything around us reflected that, from who sat on the Supreme Court, to who listened to our chests when we were sick, to who oversaw services when we went to church on Sunday.

But from time to time we encountered a teacher, or a parent, or even a book that told us that we should let our ambitions fly, that we should believe in ourselves, that the only limits we should put on what we tried for were the limits of our desires and our talents. When I told people I was going to give this speech, most had never heard of

Betsy-Tacy, and I had to describe them as a series of books for girls. But they were so much more than that to one little girl who grew up to be a woman writer and who, perhaps, learned that she *could* by the example given inside these books.

—ANNA QUINDLEN

(*Adapted from a speech given to the Twin Cities Chapter of the Betsy-Tacy Society on June 12, 1993*)

All's well that ends well.

—Wm. Shakespeare

1

A Courier with Letters

AT THE TOP OF Agency Hill, Betsy Ray turned Old
Mag off the road into the shade of an elm.

The old mare always climbed the hill at a snail's
pace. But once on the summit, out on the high undu-
lating plain that led to Murmuring Lake, she usually,
of her own accord, broke into a trot. Today she continued to walk, turning her head—ears enclosed rak-
ishly by the lacy betasseled fly net—to Betsy in the

surrey as though to ask whether speed was really necessary. Betsy guided her into the deep patch of shade.

"I know it's hot, old girl," she said, using her father's affectionate address. "And that was a long hill. Let's rest."

Old Mag flapped her tail, shook off flies languidly, and stopped.

Betsy turned in her seat and looked down the road up which she had come—a long dusty road, fringed with butterfly weed and purple vetch. It bisected residential streets which ran in parallel rows all the way down to the river. Beyond this silver streak hills climbed again, giving the town of Deep Valley its name.

Betsy's eye could pick up many landmarks—the red brick turret of the high school she would enter as a senior that fall, and near it, at the corner of High Street and Plum, the roof of her own home, a green, frame, vine-covered house where boys and girls loved to gather after school. Far to the south rose Hill Street, where she had lived as a child with red-haired Tacy Kelly and yellow-haired Tib Muller for playmates. Betsy, Tacy, and Tib had picnicked and explored over every rise of those distant, wooded slopes.

Looking down to Front Street, she found her father's shoe store, and between Front and the river, the shining rails which, less than a month ago, had carried her older sister Julia away to Boston and the S. S. *Romanic* and a summer of travel in Europe. This was to be followed by a winter of study in Berlin. Julia planned to be an opera singer.

Since Julia's departure, Betsy had been visiting Tacy and Tib. Her mother and her younger sister Margaret were settled at Murmuring Lake Inn, to which Mr. Ray drove out every night from the store. Betsy had stayed in town because Carney Sibley, a member of the Crowd, was entertaining a house guest whose visit had brought on an unexpected summer crop of parties.

Deep Valley was quiet now, almost as quiet as it looked, simmering in the heat between its hills. The Crowd was dispersing to lake cottages, and the farms of relatives, and vacations in the nearby Twin Cities of Minneapolis and St. Paul. Tib was going to Milwaukee.

A group of the boys had left that day on a canoe trip. They were paddling down the river to the Mississippi and a brief way along that celebrated stream. Joe Willard had left early in June to work in the harvest fields.

"There's hardly a soul left in town but Tony," Betsy thought. Cab, too, of course. His father had died recently and Cab was helping in the family furniture store. Tony had taken a job at the Creamery.

Betsy was glad she hadn't been forced to spend the hot day at the shoe store waiting for her father.

"You take Old Mag and go along," Mr. Ray had said with characteristic thoughtfulness. "I'll pick up a ride tonight. You might as well get out in time for a swim."

Betsy was pleased to be taking the solitary drive. She was a friendly, fun-loving girl with high spirits, touched off like firecrackers under a match by the company of others. Yet as she grew older, she liked increasingly to be alone.

She wanted to be a writer, and she had already discovered that poems and stories came most readily from the deep well of solitude. Moreover, she had discovered that at seventeen one was growing up so fast that one needed time to think, to correlate all the perplexing changes and try to understand them.

Betsy was very conscious of being on the threshold of the adult world; although, unlike her sister Julia, she did not long to enter it. Betsy had clung to every phase of childhood as it passed. She always wanted to keep life from going forward too fast.

Her friend, Tacy, was the same. They both had gallant adventurous plans for their lives out in what Julia called the Great World. But they were well content to linger in high school. Like Julia, Tacy was musical, an inheritance perhaps from her father, who played a worn, beloved violin whenever time allowed. Tacy sang in a tender soprano voice.

"You grow older in spite of yourself," Betsy thought resentfully, her gaze returning to the red brick turret. She would be graduating from high school next June, in the Class of 1910. Feeling suddenly that she didn't want to be seventeen, she pulled off her gloves and took off her large flower-laden hat.

"I wish I were a freshman again!" she exclaimed.

Bareheaded, her hair blowing, she looked younger, but she did not look like the Betsy Ray who had entered high school four years before. At thirteen, grown suddenly tall and thin, she had been plainly in the awkward age. Now she enjoyed being tall and slender. She loved high heels that made her even taller, large droopy hats, lacy clothes, perfumes, bracelets, and polished fingernails.

She curled her dark hair every night and wore it parted and pomped on the sides. Her skin was pink and white, very quick to flush. She had warm hazel eyes and a bright ready smile which was one of the things her friends liked most about her. Betsy thought it regrettable, for her teeth were parted in front, giving her an ingenuous expression. She preferred to look enigmatic.

Old Mag lurched forward as a sign that she was

ready to go on, and Betsy turned her back to the road. This was wide enough for two teams to pass and ran through fertile farm land. Corn as high as a man's waist rose beside the road, and fields of rye almost ready for the harvest. Meadows were full of tiger lilies, daisies, Queen Anne's lace—and well-fed cows.

Although distant figures could be seen in the fields, the landscape seemed empty. The houses, small and neat beside their big barns, seemed to be asleep. There wasn't a sound except the cooing of mourning doves and Old Mag's hoofs thudding steadily now.

Suddenly Betsy heard another horse coming behind her almost at a gallop. A great cloud of dust arose and poured into the surrey so that she coughed and choked. The other rig did not pass. It drew to a stop beside her.

"Listen my child and you shall hear, of the midday ride of Paul Revere—the second." The drawling voice was theatrically deep. Betsy looked, startled, into black laughing eyes.

"Tony Markham!" Betsy halted Old Mag beside his lathered animal. "Whatever are you doing here and why are you racing a horse on such a hot day? My father would certainly give you a lecture."

"Your father sent me, smarty!"

"My father sent you! Well, I'm sure he didn't

expect you to drive like that."

"Oh, I've only done it since the top of the hill. We crawled up that so slowly, it's a wonder I ever caught you."

"But why did you want to catch me? Papa sent you, you said . . ."

"Yes. Important dispatches!" Tony reached into the pocket of his shirt and produced three letters. Leaning across to the surrey, he handed them to her.

Betsy caught the flash of unfamiliar stamps.

"Letters from Julia!" she cried.

"Yep. Two." Tony looked very well pleased. He took off his hat and ran lazy fingers through his bushy black hair, which was curlier even than usual in the heat. "Your father thought your mother might as well have them . . . not have to wait until tonight."

"Isn't Papa an angel!"

"That's right!" Tony answered. "Praise your father! What about me, galloping up Agency Hill in this heat?"

"Oh, you!" Betsy answered. "How did he happen to find you anyway?"

"I dropped into the shoe store, looking for you. Thought you might go to the Majestic with me. I have two or three hours off in the afternoon, you know. I might as well be with you as with anyone else."

"Well, thanks!" Betsy answered.

"Maybe even a little better," Tony said magnanimously. He spoke in a teasing brotherly tone. He was, in fact, almost like a brother to the Ray girls.

Betsy was very fond of him. With his crest of hair, his black eyes which were bold, laughing, and sleepy all at once, his drawling voice, his lazy movements, Tony was nothing if not lovable. But she worried about him, too. She didn't always like the company he kept. He went with an older, wild crowd, and she had resolved some weeks before to get him back into the high school crowd. She thought he would be safer there, not tempted to leave school before he graduated.

Remembering her design, she smiled at him.

"I'm sorry I couldn't have gone," she said. "Why don't you ever come out to the lake? It's terribly nice out there. Come some Sunday."

"I go up to Minneapolis if the League team is playing at home. I've gone nuts on baseball."

"You go to Minneapolis? But how can you afford it . . . to go that often, I mean?"

"Oh, I don't pay. I hop a freight. I've made friends with a couple of brakemen," Tony explained grandly. "Poker-playing pals of mine."

Betsy didn't like the sound of that.

"Well, you don't go *every* Sunday," she replied.

"The first Sunday you don't go, come out to the lake. Do you hear?"

"Yes, ma'am," said Tony, "I hear and I heed. Well, I must get this nag back to the guy your dad borrowed it from."

"You walk him every step of the way," Betsy scolded. "Papa won't like it if he looks the least bit hot."

"Yes, ma'am," said Tony again. He turned his horse around, picked up the whip as though about to brandish it, then acted alarmed and put it back in the socket with a virtuous look. Betsy laughed.

"Good-by," she called. "We'll be looking for you."

Holding the reins loosely as Old Mag started to trot, Betsy studied the letters. They were postmarked from the Azores Islands, of whose existence she had been unaware until Julia's trip was planned. Julia had said in the letter she sent back by the pilot boat that the Azores would be her first stop.

Her father, Betsy noticed, hadn't opened the letters.

"He must have been dying to, but he knew Mamma would like the fun of it," she thought.

The third letter was addressed to her. She looked at it casually, for the importance of any ordinary letter was dwarfed by the arrival of mail from Julia. This wasn't, however, an ordinary letter. The handwriting on the envelope made her catch her breath.

"It is! It's from Joe! Why is he writing to me, do you suppose?" Betsy asked the empty air.

She clucked to Old Mag to hurry, for she didn't want to open the letter quite yet. She felt churned up by the sight of it. Betsy liked Joe Willard a great deal, and she had for a long time, with very little encouragement.

He was a stalwart, light-haired boy with blue eyes and a strong, tanned face. He was in Betsy's English class, where they had long been rivals. For three consecutive years he had won the Essay Contest for which Betsy herself had competed twice. He was an orphan and earned his own living. Last winter he had worked after school and on weekends for the *Deep Valley Sun*.

He had gone around then with a girl named Phyllis Brandish. He had never asked to come to see Betsy and had danced with her only once. Then, out of a clear sky last June, after leaving for the harvest fields, he had sent her a postcard!

Betsy's most loved possession was an old theatrical trunk which had once belonged to her Uncle Keith, an actor, and now served her for a desk. She had put Joe Willard's postcard in that trunk. When the family moved to the lake, the trunk, of course, could not go. But a few selected manuscripts, notebooks, and pencils, an eraser, and a dictionary had gone in a stout box marked "My Desk." The card had been included.

It had come from Texas. The letter, Betsy noticed, studying the postmark, came from North Dakota. She knew that Joe was working his way north with the harvest. But harvest wouldn't have come to North Dakota yet. It hadn't even reached southern Minnesota.

"What the dickens is he doing in North Dakota?" she puzzled.

Old Mag slowed down for a farm house known to Deep Valley folk as the Half Way House because it lay at a point half way to Murmuring Lake. Outside the gate was a watering trough full of fresh water. The farmer who lived there had had so many people stop and ask to water their horses that he had put out the public watering trough to save time. His wife, Betsy had heard, preferred the old, sociable, time-wasting stop in the farm yard.

Betsy climbed out and unfastened Old Mag's checkrein. The trough was set in the shade of a big tree and Old Mag drank long and gratefully. Slowly Betsy ran a finger under the flap of the envelope.

Joe's letter was typewritten, and the printed heading said *The Courier News*, *Wells County's Finest Weekly*, *Wells, North Dakota*. He plunged immediately into a surprising piece of news.

Last summer, he said, harvesting near Wells, he had

made friends with the editor of this paper, and his wife. Mr. and Mrs. Roberts were swell folks. He had written to them once or twice over the winter. They knew he was working on the *Sun*.

Mr. Roberts had been taken sick and sent to a hospital, and he had written to Joe. The letter had been forwarded by Mr. Root, the editor of the *Sun*, to Oklahoma, where Joe was harvesting. Mr. Roberts had asked Joe to come and help Mrs. Roberts. Under her supervision, Joe wrote with pride, he was practically running the paper.

He was living with the Robertses.

"I have a big square room with a view into a silver maple. The leaves whisper like a bunch of high school girls, but fortunately I'm not here very much. I'm down at the paper all day long. I like this job, Betsy. I even like the smell of the presses. I can learn a lot about newspaper work this summer.

"I've heard from Mr. Root. I can't do half as well as he expects me to, but I'm going to do my darndest. If you answer, as a well-bred young lady is sure to do (and besides I know you go wild at the sight of a pencil), address me here. Sincerely, Joe."

Betsy didn't hurry Old Mag away from the watering trough. She read Joe's letter twice and then put it with Julia's beside her on the seat. She looked at the windmill turning lazily above the Half Way House with shining eyes which didn't see it at all.

Joe Willard had written to her. He wanted to correspond. And what wonderful news he had to tell!

She was glad she had put sachet bags into her stationery and that she had received for her birthday a sealing wax set, colored sticks of wax and a seal with her initial on it. Scents and sealing wax were la de da, of course, but Julia had told her long ago that even with a boy of your own sort, which Joe certainly was, a little la de da didn't hurt.

"I'll write to him tonight," thought Betsy. She slapped the reins and Old Mag, refreshed by her drink and the rest, went forward briskly toward Murmuring Lake.

2

More Letters

JULIA'S LETTERS WERE READ until they were worn thin. Mrs. Ray read them first to herself and then asked Betsy to read them aloud to her and Margaret. She read them to herself again at intervals throughout the day, and after supper Betsy read them aloud to her father. After half an hour he wished to hear them again, so Betsy read them again, and over and over on succeeding evenings.

Mr. Ray usually took Margaret on his knee to listen. He was a tall, stout, very erect man with satiny black hair, hazel eyes, and a big nose. He listened with a proud fond smile. Mrs. Ray, red-haired, slim, and alert, listened in a rocker close by. The lamp threw their shadows on the unplastered wall, and frustrated moths banged unheeded on the screened door of the cottage. It was one of half a dozen cottages, each with two small rooms and a narrow porch, that surrounded the rambling, white-painted old Inn.

Both letters had been written on board the *Romanic*, en route to Naples. They were long letters. Julia remarked that people said she spent most of her time writing; but she wanted her family to take the trip right along with her. And if ever one person took four others through Europe by means of pen and paper, it was Julia that summer.

The Rays lived a double life. They rested and ate, fished and bathed at Murmuring Lake in Minnesota. But they also took the Rev. Mr. Lewis' "personally conducted tour."

Although landbound, they felt the lazy charm of shipboard life, sitting in deck chairs watching the ever-changing water. The steward prepared salt baths for them. They had breakfast at nine, broth at eleven, luncheon at half past one, tea on deck at four, and dinner at seven.

They went to church in the salon and heard the Church of England clergyman pray for King Edward and Queen Alexandra. They heard Julia, in her little black silk dress, sing at the Ship's Concert. They ate at the Captain's dinner and danced at the Grand Ball.

At the Azores they felt the intoxication of a first encounter with a tropical island—purple bougainvillea climbing over everything; narrow streets with tiny plaster houses painted white, blue, yellow, and pink; whining beggars, clamoring vendors, women wrapped in shawls.

They went on through Italy, Switzerland, up the River Rhine, into Holland, Belgium, France, and England.

Julia enjoyed everything five times as much as the average traveler, she said. "I think of each one of you and look at everything just five times as hard."

Bettina (Julia's name for Betsy) must learn languages at once. "Every cultured person should know at least French."

She was buying presents for them madly. The Rev. Mr. Lewis had promised to bring a box home in the fall when Julia went on to Berlin and her study with Fraulein von Blatz.

"Oh, I'm so happy! I can't believe it is I, Julia Ray,

who is traveling in Europe, having all her cherished dreams fulfilled."

Letters, more than anything else, characterized this summer vacation for Betsy. The Ray cottage was set out on a point with a view across the lake to Pleasant Park, where Mrs. Ray had lived as a girl. Sitting on the porch of the cottage or down on the sandy isolated Point, Betsy wrote to Julia. She wrote to Tacy and to Tib; to Leonard, the sick nephew of Miss Cobb, her music teacher. She wrote to Joe Willard.

Betsy had answered Joe's first letter with praise and encouragement. His reply came, brimming with elation. A land-swindle trial had been going on in Wells County when he arrived in June. It had started out quietly; a crook, Joe said, had been indicted. But the case had developed national ramifications when the crook was discovered to have been aided by a senator. Court was continued in session.

Joe had seen the importance of the case and had started filing the story every day for the Minneapolis *Tribune*. The stories were published, and he was paid space rates. On the day he wrote Betsy, the *Tribune* editor had telephoned, long distance.

"Ordinarily," this august personage had said, "with a story which has ballooned like this one, we would send a correspondent to Wells. But we like your stories. You may handle the case for us."

Joe had accepted with some misgivings. He had not concealed his age, but neither had he mentioned it.

"I'd just as soon they didn't find out how young I am," he wrote. "So I wish you'd keep the assignment a secret. I haven't told anyone what I am doing except you and Mr. Root."

When Betsy received that letter, she went down to the boathouse, took out a boat, and rowed to Babcock's Bay. She liked this quiet backwater, where trees grew close to the shore, making golden-green aisles when the sun shone. She read Joe's letter a second time and a third, then held it between her hands and looked off across the quiet, gleaming water.

"I haven't told anyone except you and Mr. Root." He had picked her for a confidante!

She took out her paper and a pencil and wrote an answer, reading through what she had written, correcting and interlining as she did with her stories. When she returned to the cottage, she copied it all on scented paper and sealed it with green sealing wax.

Joe's typewritten letters and Betsy's scented, green-sealed replies went back and forth regularly after that.

Betsy took to reading the Minneapolis *Tribune*. She looked for Joe's stories and one day she noticed with excitement that the story was signed at the top, "Joseph Willard."

"Isn't it a terrific honor," she wrote to Joe, "having

your name signed to a story in a newspaper?"

A few nights later, her father looked up from his reading.

"I wonder whether this Joseph Willard who writes for the *Tribune* is any relation to the Willard boy who works on the *Deep Valley Sun*?"

"Yes, he is," Betsy replied.

"Uncle, or something?"

"Something," Betsy murmured noncommittally. She felt guilty but she stood by her promise. "Joe has mentioned that case to me. We correspond, you know."

"You certainly do," Mrs. Ray remarked. "You're keeping the mails busy. I don't remember his ever coming to the house, though."

"He never has," Betsy replied. "But he will!" she thought, and smiled to herself.

She clipped all the Joseph Willard articles and kept them in the box with her own stories.

Betsy found time for stories in spite of the time she gave to letter writing. And that summer she started in earnest trying to sell to the magazines. When she finished a story she copied it neatly and sent it away with return postage enclosed to *The Ladies' Home Journal* or *The Delineator*, *The Youth's Companion* or *St. Nicholas*. As regularly as she sent them out, they were returned.

But Betsy was stubborn. If a story came back in the morning from one magazine, it went out in the afternoon to another. She kept a record in a little notebook of how much postage each manuscript required, when it went out, and when it came back. She was not at all sensitive about her campaign and the family took a lively interest in it.

"Uncle Sam ought to manufacture round-trip postage stamps," Mr. Ray chuckled. "They would certainly be a convenience to Betsy."

"My stories will start selling some day. You'll see."

"Of course they will," Mrs. Ray put in, with her usual monumental confidence in her daughters. "The magazines are full of stories not half so good as Betsy's."

"I like them just as well as the stories in my fairy books," said Margaret.

Margaret, eleven years old now, was up to Betsy's shoulder, and as straight as her father. She was immaculately neat, very quiet and self-contained. She wore her braids crossed in back with big taffeta bows behind her ears. Her serious freckled face was illumined by star-like eyes.

She and Betsy liked to take books down on the Point. The steep bank hid the Inn from their view. Little white-edged waves lapped at their feet, small stilt-legged birds ran along the sand, and reeds at the water's edge made a forest for a Thumbelina.

Margaret read from her fairy books and Betsy read *Les Miserables*. She had begun Victor Hugo's tome in a zest for self-improvement, having heard it called the greatest novel in the world, but she soon became deeply engrossed.

She was following Jean Valjean's adventures one Sunday afternoon, with Margaret deep in the *Blue Fairy Book* beside her, when she heard a rustling on the bank and looked up to see Tony descending.

He had come several times since the day he gave Betsy the letters and she was pleased to be succeeding in her enterprise. It was fun, too, to have a cavalier. There weren't many young people at the Inn this season. She jumped up to greet him and Margaret followed, her face wreathed in smiles.

"Something for you, Margaret," he said carelessly, thrusting a box of candy into her hands. He always gave Margaret the candy he brought. Tony's visits seemed to be to the entire family, although he was Betsy's classmate.

They went up to the cottage to dress for a swim. Betsy and Margaret put on blue serge bathing suits, trimmed with white braid around collars, sleeves, and skirts, long black stockings, laced bathing shoes, bandanas on their heads.

"Very skippy," Tony said.

In the water he romped with Margaret, who was paddling about on water wings. Betsy swam with a joyfully vigorous breast stroke. Then she found a sun hole and floated, staring up at faraway swirls of cloud.

Tony was playing croquet with the family when Betsy emerged from the cottage, dressed for supper. She had put on a filmy pink dress and wore flowers in her hair. Tony leaned on his mallet, his dark eyes teasing.

"Look at Betsy! I swear she's gunning for me. It's no use, girl. I'm hooked. Margaret's got me."

He stayed for supper, of course, and although the Inn had provided a gigantic Sunday dinner, supper was also an abundant affair, with cold ham and chicken, potato salad, green corn on the cob, baking powder biscuits, and plum cake heaped with whipped cream.

Mr. Ray and Tony talked baseball. Mr. Ray enjoyed Tony's accounts of the Minneapolis League baseball games.

"But I don't like your transportation, Tony," he said. "You might lose a leg some day, hopping a freight."

"Oh, they slow down for me!"

"What do you do with your time up there in the cities after the game is over?"

"I hang around with Jake and Harry. They're my brakemen pals."

"Aren't they a lot older than you are?"

"Sure. Ten years or so, but I like to hear them talk. They're full of the darndest yarns."

Betsy was listening intently. She could tell her father was troubled. Tony turned and tweaked her nose.

"What makes you listen so good?" he asked in affectionate derision. "You don't understand about baseball or railroading, either."

After supper, Tony asked Betsy to go rowing. They went down to the boathouse and Old Pete gave them a boat. Tony took off his coat and folded it over the seat, fitted the oars into the oarlocks, and rowed to the middle of the lake.

The water was as smooth as glass. Now and then an insect skimmed along the surface, making a crack in the mirror. Tony rowed lazily, while the sun sank out of sight and diaphanous clouds all over the sky turned pink.

He crossed the oars, looked up and around him.

"Nice. Isn't it?" he said.

Tony never talked much. He teased, joked, and clowned, but he seldom talked about anything important to him. Betsy thought sometimes how little she knew of Tony's life. Other boys talked about school and sports, their larks and scrapes, their girls, books they were reading. A few of them talked about ideas that stirred them. Tony was either fooling or he was silent.

He could listen, though. Betsy talked more about herself with Tony than with any boy she knew. He understood what her writing meant to her. He had shown the same sensitive insight into Julia's music.

Tony loved to sing himself and had a fine deep voice. Basso profundo, Julia called it. Julia had been quite excited for a time by Tony's gift as a singer. But he had no ambition to sing professionally or to do anything else except enjoy life as it passed.

Betsy told him now about the story she was working on. It concerned a New York debutante.

"Sort of a Robert W. Chambers story," she explained.

"But you don't know anything about New York debutantes, Betsy."

"That doesn't matter. I make it up."

He started rowing again and they found themselves near Pleasant Park. The old house was surrounded by tall trees that almost hid it from view. The lawn was enclosed on three sides by a white picket fence. On the fourth side, the land sloped to the water, and there were a boathouse and docks.

"Just think!" Betsy said. "That's where Mamma

grew up. A farmer lives there now."

"Your grandfather is in California, isn't he?"

"Yes. He's Mamma's stepfather. Hers and Uncle Keith's. She was married in that house."

"Well," Tony said. "It was some marriage! I don't know another family that gets along as yours does, Betsy. Honest to gosh, I've always been sort of glad I got acquainted with you Rays!"

And then, having been betrayed into what he considered sentimentality, he changed the subject.

"Let's sing," he said.

They sang while the stars came out and the color of the sky deepened to a rich dark blue. The first sprinkle of stars was followed by armies of them.

They sang everything they knew, beginning with old songs like "Annie Laurie" and "Swanee River"; going on to "What's the Use of Dreaming," Mr. Ray's favorite, and "My Wild Irish Rose," which the beloved Chauncey Olcott had brought to Deep Valley every autumn since Betsy could remember. They sang the songs associated with each high school year.

> "*Dreaming, dreaming,*
> *Of you, sweetheart, I am dreaming. . . .*"

That had been the hit of their freshman year. From the sophomore year they sang:

> *"Come away with me, Lucille,*
> *In my merry Oldsmobile. . . ."*

They sang last year's "Howdy Cy, Morning Cy," and finished in style with the duet from "The Red Mill":

> *"Not that you are fair, dear,*
> *Not that you are true. . . ."*

They had sung it many times beside the piano at the Ray house. Their timing was perfect, and their voices blended warmly. Someone sitting in darkness on the distant point applauded.

"Say," Tony exclaimed. "We're pretty good. Broadway doesn't know what it's missing!"

"Yes," Betsy agreed, "you and I make a good team."

Tony didn't answer, and her words lingered in the air as words do sometimes, taking on undue significance by reason of the fact that they are left suspended. He picked up the oars and started rowing toward the lights of the Inn, gleaming through the trees.

The next afternoon, when Betsy and her mother were rocking and mending on the porch of the little cottage, Mrs. Ray said suddenly, "Betsy! I think Tony is getting a little . . . well . . . sweet on you."

"Heavens, no!" said Betsy, startled. "Tony is just like a brother."

"He used to be," said Mrs. Ray. "But . . . I have intuitions sometimes where my children are concerned. I think Tony's feeling toward you is changing. I don't like it."

"Why don't you like it?" asked Betsy. "Why wouldn't you like it, if it were true, I mean? Lots of boys have had crushes on me and you never minded."

Mrs. Ray answered slowly, "We're all so fond of Tony."

"Of course!" cried Betsy. "Papa likes him better than any boy that comes to the house. In fact, we all do. So what's wrong?" Her mother didn't reply and Betsy added, "I suppose you don't like those freight-hopping trips to Minneapolis? I don't myself. Maybe I can talk him out of them."

"How do you feel about Tony, Betsy?" asked Mrs. Ray. "You aren't . . . serious . . . are you?"

"Heavens, no!" said Betsy again, and felt suddenly very old. Her mother's tone was the searching one Betsy had heard her use with Julia. It seemed strange to think that she was old enough so that her mother worried about one of her crushes being serious.

"I haven't a crush on Tony or on anyone else," she said, but she felt herself blushing and jumped up hurriedly, pretending to have lost her thimble. She had thought suddenly about Joe Willard's letters, how she looked forward to them, how hard she worked over her answers. She hoped that her mother would not extend her questioning to Joe.

Happily, perhaps deliberately, she didn't.

"Betsy," said Mrs. Ray briskly, when her daughter had shaken her skirts and sat down. "What do you think of the new, long-sleeved tucked waists? Would you like one to go with your suit?"

"Yes," answered Betsy, "I think I would."

3
Back from the Lake

BETSY ALWAYS LOVED the late summer return from Murmuring Lake to the house on the corner of High Street and Plum. Mr. Ray had always mowed the lawn. He had clipped the hydrangeas and bridal wreath and set the sprinkler going. Anna, the hired girl, had usually come back a few days earlier, so the house was aired and clean. But it never looked like home until Mrs. Ray had scattered books and magazines about, and the girls had cut flowers for the vases.

This year there was no Julia to run to the piano, but Betsy unlocked it and dashed off a few scales just to let the neighbors know that the Rays were back.

The piano had photographs of Julia at all ages ranged along the top. It stood in a light, square hall which Julia had grandly named the music room. To the right, a golden oak staircase curved upward. To the left, an archway led into the parlor, a warm, friendly room, with crisp lace curtains, sofa pillows, pictures and books, a green-shaded lamp, and a brass bowl holding a palm.

The dining room was just behind. It was papered in a dark, fruity pattern above a well-filled plate rail. A gold-fringed lamp hung by a chain over the center of the table. There was a fireplace in one corner, a gong in another, and a fine display of cut glass and hand-painted china on the sideboard. A swinging door led to the pantry and Anna's kitchen.

Anna had already started baking cookies, wearing a broad, pleased smile. Margaret was smiling, too, as she wandered through the house with Washington, the cat, in her arms.

Washington and his companion, Lincoln, the Spitz dog, had spent the summer on Anna's brother's farm.

Abe Lincoln had been excited by the return. He had run around barking sharply, jumping upon forbidden chairs. Washington had relaxed on his favorite pillow with a supercilious air. But he had started purring when Margaret picked him up.

Betsy began joyfully to telephone. It was fun getting back to the Crowd. Carney, who had been graduated from high school in June, was busy getting ready for Vassar.

"Mother and I are going up to the Cities to buy my clothes," she said.

"What joy! When?"

"Tomorrow. So let's go riding tonight. We'll pick up the bunch."

Tacy suggested an afternoon picnic.

"All right. I'll bring my Kodak. And I'll stop by for Tib."

"I'll 'phone her you're coming so that she can have a lunch packed."

"Do. The Mullers are such good providers. What's the state of the Kelly larder?"

"Oh," said Tacy, "fair. I'll put some cocoa in the pail." They had a special, battered, smoke-blackened pail in which they always made cocoa on their picnics.

Walking toward Hill Street, Betsy thought how long she and Tacy had been having picnics.

"It's thirteen years now since we met each other at

my fifth birthday party. And we started picnicking the very first summer."

There was nothing like a picnic! she reflected. If you were happy, it made you happier. If you were unhappy, it blew your troubles away.

Passing Lincoln Park, she arrived at Tib's chocolate-colored house. When she and Tacy were children, they had thought this a mansion, and its ornate style had indeed been the height of elegance. It had a wide porch, a tower, numerous bay windows, and a pane of ruby glass over the front door.

Tib had seemed like a story-book princess, and she seemed so still, Betsy thought, when Tib came running over the green lawn. She was slender and swaying, above ankle-length skirts which fluttered as she ran. Her clothes were fragile, lace-trimmed, and beribboned. Her blond hair, bleached by the sun to a straw tint, was dressed in little puffs which were held in place by a wide band tied around her head. This band was the very newest fashion.

"*Liebchen!* I'm so glad you're back!" She hugged Betsy warmly. "I've been making such a lunch! Deviled eggs, *Kartoffel Salat, Leber Wurst.* . . ."

"You're the most deceptive character," Betsy interrupted. "You look as though you lived on butterfly wings and you talk about *Leber Wurst.*"

They went inside, where Betsy greeted Mrs. Muller

and Tib's brothers, Fred and Hobbie. Mrs. Muller was blond and stocky; Fred was blond and slender; Hobbie, blond and dimpled. Betsy went into the kitchen to speak to Matilda, the hired girl.

Tib brought out a bulging basket. Betsy picked up her own basket and the Kodak, and they started for Hill Street.

Tacy, smiling radiantly, met them in the vacant lot. She looked tall, approaching. She was, in fact, taller than Betsy. Her auburn hair was wound about her head in coronet braids, not so fashionable as pompadours or puffs, but very well suited to Tacy. She had large blue eyes which could brim with laughter one minute, and the next be wistful or shy. Real Irish eyes, Mrs. Ray often said.

"Tacy," said Betsy. "Do you know that you're getting awfully pretty?"

"I was thinking that, too," cried Tib. "Why, an artist would like to paint your picture the way you look right now!"

"I'll snap it after we get up on the hill," said Betsy.

"*Be Gorrah!*" cried Tacy. "It's a *foine* picture they'll be taking of the Colleen from Hill Street."

Tacy affected an Irish brogue when she felt especially silly. She and Betsy loved to act silly, and Tib laughed at all their jokes, which made her a gratifying third.

The Kelly house at the end of Hill Street had seemed big to Betsy once because it was so much bigger than the yellow cottage across the street in which she had grown up. But looking at it now, low and rambling, its white paint fading under the reddening vines, Betsy realized that it was somewhat small for the big family it had to house.

She had always loved the merry crowded house. Warmth and comfort enveloped her whenever she entered the door. All the Kellys loved her; they petted and teased her as though she were still a little girl.

Today only Mrs. Kelly was at home. A large, gentle woman with a tender mouth like Tacy's, she sat with her mountain of darning in the window of the dining room. This big bow window was the heart of the house. Here Mr. Kelly sat in the evening with his newspaper, here on Sunday he played his violin. Here Betsy and Tacy used to cut out paper dolls, looking up at the overhanging hills.

The Kelly house had few of the so-called modern improvements. It was lighted by lamps, there was a pump in the dooryard. But the views from the windows would have graced a castle.

"Mrs. Kelly," Betsy said, when she had kissed her, "I never realized when I was little that your house had such lovely views."

"I've heard Papa say that he bought the house for

the views," Mrs. Kelly replied.

"Well, I'm certainly glad he bought it," said Tacy. "What if we hadn't moved to Hill Street? What if we still lived in Mazomanie, Wisconsin? Why, Betsy, we might not even know each other!"

"*I* lived in Wisconsin," Tib observed. "You might have known me, anyway."

"And I suppose you wouldn't have missed me at all!" cried Betsy. "Listen to them, Mrs. Kelly! Heartless creatures! Practically plotting to get rid of me."

Mrs. Kelly laughed indulgently.

Tacy brought out the pail and Tib said it was too hot for cocoa, but Betsy and Tacy shouted her down.

"No respect for tradition."

"We always have cocoa."

Laughing and wrangling, they started up the steep road behind Betsy's old house, the road which had once seemed the longest, most adventuresome in the world. There had been just one white house on the Big Hill in those days. Now there were several modern cottages. Change had not yet touched The Secret Lane, however. This ran along the summit, a twin row of thickly leaved beech trees.

Beyond it, they came out suddenly on a wide, bright view. The hilltop overlooked a valley so capacious that it seemed empty, although it held scattered farms and a huddle of small houses known as Little

Syria. In the distance, the river wandered.

"Of all the places we used to play when we were children, I love this the most," Betsy said.

They stretched out on the hillside, a slanting coppery sea of goldenrod. A vireo far above them sang continuously and monotonously, like a dull woman talking.

Betsy, Tacy, and Tib began to talk. They talked about their summers—Milwaukee, Mazomanie, and Murmuring Lake. They talked about being seniors. They talked about boys. At least, Betsy and Tib talked about boys. Boys didn't interest Tacy.

However, she volunteered the information that a famous athlete named Ralph Maddox was coming to high school this fall. She had heard her brothers say so. He was coming from St. John, where he had been the star of the football team.

"I hope we can get him for the Zets," she said.

"You want him for the Zets? I'll make a note of it. Just leave it to me," said Tib, patting her yellow hair.

Betsy told them she had been corresponding with Joe Willard.

"How did that happen?" asked Tib.

"How did it happen? He wrote to me, of course. You don't think I'd write to him first, do you?"

"Do you think you'll be going with him this year?"

"No idea," said Betsy. She had announced last year

that she was going to do just that, and then he had gone with Phyllis Brandish! She wasn't going to tempt fate again.

"There's a Joseph Willard who writes for the Minneapolis *Tribune*," Tacy remarked.

"May be related. Do you think so, Betsy?"

"Um hum," answered Betsy, feeling uncomfortable. She wasn't accustomed to keeping secrets from Tacy and Tib. She jumped up. "Let's get some pictures. Maybe we ought to start the fire first. Background for your portrait, Tacy."

They gathered dry wood and made a fire which poured smoky fragrance into the air. While Tacy adjusted the pail, Tib spread a red cloth and set out the contents of the baskets.

Betsy focused her camera. "Get set now!"

Tacy jumped up and put one hand behind her head, the other on her hip.

"No! No!" cried Betsy. "You're not Carmen. You're the Irish Colleen. Remember?"

"Be jabbers, that's right!" said Tacy, and put both hands on her waist, arms akimbo.

Tib pushed her down. Tacy's long red braids came loose. Around her face little tendrils of hair curled like vines. She looked up at Betsy, her eyes full of laughter, the skirts of her sailor suit cascading about her. Betsy snapped.

"Tacy Kelly at her silliest!" she said.

She snapped Tib on a rock, holding out her skirts. Tacy snapped Betsy tilting the jug of lemonade. Tib snapped Betsy and Tacy feeding each other sandwiches.

When the film was used up, they collapsed in laughter.

"Gosh, how silly!"

"Does us good. We're getting too darned serious."

"We're getting too darned old. Gee, seniors this fall!"

"Let's eat. We have to get back early, you know. Carney's taking us riding."

Carney, informed by telephone of Betsy's whereabouts, picked her up at the Kellys'. Tacy and Tib piled into the Sibley auto, too, and they went in search of the rest of the Crowd . . . the feminine portion of it. This group continued the same in character—lively, exuberant, loyal—although its personnel changed from year to year.

Carney, this fall, was going out of it. The Crowd would miss Carney, with her twinkling eyes. Her side lawn was a gathering place; her automobile dedicated to the Crowd.

Hazel Smith was just coming into the group. She was a plain, freckle-faced girl, mirthful and breezy.

Alice Morrison was tall, with rosy cheeks and thick blond hair. She was quiet, but no one in the Crowd enjoyed fun more wholeheartedly than Alice.

Winona Root was tall, dark, and debonaire. She had magic in her fingers at the piano.

Irma Biscay was rounded and alluring. She was a sweet-tempered, merry girl, but the attraction she held for the opposite sex kept her from being very popular with girls. She had not yet returned from her vacation, and the Crowd, cruising along the shadowy streets, discussed the source of this attraction. Betsy, whose hair was straight, laid it to her curly hair. Tib, who was tiny, felt sure it was her lovely figure.

"It's her form," Tib asserted vehemently. "Her form is like that Miss Anna Held's who takes the milk baths."

Alice suggested that Irma's success might spring from the fact that Mrs. Biscay was such a good cook. But Betsy scoffed at that.

"Look at Anna! The boys come to our cookie jar as though they owned it. Yet I don't slay everyone. Irma makes me think of the Lorelei. You know, Tib, in that German song. Let one of our beaus see much of Irma and . . . good-by! He's gone, just as though he had been dashed against a rock."

Tib started to sing.

"Ich weiss nicht was sol es bedeuten. . . ." And the rest joined in, making up English words. The Crowd loved to sing, rolling through the night in Carney's auto. Winona started "I Wonder Who's Kissing Her

Now" and they were singing this with enthusiasm when the auto broke down. (They seldom took a ride anywhere without the auto breaking down.) Fortunately they were near the Rays', and the girls pushed the machine to Betsy's door, singing at the tops of their voices.

They found an indignant group on the porch. Tony was there, sprawled in the hammock, and Dennis Farisy, who looked like a cherub but was not at all cherubic, and Cab Edwards, who had once been Dennie's inseparable companion . . . but Cab seemed older and more mature since he had started work at the family furniture store.

"What do you mean, not being around tonight?" he shouted now, indignantly.

"We were just going home, and it would have served you right," yelled Dennie.

"We wouldn't have stayed five minutes more," drawled Tony, swinging luxuriously.

Winona ran up the steps and dumped him out of the hammock. They started tusseling. Everybody went inside and Winona sat down at the piano. They made fudge. They stood around the piano and sang. They rolled up the rugs and danced.

"All out by ten o'clock," Mrs. Ray called down the stairs.

The Ray family was really back from the lake.

4
The Rays' Telephone Rings

IRMA CAME BACK, as bafflingly attractive as ever. Tom, who had been vacationing in the East, returned to get ready for Cox Military. Dave, Stan, and Lloyd, who had gone down the Mississippi in canoes, reappeared, tanned and full of stories. And at the Majestic Motion Picture Theater, at Heinz's Ice Cream Parlor, and the other haunts of the young, Betsy looked around for Joe. His letters had stopped coming as abruptly as they had started, and the series of stories in the Tribune had ended, too. Probably, she thought, he was out at Butternut Center with his uncle and aunt. She wondered why he didn't call her up.

All the talk was of being seniors.

"It's going to seem queer to be seniors," the girls agreed, looking ahead to that day, not far off now, when they would pass through the wide, arched doorway of the high school wearing their new dignity.

"Poor me! I'll be a freshie again," Carney mourned.

She and her mother had returned from Minneapolis, where they had stayed at a hotel and had bought clothes in the city stores. The girls flocked to her house to hear all about it, Betsy accompanied by Margaret, whom she was taking to Miss Cobb's house for her first piano lesson.

"What did you buy?"

"Oh, a tweed suit with a brown velvet collar and a brown velvet tricorn Gage hat."

"Any new party dresses?"

"I have," announced Carney grandly, "a store-bought party dress! It's pale pink silk with elbow sleeves and a square neck. It's a dear. Come on! I'll show it to you."

There was a rush for the stairs.

Ascending, they heard the hum of a sewing machine.

"Miss Mix is making my school dresses and under-wear. I wish you could see the underwear! It's made of sheeting!" Carney giggled. "Mother wants it strong so it can stand a college laundry. That's what it is to have a New Englander for a parent."

"Good thing it isn't your trousseau," said Tib, who liked lingerie as delicate as cobwebs, lace-trimmed and strung with ribbon.

They piled into Carney's room, where the store-bought party dress was reverently inspected. The suit was displayed, too, and Winona tried on the brown Gage hat, setting it at a ridiculous angle and parading up and down. Margaret struggled to keep her smiles from turning into undignified chuckles when Winona, pretending to be Carney, snatched Larry Humphreys' photograph from the bureau and pressed it madly to her middy blouse.

Betsy jumped up and spoke in a bass voice, obviously representing a Vassar dignitary.

"No, Miss Sibley," she said. "Do not bring that Howard Chandler Christie profile inside the sacred portals of Vassar."

"I always turn it to the wall when I'm studying, your honor," squeaked Winona.

"It makes no difference. Vassar is a girls' college. Leave men behind, all ye who enter here!"

Carney made a dash for Winona and succeeded in

wresting the picture away.

"You're just too silly!" she cried.

"Silly, am I?" said Winona. "Just for that I'll go home and wash my hair." That broke up the party.

"Margaret and I are going to Miss Cobb's," said Betsy.

"I'll walk down with you," Carney volunteered. "I'm going that way, matching ribbons. Heavens, I never thought that going away to college involved so much matching of ribbons!"

Carney, Betsy, and Margaret started down Broad Street under the high trees.

"It's funny to be teased about a boy you haven't even seen for three years," Carney remarked.

Larry and Herbert Humphreys had moved from Deep Valley three years before. Herbert and Betsy were great friends. But there was no romantic feeling between them such as had always existed between Larry and Carney. Carney had never liked any other boy so well.

"Have you heard from him lately?" asked Betsy.

"We still write every week." Carney had a dimple in one cheek which flickered mischievously now. "He wishes he was going to West Point."

"Ah ha!" said Betsy. "Across the river from Vassar."

"But," said Carney, "he's going to Stanford, all the

way across the continent and bursting with girls."

Her smile vanished and she turned to Betsy, frowning.

"I want to see Larry," she said firmly. "I have to find out whether I still like him. Maybe he's changed. I feel as though I couldn't ever . . . get married to anyone else until I know."

"Have you told him that?" asked Betsy.

"No, I haven't. But I should think he'd feel the same way . . . about seeing me, I mean."

"I'd like to be a mouse under a chair when you two meet," said Betsy.

They reached the long flight of wooden steps which led to Miss Cobb's cottage and Carney turned to Margaret, whose eyes were shining with excitement at the prospect of beginning music lessons.

"Good luck!" Carney said. "I'll bet you begin with middle C."

Carney had studied with Miss Cobb, of course. Most of Deep Valley's boys and girls began their piano study with Miss Cobb, a large stately woman with light hair combed smoothly down on either side of a calm, kindly face. There had been a girl and three boys in the little cottage once, children of Miss Cobb's sister who had died. Miss Cobb had broken her own engagement to marry and had taken the whole brood to raise. The two oldest had passed away with their mother's complaint. Leonard was ill with it now, out in the Colorado mountains. Only Bobby, the sturdy pink-cheeked youngest of the lot, lived on with his aunt.

Betsy was glad to be back in the little low-ceiled parlor with the upright piano and the grand piano and the scent of geraniums. Miss Cobb told her that Leonard had enjoyed her letters.

"I've enjoyed his letters, too, Miss Cobb," Betsy replied. She had learned from Leonard's letters—she had learned about courage.

He was not, Betsy suspected, getting any better. But there weren't any complaints about the pain or the discomfort or the boredom. He told instead about the funny things that happened around the sanatorium.

He was interested in music. His letters were full of comments on phonograph records, musicians, and musical compositions. There wasn't a word about not being able to develop his own talent, about how sad it was to be young and full of plans and have a curtain drop across your future like the curtain of a theater . . . only that, Betsy thought, always came at the end of something and Leonard's life had just begun.

A shadow crossed Miss Cobb's face, but it was like the shadow of a cloud passing over a mountain. Smiling, she turned to Margaret. She whirled the piano stool until it was the proper height and Margaret sat down, her back very straight. Miss Cobb struck a note and said, as she had said in previous years to Julia and Betsy, "This is middle C."

Betsy liked that. She always liked things to go on as they had gone before.

She was glad on Sunday to be back in the choir of St. John's Episcopal Church. Tib, Winona, and Irma were all in the choir and there was hushed gossip and laughter in the robing room as they put on their long black robes and the black four-cornered hats. Reverence descended as they formed into a double line, and glory burst, as always, when they marched down the aisle singing.

There was a substitute preacher, for the Rev. Mr. Lewis had not yet returned. He was on his way home. Julia had left the party in London.

"I left London," she wrote, "with Big Ben chiming in my ears. You know that famous clock; it plays a hymn tune at the striking of the hours:

> "*Oh, Lord our God,*
> *Be thou our guide,*
> *That by thy help,*
> *No foot may slide.*"

That's the prayer I'm taking with me to my wonderful experience in Berlin."

"I know the tune those chimes sing," said Betsy. "They have it in chime clocks. I never knew the words before, though."

"They're called Westminster chime clocks. We ought to get one," Mrs. Ray said.

The next letter came from Berlin.

"The moment I arrived," Julia wrote, "was the most ecstatically happy moment of my life. Oh, oh, oh, I'm going to work so hard! Fraulein says I'm too nervous and exuberant. I must calm down, get strength, and then do things."

She added that Fraulein wished her to stay on a few days before going into a pension.

"I'm glad. Her house is so interesting . . . musicians, critics, and artists coming and going. I have only one worry—my trunk hasn't come! So far, I haven't had to dress up, and it's fortunate, for I'm still wearing the suit I wore when I arrived. I wash out my waist every night."

"For heaven's sake!" said Mrs. Ray, when she read that. "What's the matter with the Germans that they can't do a simple thing like deliver a trunk?"

"Probably Julia was so excited that she sent it to Kalamazoo," said Mr. Ray.

"Never mind!" Betsy consoled her mother. "Julia looks pretty in anything." But Mrs. Ray worried about Julia meeting the Great World in a travel-stained suit.

"All the pretty clothes there are in that trunk!" she mourned.

The next night, when the Rays were at supper, the telephone rang. Anna said that a gentleman wished to speak to Mr. Ray. He returned to the table, smiling.

"It's the Rev. Mr. Lewis," he said. "He reached town this afternoon and wants to come right up."

There was an outcry of delight.

The family rushed through peach cobbler—Mrs. Ray left hers untouched upon the plate—and was waiting in the parlor when the Rev. Mr. Lewis arrived.

"You may not have holly around, but it's certainly Christmas for this family," he announced, putting a large box on the table. He wiped his face. "That daughter of yours! When she wasn't writing letters to you folks, she was buying presents."

"For you to carry home!" put in Mr. Ray.

"Glad to do it," said the Rev. Mr. Lewis, grinning. "Glad to do anything for Julia."

"Before we look at a single present," Mrs. Ray said, "we want to hear about her. Exactly how was she when you left her?"

"Exhausted but blissful," he replied. "That puts it in a nutshell. She didn't miss a church or an art museum or an historical monument. She asked so many questions that I was hard put to find answers. She wants to learn, that girl does."

"Did she drive you crazy," Mr. Ray asked, "being late for everything?"

"Frankly, yes." The Rev. Mr. Lewis grinned again. "She caught every boat and train just as it was pulling out. But she was so sweet, so helpful, taking care of people who were seasick, rubbing heads, mending clothes, doing the ladies' hair new ways. . . . She found me the one thing Mrs. Lewis had asked me to bring back, a little mosaic chest, from Rome. Everybody in the party loved her, including me."

The whole house was suddenly lonesome for Julia. Mrs. Ray wiped her eyes.

Mr. Ray spoke briskly. "Well, now that we've heard all about her, how about opening the box?"

It was indeed like Christmas when Julia's box was opened. Most of the presents were already familiar, for Julia had described them in her letters. She had bought Betsy's Class Day dress in Lucerne, which was famous, she said, for embroidered dresses. It was pale blue batiste, heavy with embroidery. Betsy got a blue plume, too, from Paris, for the dress hat she would have in the spring, and white gloves from Paris, and exquisite blue and gold Venetian beads.

While Betsy exulted over these, Mr. and Mrs. Ray, Margaret, and Anna were unwrapping and exclaiming. The Rev. Mr. Lewis was almost as happy as they were.

"Am I Santa Claus or am I not?" he wanted to know.

The night before school began, when Mr. Ray came home, he called Betsy down to the parlor. He had a pleased look on his face.

"See this picture?" he said, handing her a folded copy of the Minneapolis *Tribune*. "Isn't this the Willard boy who goes to Deep Valley High School? The one you've been getting letters from all summer?"

Betsy took the paper, and Joe's eyes looked out at her under their heavy brows. His lower lip was outthrust as usual, giving his face a look of good-humored defiance.

The story beneath the picture said that this was the Joseph Willard who had written such a fine account of the North Dakota land-swindle trial. It made much of the fact that he was only seventeen.

"I saw Mr. Root on the street tonight," Mr. Ray said. "You never saw anyone so pleased. He kept saying, 'That Joe Willard is going to be a top newspaper man, and I taught him all he knows.'"

"Mr. Root is an awfully good friend of Joe's," Betsy replied. She was bursting with pride.

After supper, when Anna was doing the dishes and Mr. and Mrs. Ray and Margaret were reading in the parlor, Betsy sat down at the piano. She played a few jubilant scales, then opened her book of Beethoven sonatinas. She was pounding through the first one when the doorbell rang.

"I'll answer it," she called, jumping up. She opened the front door and there on the porch stood Joe Willard, hot and rumpled but smiling, his hair looking the color of silver above his tanned face.

"Why, Joe!" cried Betsy.

"I came right from the train."

"I've just been reading about you. Papa brought home the paper."

"Of course, the picture doesn't do me justice."

He smiled at Betsy and Betsy smiled at him. A full minute passed before she remembered to ask him in.

"Papa and Mamma will be so glad to meet you," she said quickly then. "Papa has been reading your stories all summer."

As she led him into the parlor, Betsy felt very conscious of the fact that this was the first time he had been in her home. The other boys in her class had swung in the hammock and sat on the front steps. They had sung around the piano in the music room and sprawled all over the parlor and sat in front of the dining room fireplace eating her father's sandwiches. They had danced to the two tunes, one a waltz and one a two-step, Mrs. Ray knew how to play on the piano, and had raided Anna's kitchen time and again. But Joe Willard, the most important boy of all, had never been inside her house before.

He was following her now with the swing in his walk more pronounced than usual, as though he were stirring up courage. When she stopped at the archway, he drew himself erect and his smile was a little fixed. Betsy was amazed, and flattered, too, that the great Joe Willard should be nervous at meeting her parents. She smiled reassuringly.

"Mamma," she said, "Papa, it seems ridiculous that you don't know Joe Willard, but I don't believe you do."

Mrs. Ray stood up. She gave him the gay smile all the young people loved.

"I don't know whether I'll let him come in or not," she said. "He's the boy who always wins the Essay Contest away from my Betsy."

"Oh, let him come in, Jule," Mr. Ray returned. "He's quite a fellow, his picture in the paper and all."

And then Mr. and Mrs. Ray were shaking his hand and Margaret was greeting him, too. She looked grave and appraising, as she always did with her older sisters' visitors. None of them ever quite measured up to Tony, in Margaret's opinion.

Old Mag was hitched out in front, for Mr. Ray had planned to take the family riding that night. Mr. and Mrs. Ray and Margaret left without Betsy, and Betsy and Joe sat down on the porch steps. Betsy hoped that casual visitors like Cab, Dennie, or Tony would have sense enough not to come in when they saw them sitting there.

The twilight was crisp, filled with the smell of burning leaves. The sky above the German Catholic College on the hill was tinted by the afterglow.

Betsy asked Joe about the *Tribune* story, and he explained that the city editor had asked him for a photograph, and when Joe sent it he had found out that Joe was only seventeen. Then he had written another letter which Joe now pulled out of his pocket and showed to Betsy.

"You did a fine job. Privately, you never would have had the chance if I had known how young you were. But you wrote like a veteran. There's a place for you on the Minneapolis *Tribune* when you finish high school and come up to the U."

"Joe, that's wonderful!" cried Betsy. "You're going to the U?"

"I'm going to start there," answered Joe. "Say, you told me you thought *Les Miserables* was the greatest novel ever written. I think *Vanity Fair* is the greatest. Let's fight."

Betsy accepted the change of subject. Joe would be slow to let her or anyone else look through the door of the room where he kept the problems he had met in the past, his plans for the future. Joe Willard wasn't easy to get acquainted with. But Betsy felt a sweet, strong certainty that she would succeed in time.

They sat on the porch and talked while stars appeared above the college and a pearly glow announced that the moon would join them soon. No one else came, or if they came they went away. Betsy and Joe watched the moon rise.

"How do you like being a senior?"

"I like it."

"I have an idea that this year is going to be perfectly wonderful."

"I have the same idea," Joe Willard said, looking at the moon.

5

The Last First-Day of School

As Betsy wound her hair on Magic Wavers, preparing for her last first-day of high school, the importance of that event was dwarfed in her mind by Joe's call. In a way it was dwarfed, in another way it was glorified. The fact that Joe had sought her out, that they were obviously going to go together, put a crowning touch to her joy in being a senior.

She wound her clock briskly and set the alarm

for six. She wanted to get into the bathroom early next morning, to have time to prink. She and Tib had planned exactly what they would wear for the great day. Betsy had decided on her pink chambray dress with a wide pink band around her hair.

She slipped a kimono over her nightgown and threw a pillow to the floor beside Uncle Keith's trunk.

"I guess I'll read over my old diaries, and start the new one tonight," she said aloud.

She got out the three fat notebooks which held the story of her first three years in high school, and the fourth one with its tantalizing empty pages. As she read, the quality and mood of each year returned like a tune.

Her freshman year, and her joy in finding a crowd, her discovery about her writing, and her yearning for Tony.

"I've never been so much in love with anyone as I was with Tony when I was fourteen."

Her sophomore year, and her trip to Milwaukee to visit Tib, the attempt to be Dramatic and Mysterious in order to captivate Phil Brandish, Phyllis' twin.

"After I got him, I didn't want him."

And last year, her junior year, when she had been all wound up in sororities, and going with Dave Hunt.

"That was funny. We were really just friends. Not a bit of a crush."

Through all three years, Joe Willard had stood in

the background, a figure of mystery and challenge, and now in her senior year they were going to go together. How completely and utterly satisfactory!

Betsy dipped her pen in ink.

"Three years ago this fall," she wrote, "I began my first diary and my four years of high school loomed ahead so bigly that the start of my senior-year diary seemed but a vague possibility. Yet here I am starting it!

"How different I feel! One begins one's freshman year wild with anticipation, eager for the days to pass, radiantly happy! But one begins one's senior year with a sense of looking back, a longing to enjoy each minute to the full, a little touch of sadness."

She didn't feel at all sad but she thought that sounded good.

"I would like to stop the clock right here and take a little breathing spell. As Mary Ware said, 'It's so nice to be as old as seventeen, and yet as young as seventeen.' But time goes on, on, on. . . ."

She meant to develop that but she couldn't think just how. Besides, she was getting hungry. She always got hungry when she stayed up late. She opened the door of her room into a dark sleeping house, and crept softly down the stairs.

Out in the kitchen, she lit the gas light and foraged. Finding milk, cold sausages, and part of a chocolate cake, she tiptoed with them back up to her room.

How handsome Joe had looked! How thrilling that he had come to see her on his first night home! When her lunch was eaten, she turned out the gas, opened her window wide, and crept into bed.

The next thing she knew the alarm clock was shrilling and she jumped to her feet, remembering drowsily that if she wanted a leisurely time in the bathroom, it behooved her to get there. After her father started shaving, she wouldn't have a chance. And if she got in just ahead of him, he was sure to rap on the door, saying, "Hurry, Betsy! Remember, I must shave."

She was amply early, and when the breakfast gong sounded she emerged from her room looking as she had planned to look, in the pink chambray dress which was made in princesse style, long and close-fitting, trimmed with white rickrack braid. The wide pink band was tied around her Magically Waved hair; her fingernails were buffed to a pink shine.

Margaret joined her in the hall. It was hard to know whether Margaret, too, had been up early prinking, for she was always so fastidiously neat. She wore a new white middy blouse with a red tie, and the red bows which tied her braids behind each ear were gigantic. She carried a pile of last year's books under her arm.

The tempting smell of muffins filled the air. Anna always made muffins for the first day of school. A plateful of the fragrant, tender pyramids was already on the table, and she brought another shortly, for Tacy and Tib dropped in to call for Betsy. The two girls were full of excitement about Joe Willard's picture in the paper.

"He's back. He dropped in last night," Betsy said, offhandedly.

"He dropped in?" cried Tib. "Betsy Ray! Tell us about it."

"What is there to tell?"

"Do you like him as well as you thought you would?"

"I like him as well as I always did. I've known him for three years."

"She's just being irritating," Tacy said. "You tell us what happened, Mrs. Ray."

"I don't know," answered Mrs. Ray. "We tactfully retreated, didn't we, Margaret?"

Margaret nodded, beaming.

"There's a poem I learned in school," said Mr. Ray. He threw back his head and began a sing-song chant:

> *"New hope may bloom,*
> *And days may come,*
> *Of milder, calmer beam,*

But there's nothing half so sweet in life,
As love's young dream,
Oh, there's nothing half so sweet in life,
As love's young dream."

"Papa!" protested Betsy, blushing. But she wasn't annoyed. "We just had a nice sensible time."

"On the porch in the moonlight," put in Mr. Ray.

"He's so handsome," said Mrs. Ray, "I could have a crush on him myself if I didn't have such a crush on my husband."

"He's not so nice as Tony," said Margaret, in a distant tone.

"Oh, but Tony's different, Margaret," Tacy replied. "There's no fun teasing Betsy about Tony. He hasn't a crush on her."

"And she hasn't a crush on him," Tib added. "You'll understand when you're older."

"Perhaps," said Betsy, "we'd better go to school."

They called out to Anna that the muffins were marvelous and descended the porch, arm in arm, into High Street. The vine over the porch was turning red; and in spite of the summerlike green of the trees, the petunias, zinnias, and nasturtiums still blooming in the borders, Betsy felt the impact of the coming season, the melancholy of September.

For the first time, she missed Cab.

"It'll seem funny not to have Cab walking to school with us," she said, and tried to imagine what it would be like to be giving up school in your senior year. She wondered how Cab was feeling about it, down at the furniture store.

"We'll miss Carney, too," said Tacy.

"She's coming to visit today," Tib announced. "She's going to classes with us."

The school-bound parade surged along High Street: freshmen looked frightened and eager; sophomores, proud; juniors, complacent. Betsy wondered whether she and Tacy and Tib betrayed their consciousness of being seniors as they chatted loftily, well aware of admiring eyes.

They went through the big doors, climbed the stairs past their old friend Mercury, so lightly poised that Betsy never quite believed he was made of stone, and paused in the upper hall. Here was the case which held the silver trophy cups for which the school societies, Philomathian and Zetamathian, competed annually—in athletics, in debating, and in essay writing. The Essay Cup made Betsy think of Joe.

"How will we feel competing against each other this year . . . when we're going together," she wondered.

He didn't appear in the Social Room. He seldom came there. Having a job in addition to his school work, he usually reached school with the last gong and hurried away at the end of each session.

Ralph Maddox appeared, however. The new senior athlete from St. John caused a sensation.

"He's beautiful!" cried Winona.

"He's ravishing!" cried Hazel Smith.

"He's absolutely pulchritudinous!" cried Betsy—all this in hushed voices, of course.

"Hmm," said Tib. "I don't mind getting *him* for the Zets."

Tall, broad-shouldered, with dark washboard curls rising above a classic profile, he looked kin to Mercury out in the hall. He moved a little self-consciously through the buzzing room. Of course, thought Betsy, if you were that handsome you couldn't help but know it.

Carney joined the girls just as the gong rang and accompanied them into the Assembly Room.

"Gosh, I feel superior," she said, "watching the rest of you start the same old grind!"

As usual, Betsy, Tacy, and Tib headed for back seats and found three together. Miss Bangeter announced the opening hymn. Boys and girls stood and sang with a will. They sat, with much banging of seats and scraping of feet, and Miss Bangeter read from the Bible.

She read from the Bible every morning and it was

one of the things, Betsy realized, she would remember from high school. She liked the magnificent prose as it rolled from the lips of the principal, who was magnificent herself, in a dark, austere way.

"I'm sorry for high schools that haven't Miss Bangeter for principal," Betsy thought.

Miss Bangeter read this morning from the thirteenth chapter of First Corinthians.

"'Though I speak with the tongues of men and of angels, and have not charity, I am become as sounding brass, or a tinkling cymbal.'"

Betsy was listening dreamily when the familiar words flashed out with sudden meaning.

"'When I was a child,'" read Miss Bangeter, "'I spake as a child, I understood as a child, I thought as a child: but when I became a man, I put away childish things.'"

Betsy looked across the aisle at Tacy and saw that Tacy was looking at her. She reached for a tablet and a pencil and thought she would write the words down, but she stopped, for she knew she would remember them. They were so apt, so significant, at the beginning of the senior year.

"I put away childish things." You didn't want to, perhaps; but you did. She would have to, and so would Tacy and Tib and all of them.

Betsy felt a wave of that sadness she had not felt at

all last night when she told her diary she felt it. But it was soon dispelled. They went the round of their classes, Carney making derisive remarks.

Spurred by Julia's constant references to the need of modern languages out in the Great World, Betsy had registered for German. Her father had been pleased.

"We have so many Germans in Deep Valley, all over the county, in fact. Lots of them who come into the store can hardly speak English. It's a language you can really use, Betsy."

"That's right," Betsy said. "Why, Tib's father and mother often speak to each other in German. I can talk it with them. And I can talk it with Tib. And I can go to hear sermons at the German churches."

"Besides," said Mrs. Ray, "you can speak it with Julia when she comes home."

"And I can teach it to Margaret. *Nicht wahr*, Margaret?"

"Say *Ja*, Button," Mr. Ray advised.

"*Ja, ja*," said Margaret, full of laughter.

These fine plans filled Betsy's mind now as she left Tacy, Tib, and Carney and went alone into the first-year German class. Her classmates were mostly awe-struck freshmen. Her teacher was the blond Miss Erickson, who had tried to teach her Latin.

Tacy and Tib joined her for physics under Mr.

Gaston. They knew this subject would be hard and had dodged it in their frivolous junior year.

They could relax in the civics class, next on the schedule. Miss Clarke, who had taught them Ancient History, Modern History, and United States History, was a girlish, indulgent teacher.

Last of all came Miss Bangeter's Shakespeare class.

Miss Bangeter didn't teach many subjects. But her senior Shakespeare class was famous. She loved Shakespeare; she had specialized in his works in college. Her class read some of the comedies and tragedies aloud, parts being assigned to the various students.

Betsy had looked forward to it ever since Julia had taken it two years before, and she welcomed it also for another reason. Joe would be there. Even when they hadn't been friends, held apart by that curious hostility which, for a time, had stood between them, they had always enjoyed being together in English class.

He came into the classroom now with that swinging walk which was so much a part of him, and looked around at once for Betsy, who was also looking for him. They smiled at each other.

As soon as class was dismissed, he came over to her.

"I have to get down to the *Sun,*" he said. "But not

until I settle something important. When am I going to see you again?"

Betsy thought quickly. Winona was entertaining the girls Friday night for Carney. Saturday night she was going to the Majestic with Tony.

"Why don't you come up Sunday night?" she asked. "Come to lunch. That's what we call Sunday night supper at our house. I don't know why, but we do."

"Seeing as how it's lunch and not supper, I'd love to come," answered Joe. He smiled at Tacy, Tib, and Carney and went out of the room.

The three girls looked at each other.

"Well!" said Tacy.

"About time!" said Tib.

"Hurray!" cried Carney. "I'm glad it happened before I went to Vassar. Betsy's going to go with Joe Willard, *at last*!"

"Don't be silly!" Betsy answered, blushing as pink as the pink chambray dress.

6

The Senior Class President

THE PARTY FOR CARNEY was a noteworthy affair. Of course, her impending departure was noteworthy. She was going so far—half way across the continent—and she was the first Deep Valley girl to go east to college. And she would leave a yawning gap in the Crowd. No more on warm September days would they sprawl on the Sibley lawn. No more on moonlight nights would they go rattling about the country, singing, in the Sibley auto. The girls brought letters to be read on the train and small gifts for the trip. Winona presented a corsage of carnations which Carney popped into the ice box so that she could wear it on the morrow.

They played five hundred. Five hundred was almost as much the rage as bands around the hair. There were dishes of candy kisses on each table, there were prizes, and superlative refreshments—crab meat salad, home baked rolls, cocoa, an enormous sunshine cake. The boys raided and were invited in, which made the party perfect.

It was well that the Crowd got its innings on Friday night, for at the train next morning they were far outnumbered by Sibleys. Carney's own family was reasonably small, but there were Sibleys all over the county. The station swarmed with grandparents, uncles, aunts, and cousins, so that the Crowd got only a glimpse of Carney in the tweed suit and the brown velvet tricorn, with the big bouquet of carnations. Her eyes were shining behind her glasses. The dimple stood out in her round pink cheek.

"Write to us!" the Crowd called when she came out on the observation platform.

"I will, I will."

The whistle blew, the bell began to ring, and the

great oily black wheels started turning. Carney waved with vigor but her lips were set as though it were an effort to keep calm and matter-of-fact.

"I wonder whether college will change Carney," Betsy said, when the train was gone.

"Maybe she'll come back with an eastern accent."

"Carney never 'put on' in her life."

"Some people do, though, when they're in the East only a little while."

"Well, Carney will come back with her same old Deep Valley accent," Winona said positively, and everyone agreed.

Betsy and Tony discussed her departure that night, eating pineapple sundaes at Heinz's after the picture. Tom had already left for Cox, and Al and Squirrelly would soon be leaving for the U.

"You and I will be going off to college next year, I suppose," Betsy said.

"Heck! I probably won't even graduate."

"What do you mean? Of course you'll graduate!" Betsy was indignantly emphatic. "Probably," she added, "you'll go to the U at Minneapolis."

"Well, I'm going up to Minneapolis all right . . . tomorrow," he said wickedly. "The team is playing at home."

"How are you going?"

"In my private car."

"Tony," said Betsy, "you ought not to do that."

"Why not?"

"Papa told you. You might lose a leg. Besides, those railroad men are all too old for you."

"They suit me fine."

"I wish you wouldn't do it," Betsy said.

Tony looked at her across the metal table, his laughing black eyes growing suddenly somber.

"Do you really wish I wouldn't?" he asked.

"I certainly do."

"I might stop it," he said enigmatically.

"I wish you would," Betsy replied. "I worry about those trips, Tony. I like it so much better when you just hang around with the Crowd."

"And with you?" Tony asked. His tone was low. Betsy was hardly sure she had understood what he said. Although Tony was so bold and breezy, he was intensely reticent. He was not given to personal remarks, or at least not with her. And if he had really said what she thought he had said, he wouldn't like having said it when he found out about Joe. She decided to pretend she hadn't heard.

"If you don't go to Minneapolis," she replied, "we'll expect you for Sunday night lunch."

He did not appear on Sunday night, but Joe came early, his blue suit neatly pressed this time, his pompadour burnished by much brushing. He and Mrs.

Ray started talking about books. It seemed to Betsy that he had read everything, beginning with *The Iliad* and *The Odyssey*. But Mr. Ray had never even heard of *The Iliad* and *The Odyssey*. He liked people instead of books. He was wary of intellectuals and Betsy could see that he acted a little guarded with Joe. Joe also seemed a little guarded with him.

Shifting from books, Mrs. Ray told him the news of Julia, whom Joe had known slightly. She showed him Julia's pictures and chatted on about the difficulties with her trunk.

"If I remember Julia," Joe said gallantly, "she doesn't need to worry if that trunk never comes."

He got on famously with Mrs. Ray, but Betsy felt a little fearful when he pushed his way deliberately through the swinging door to the kitchen where her father was making sandwiches.

Mr. Ray always made the sandwiches for Sunday night lunch. They were a family institution. He sat down to make them, looking dignified and benevolent, as he went about his invariable rites—buttering bread, arranging slices of cold meat, cheese, or onions, seasoning them expertly while the coffee he had earlier set to boil exuded its inviting fragrance. He liked to have lookers-on but Betsy wondered what under the sun he and Joe would find to talk about.

As she chattered with Cab at the fireplace, she

kept an ear turned to the kitchen. Certainly a hum of conversation was issuing therefrom. At last she found courage to saunter out, and she found Joe watching the sandwich-making intently, but not half so intently as he was listening to Mr. Ray's story about an old Syrian couple who had come into the store to buy shoes.

When Joe was helping Betsy arrange the cups and saucers on the dining room table, he said, "I always thought it was just people who want to write, like me, who enjoyed analyzing people. But your father is a far better student of human nature than I'll ever be. He likes people better."

Betsy was delighted and even more delighted later when her father remarked, "That Joe's a nice boy, a fine boy, and he certainly does like my stories."

A letter came from Julia the next day, and to Mrs. Ray's dismay, she was still without her trunk. Moreover, she had needed it badly for an event which she dramatically described.

Fraulein von Blatz had taken her to a reception given by the Kaiser . . . no less . . . for an American who was coming to Berlin in a balloon. His name was Wright.

"I asked Fraulein whether it was perfectly all right for me to go as I was. She said, 'Of course, of course,' in that vague way of hers. She doesn't care a thing about clothes and wears a suit and a man's old hat wherever she goes. It doesn't matter, for she's a celebrity, but I'm not—yet.

"We drove clear out to the end of the city to a magnificent estate. Our host was a pompous old officer. He couldn't speak any English and you know my German! But I smiled my most elegant smile.

"Over the garden wall was the field where the Emperor was to greet the balloonist. There were hundreds of troops at attention. The garden was swarming with grand ladies, to some of whom Fraulein introduced me before she disappeared. They wore jewels and trailing dresses and plumed hats and white kid gloves. I didn't even have gloves.

"I began to be conscious of my rags and tatters. In fact, I was fussed. For how could I rise above clothes—as I pride myself on being able to do—when my vocabulary was limited to '*Ach, ja, sehr schoen*'? Bettina, you learn languages!

"I fumed and cussed until my sense of humor came to the rescue. Then I began to play with a little girl Margaret's age. (They give such cute curtseys when they are introduced.) She and her sisters, about fourteen and eighteen, were with their governess. Their mother, the Countess von Hetternich, was at the Royal Palace in the Empress' party.

"The youngsters laughed at my German and I tried to help their English. We had lots of fun. The balloonist broke his propeller or something about fifty miles away, so we all had cakes and coffee and went home."

Mr. Ray was interested in the balloonist, but Mrs. Ray could think of nothing but Julia's predicament.

"She must have been embarrassed or she wouldn't have told us about it. Ordinarily Julia never thinks about clothes."

"She thought it was a joke," said Betsy. "And so do I. Imagine her, after all the trouble you took with her clothes, going to the Kaiser's reception without gloves!"

"Tell your mother that Julia's entrée into Berlin society wasn't half so much of a fiasco as Mr. Wright's," said Joe, when Betsy told him about it at school.

School activities were getting under way. Philomathians and Zetamathians were approaching the day when newcomers would be asked to choose societies. Last year on this occasion, Dave Hunt had put the Zetamathian banner on the cupola, thereby goading the rival society, the following spring, into painting Philomathian on the roof.

Miss Bangeter gave advance warnings that there would be no more such goings-on.

"The boys who went up there last year were suspended; if anyone tries it again, he will be expelled."

That settled that, and with roof climbing out of the question, excitement centered on the rushing being given Ralph Maddox.

He was sure to be a Philo, gossip said. He had Philomathian cousins.

"Why, they got him to come to Deep Valley," Winona explained.

"He's practically a Philo now," said Joe. "Boy, boy, this cinches the athletics cup!"

Betsy and Tacy hurried off to Tib. "You promised to get him for the Zets, remember?"

"I remember, I remember," said Tib.

Watching her chance in the Social Room, she gazed up at him naively. "I just have to tell you. We're so thrilled about your coming to Deep Valley. You know, our big football star, Al Larson, graduated. We just needed another football star."

After that wherever you saw the tall, dark, handsome Maddox, you saw Tib, small, blond, and enchanting, smiling up at him.

"Is he practically a Philo now?" asked Betsy.

"Sure," said Joe. "Blood is thicker than water."

"I'll bet you a box of candy Tib gets him for the Zets."

The next day Tib, standing on tiptoe, pinned a blue ribbon into Maddox's lapel, and Joe brought a big box of candy to the Social Room.

Busy as he was, Joe was mingling more with the high school crowd this year. Betsy was glad, for he had always been something of an outsider. Working after school, he had been unable to take part in athletics, and until last year he had not had the money for social life.

He had always found time for the Essay Contest, of course, and last year, as a reporter for the *Sun*, he had attended football and basketball games. He had headed the program committee for the Junior-Senior Banquet and had helped to paint that fateful Philo-mathian on the roof.

These things had drawn him into the current of school life, and it was good for him, Betsy thought, to ride that giddy current. His experiences had matured him, just as different, less sober, experiences had matured Tony. Like Tony, Joe needed a crowd, needed fun, needed to go with a girl who thought high school affairs were important.

When class elections came along, he arranged with Mr. Root to be late getting down to the paper.

"I'm really interested," he confided to Betsy. "I'd really like to know who's going to steer us through this year of glory. It will be Stan, I suppose?"

Stan Moore had been president through the sopho-more and junior years.

"He would be a good one," Betsy answered. "But some kids think that the offices ought to be passed around."

"You've been secretary for two years, haven't you?"

"Yes. And I wouldn't accept it again. Last year I thought I wanted it awfully, but now I can see that it wouldn't be fair. And I'm going to be plenty busy."

They walked together into the Assembly Room and Betsy took her place on the platform with last year's officers. Stan took charge. Hazel started the election ball to rolling by nominating him.

Stan jumped up. "Thanks very much," he said, "but I've had this office twice and I think it's time someone else had it."

Dennie rose. "I want to nominate an outstanding boy and a swell athlete, Dave Hunt." There was a burst of applause. A voice in the rear of the room cried, "I second the nomination."

Alice stood up. "I think," she said, "that we might have a girl president for a change. I have a girl in mind who would be just the one. She's a leading senior and the best girl debater in the state. Hazel Smith." There was another burst of applause even louder than the first, and again a prompt seconding voice.

"We have two nominations," Stan said. "Dave Hunt and Hazel Smith. Does anyone else have anything to say?"

To the surprise of the class, Tony pulled himself lazily to his feet. He had always taken even less interest than Joe in school affairs. He didn't make a speech now, but he stood, for long seconds, in silent scrutiny of all the class. It came to Betsy that he was challenging them. He was, she realized, about to make a nomination which, in his opinion, would test them, and his gaze as much as said that he doubted how well they would come off. That bold, scornful gaze circled the room for a last time, then he drawled in his deep voice, "I nominate Joe Willard," and sank back into his seat.

There was no applause whatever. When Betsy realized that, it was too late to start any. A confused silence had fallen on the room, broken only by Tacy's, "I second that nomination."

Joe Willard! He wasn't an athlete. He had never held a class office. No one had ever thought of him in such a connection.

Yet, Betsy thought defensively, he had always been a credit to the school. Among grown-ups in Deep Valley, he was, without doubt, the school's outstanding student. Men and women knew Joe Willard; they admired him and said he would make his mark. And in school, when you came to think of it, who had been a bigger help to his fellow students? He had written of school events in the *Sun* as no one ever had written of them before. And although he hadn't had time for athletics, his three-time victory in the Essay Contest had been, she assured herself doggedly, as good as winning touchdowns any day.

But, she wondered, was there time for Joe's achievements to impress themselves on the minds of the boys and girls waiting dumbfoundedly to vote? If they had time, she knew that his chance would be good. If time was lacking, she feared that, like sheep, they would ignore Hazel Smith because she was a girl and vote unthinkingly for "an outstanding boy and a swell athlete, Dave Hunt."

Betsy couldn't, she told herself desperately, bear to have Dave win, even though she liked him. Dave already had so much. Joe must win! He must! She looked toward him and saw proudly that he was taking the issue in stride. He looked poised and cool. But she knew that he must have been surprised by Tony's breath-taking nomination, and cut by the silence in which it was received.

Someone moved that the nominations be closed. Ballots were distributed, written, and collected. Excitement played like lightning over the room when Stan stood up to announce the results. He was grinning widely.

"The new class president . . ." he said, and paused. "The new class president," he repeated, speaking slowly, "is Joe Willard."

The applause, which had been lacking before, broke out wildly then. Joe looked flustered, although he was still in command of himself. In response to the cries which rose above the clapping hands, he got to his feet, smiled, and nodded.

Then, in a quick, boyish, heart-warming gesture of gratitude and pleasure, he flung both arms above his head and waved his hands. The applause changed as though at a signal from handclaps to yells, the shrill sweet treble of the girls, a deep chorus of "Yee-ah, Joe!" from the boys.

Betsy's heart swelled. Joe, who had never had time for school politics, who had never had a home to entertain in or parents to entertain for him, who had always held proudly aloof from social life because he was poor. Joe had received the greatest honor his class had to offer. She was grateful to Tony for having thought of it. The idea had never once entered her own head.

After the meeting ended, she sought out Tony.

"That was wonderful, Tony. I don't know why we've never thought of Joe before for a class office," she said.

"I think, myself, it was smart," Tony answered, looking pleased with himself. "He's got more sense than most of these small-timers. He's been around."

That, Betsy thought, was the explanation of why Tony had nominated Joe. He was pleased to see a fellow outsider take command. He had known that Joe only needed to be presented, to be recognized as a leader.

Tony didn't know, she felt sure, that she had any special feeling for Joe. He hadn't done it for her sake, which made it all the nicer.

"It was wonderful," she repeated, smiling at him warmly, and crossed the room to congratulate Joe.

7

The Rift within the Lute

IF ANYTHING HAD BEEN needed to make the start of the senior year happy, Joe's new honor supplied it for Betsy. She was gloriously happy. She had never, she thought, been so happy in her life.

Joe started class business rolling by appointing a committee on class pins and caps. Oddly enough, Betsy Ray was on the committee. As president, Joe was ex-officio member of all committees, and so he joined the group which went down to Alquist's Clothing Store looking for caps. After much hilarious trying on, the committee decided to recommend skull caps made up in the class colors of violet and gray. The committee then renewed its strength at Heinz's, with ice cream swimming in syrups, topped by whipped cream, nuts, and cherries.

The next day, Joe called a class meeting and the committee reported. The skull caps were approved, so the committee, and president, went back to Alquist's and ordered them, with more nourishment at Heinz's.

Still later they were obliged to go down to collect the caps, not neglecting Heinz's, of course. The caps were distributed, causing quite a flurry around school. Cameras snapped as seniors posed, singly and in groups.

"Dearest Chuck," Tacy said to Tib, "you're a sensation in that cap."

"Maddox will adore it, Sweet My Coz," said Betsy.

"By my troth thou sayest true," said Tib, placing the cap at an even jauntier angle.

All the seniors were talking in that vein, for Miss Bangeter's Shakespeare class had started to read *As You Like It*.

They wore the skull caps to the first football game,

the battle with Red Feather, and Maddox, bulking large in his fame and shoulder pads, did indeed cast appreciative glances. The girls went in a crowd, for most of the boys they knew were on the team, except Joe, who, of course, was covering the game for the *Sun*.

Joe didn't have much time for girls at football games. Bareheaded, enveloped in an ancient sweater, pencil in one hand, copy paper in the other, he jogged up and down the sidelines.

The girls did plenty of yelling, but all of it was in vain. In spite of Maddox, Deep Valley went down to ignominious defeat.

The team was weak this year. It did, indeed, miss Al. Dave Hunt was a fine player, but although tall he was very thin, and his long legs helped more at basketball than at football. Maddox had been good in practice, and early in the game he made one flashy touchdown. But he didn't do it again, and he didn't seem able to keep the Red Feather team from piling up a twenty-to-six score.

The home-going crowd was optimistic, however.

"Oh, Maddox just didn't get going!"

"That touchdown showed what he can do."

"Didn't he look gorgeous running down the field?"

"We just have to have a good season," said Betsy, "in our senior year."

She was an incorrigible senior. About everything

she did, she kept thinking whether or not she would do it again.

There was something so familiar about September—golden fields clean-swept by harvest, sumac reddening along country roads, birds in great sociable flocks ready to fly south. The Crowd amused itself in the now time honored ways—going riding, going serenading, going on wiener roasts and beefsteak fries. Betsy kept thinking how different everything would be next year.

A pattern was breaking, never to be re-established. Part of it had already broken. Chauncey Olcott didn't come to Deep Valley this year.

His visit had been a regular autumn event as long as Betsy could remember. The Ray family had always gone in a body to hear him. This year an interloper named Fiske O'Hara came, in a play called *The Wearing of the Green*. Like the Olcott plays, it was an Irish romance full of ballads, which young O'Hara sang as Chauncey Olcott used to sing them.

The loyal Rays boycotted *The Wearing of the Green*. Anna would not go with her Charley. And although those fickle people who attended said that the newcomer was very handsome, with a sweet tenor voice, the Rays would have none of him.

"Don't bring those songs up to the house!" Betsy said to Tony.

"The copycat!" muttered Anna, rolling out cookies

as though she had Fiske O'Hara under the rolling pin.

The pattern was broken, too, because Julia was so far away, and in such strange surroundings.

A brief note had followed her letter about the Kaiser's reception.

"Darlings: Fraulein just came in from the 'phone, to tell me the biggest joke! I made a hit yesterday after all. One of the girls I met, the oldest of those three Von Hetternich sisters, wants to perfect her English, and her mother telephoned Fraulein to ask if I would come and stay with them awhile. Fraulein said it would not only give me a chance to learn German; it would enable me to get to know one of the first families in Berlin. Did you ever hear of such luck? P. S. My trunk has come."

The next letter told about the Von Hetternichs' home.

"You could get lost wandering through it. There are drawing rooms, libraries, separate rooms for every meal, and every member of the family has a suite. I have a huge bedroom and share a little study with Else, the daughter of eighteen. I have a bathroom all my own, and a maid draws my bath every morning. Imagine that, Bettina!"

Julia described the three daughters, Else, Emma, and Eugenia. A brother, Else's twin, had left for boarding school. It was like living in a novel, she said.

To the Rays it was like a serial story. They could hardly wait from installment to installment, as Julia wrote of being petted and showered with presents, sent in a car to her lessons, to the theater, and opera.

The Rays were excited, but none of them was surprised when Julia wrote that the Von Hetternichs wished her to stay on as long as she lived in Berlin. The Countess wrote the formal invitation to Mrs. Ray. Else wrote a letter to Betsy which Julia enclosed in one of hers.

"Please, Bettina, when you reply, be careful to write plainly. English script is hard for her to read. And for heaven's sake, don't shock the dear prim soul! She never sees a man unless chaperoned to death and listens to my accounts of dances with awe."

Betsy and Tacy were enthralled by Julia's adventures, but Tib was unmoved.

"I don't envy that Else," she said. "Living in a palace, being chaperoned to death, isn't half so much fun as going to high school."

Betsy thought she was right as the first senior party began to be talked of. Joe called a class meeting to discuss it. It would be a dance, of course. He appointed a committee to work out details, then gave Dave the chair and went off to the *Sun*.

Tony walked home with Betsy. The weather was

cool, with a spatter of rain in the air. They were glad to find a fire in the grate, and bringing in handfuls of cookies from the kitchen, they settled themselves on the hearth.

Tony had stretched out in a chair and Betsy was pulling a cushion as near to the fire as flying sparks permitted, when he said casually, "This dance they're planning . . . I'll drag you to it if you want to be dragged."

Betsy felt a cold streak sinking through her body. Her disappointment was so intense that it almost brought tears to her eyes. She knew Joe would ask her to the party. In fact, she knew he took it for granted that he was going to take her. And it would be such joy to go with him! She would be proud, too, to show the school that they were going together.

But if she turned Tony down, he probably wouldn't go at all. He would hunt up some of those wild friends of whom her father disapproved. Besides, Tony had asked her first, and the rule required that she accept him.

She jumped up and started poking the fire.

"Why, that would be grand, Tony," she said, her tone as casual as his had been. Tony was keen where people's feelings were concerned. She would have to be careful.

Fortunately, Margaret came in just then from her

piano lesson. She told Tony gravely that she had learned to play "Little Birdie Is Dead." Tony asked her to play it for him, and she complied, which showed how much she liked him. Margaret detested performing.

Unlike Betsy, Margaret showed talent for the piano, and she was a better student in school than either of her sisters had been. But she had none of the ambition which burned in their breasts.

People were always saying to Margaret, "Well, Julia sings and Betsy writes. Now what is little Margaret going to do?"

Margaret would smile politely, for she was very polite, but privately she stormed to Betsy with flashing eyes, "I'm not going to do anything. I want to just live. Can't people just live?"

"Of course," Betsy soothed her. But she could never understand.

Tony understood. He understood Betsy's ambition and Margaret's lack of it. Tony was such a darling, Betsy thought, watching his sleepily benignant look as Margaret played. She was glad she hadn't hurt his feelings, but she passed the rest of the afternoon with a sickish feeling inside.

Joe was both sensitive and proud. Once he had asked to take her home from a party, and again, to walk home from the library with her. On both occasions she had had to turn him down and for months after-wards he had made no gesture toward her. Now they were so close, so happy together. She didn't think he would act like that, and yet . . . she didn't know.

About supper time Joe called up. His voice sounded cheerful.

"I've got an assignment tonight. Bell ringers. Down at the Presbyterian Church. Don't you think you could go, even though it's a school night? Bell ringers are highly educational."

Betsy ran to ask her father and to her surprise he assented.

"I'm glad to have you hear some bell ringers, Betsy. There aren't very many of them any more. They're going out of style, like minstrel shows."

This was astounding luck. Betsy would have been overjoyed except for that dread hanging over her.

They had a very good time. After the entertainment they went to Heinz's, and they talked hard and fast over their cocoa and on the cold walk home. They never seemed to tire of talking. In fact, they never seemed to tire of each other.

Betsy knew he enjoyed her, and she admired him beyond words. He had the beginning of a genuine culture based on his prodigious reading. He had read, she thought, everything. Not only older writ-ers like Dickens, Thackeray, Balzac, Hawthorne, and

Washington Irving, but the stimulating newcomers: Jack London, Frank Norris, O. Henry. Tonight he was telling her about O. Henry's stories; his enthusiasm swept her along like the wind.

It wasn't until they reached her home and the fire that Joe brought up the senior dance. They had hung up their wraps and both were on cushions close to the dying embers. Joe had wanted to put on another log, but Betsy reminded him that the morrow was a school day.

"You can only stay until that last stick breaks in two, which it's just preparing to do."

"Then," he replied, "we must do some talking about the class party. By the way, Miss Ray, I'd like to have the honor of conducting you."

Betsy felt herself flush. She swallowed and tried to keep her tone light.

"By the way, you're too late. Somebody asked me this afternoon."

"What!" Joe started up sharply. "Who is it?"

"Tony."

"Well, of all the nerve!" He sounded really angry, but then he said, "That Markham!" and his tone was milder, almost admiring. "Darn the guy!"

He was silent, frowning thoughtfully into the flickering fire. Then he turned and looked at her with teasing bright eyes.

"All right," he said sternly. "Tony got ahead of me. And there's nothing I can do about it, except go to the dance stag. But after this, Miss Ray, you're going to go to all of the dances with me. This is a blanket invitation. I'll ask you separately, for each party, too, but remember, if someone gets ahead of me while I'm out earning my living, you have already been asked."

Betsy laughed, but tremulously. "Why, Joe!"

He seemed pleased with himself. "Tony hasn't made any such proposition, has he?"

"No, but . . ."

"Then what's wrong with it? I have to protect myself, since I'm working every night and most of the weekends. Tony didn't think to make such an invitation or he'd have made it. Willard is smart, that's all. Well, what are you waiting for? You're going to accept, aren't you?"

Betsy was laughing, but she was so perilously close to tears that she stopped. She couldn't possibly agree to this plan, but how could she best explain the impossibility of it?

She looked away from him into the fire.

"I can't do it, Joe," she said. "It isn't that I wouldn't like to. Please listen awfully hard and try to understand."

She paused again, for loyalty to Tony would keep

her from telling the real reason. She couldn't mention her fears for him.

"Tony," she said slowly, "is sort of a brother to us. He comes to our house as though it were his own. And we've been going to parties together off and on for years. I just couldn't freeze him out . . . of everything . . . like that."

She stopped but Joe was silent.

"You know, don't you, Joe," she said honestly, "that I'd rather go with you than anybody? I like Tony . . . too well to hurt him . . . but in a different way from the way I like you."

As Joe still didn't reply, she added, "Take back that blanket invitation. You ask somebody else to the dance and we'll go to plenty of parties this winter if you'll just ask me quickly."

Joe looked at her and slowly his clouded gaze cleared.

"All right," he said, and laughed. "I'll play the field. I'll invite some other girl for this party and still another for the next one, unless you'll go with me yourself to the next one. Would it be fair to ask just one ahead?"

"Perfectly fair," Betsy said.

"All right," Joe repeated. "It's a date."

The slender graying stick broke in the center, sending up a shower of sparks. Again Betsy and Joe felt that accord between them. It would take more than a misunderstanding about Tony, Betsy realized, to break it up.

She felt happy again, but when she thought of going to the senior dance with Tony and of Joe taking some other girl, she didn't feel quite so happy as she had felt before.

She remembered a poem from Junior English about the little rift within the lute.

8

Two Model Young Men

THE DANCE, HOWEVER, was wonderful. Even if she had gone with Joe, Betsy thought, it could hardly have been nicer. The great Maddox invited Tib, to the dismay of Lloyd and Dennie, her last year's cavaliers. Cab, attending by special request of the Class of 1910, invited Tacy to go with him.

Joe, after all, went stag.

"Don't think I'm breaking my promise," he said to

Betsy. "I'm just so darn busy that it doesn't seem worth while asking someone I don't give a . . . Never mind! Never mind! I'll always ask someone else when you go with someone else if you'll let me off this time."

Gladly, Betsy let him off.

It was a wonderful party. Tib and Tacy came to dress at the Ray house, lugging satchels, for they planned to sleep that night in Julia's bed. They laced one another's corsets, tied the fashionable bands around one another's heads. Tib, of course, made Betsy's puffs.

In their pastel-tinted dresses, cut princesse, flaring at the ankles to reveal colored stockings, they looked as modish, Mrs. Ray said, as girls in a fashion magazine.

"You look as pretty as posies," Mr. Ray declared.

"You look puny," cried Anna, coming into the parlor where they were revolving for family inspection. Puny was Anna's word for handsome. She turned to Mrs. Ray. "Don't it make your heart ache, lovey, to think how they're growing up? They'll be leaving us soon."

"Oh, we'll have Margaret," said Mr. Ray. "She'll be starting off to dances."

Margaret was watching with sparkling eyes. She had sat in Betsy's room, quiet as the cat in her arms, all the while they were dressing. She liked it that Betsy was going with Tony, and when Tony came in, his curly black crest brushed to a glitter, a new necktie, an immaculate shirt, his suit pressed to knife-edge sharpness, Margaret smiled delightedly.

Betsy was pleased and a little touched by Tony's splendor.

"He's proud to be going out with me," she thought. "It's very good for him."

The resplendent Maddox arrived with Cab. Tib's light little laugh sounded continuously as the boys helped the girls into their coats and slung the ties of slipper bags over their arms. Tib had not lost her heart. She had a very cool, dependable heart. But she was elated to be escorted by the sensation of the football season. She slipped her hand possessively into his arm and tripped proudly beside him through the pungent autumn evening.

At Schiller Hall, they climbed three flights of stairs, and the girls hung their wraps in the dressing room, changed into slippers, powdered their noses, and went out into the ballroom. Mamie Dodd, who played the piano, tantalized them with chords and snatches of music while programs were being filled. Then she swung zestfully into "I Wonder Who's Kissing Her Now" and couples whirled out over the shining floor.

Waiting for Tony to find her, Betsy watched Tib and Maddox. His dark curls and tall figure, Tib's delicate blondness, made an arresting contrast. Many people were watching them, including the chaperones.

"Aren't they sweet!" Betsy heard Miss Clarke exclaim to Mr. Stewart, who coached the football team and was familiarly known as Stewie.

"Handsome is as handsome does," said Stewie.

"He ought not to play football," Miss Clarke replied indignantly. "Think of that classic nose being broken!"

"He took pretty good care of that classic nose at the Red Feather game," Stewie replied.

Betsy was surprised by that remark. Hadn't Maddox made the only touchdown against Red Feather? But she forgot it as Tony came up. She had always loved dancing with Tony. He was not only light and rhythmic, but gaily inventive.

"You could dance on the stage," Betsy told him as they wove new patterns of movement to match the lilting tune.

Betsy saw Joe watching them and smiled a little anxiously. He smiled reassuringly back.

Joe had approached her as soon as she entered and asked for two dances, all it was proper to ask from another boy's girl. Except for those dances, a waltz and a two-step, he was scrupulously careful to leave her and Tony alone.

Through the whole evening, he didn't dance more than once with anyone but Betsy. He didn't stay with one girl a minute longer than he stayed with any other girl, and he ate supper with Miss Bangeter, Miss Clarke, and Stewie, seeming to enjoy their august company. In fact, he was a model, a perfect example of how the young man turned down by his girl ought to behave . . . if he wanted her to have a wonderful time.

Tony had somehow got wind of the fact that Joe had asked Betsy to the party. He was beginning to be aware of Joe's feeling for Betsy, but he had no inkling of Betsy's feeling for Joe. He took the matter lightly, being well accustomed to rivals at the Ray house. He liked Joe and beckoned him good-naturedly to their circle at supper, but Joe couldn't be won away from the faculty.

Tacy and Tib praised both boys' attitudes as they talked the party over in Betsy's room. Betsy was winding her hair on Magic Wavers and Tib was rubbing cream into her satiny face while Tacy watched benevolently, doing nothing to make herself more beautiful. Her thick auburn braids hung over her shoulders down the blue-striped flannel nightgown.

"Joe and Tony were absolutely noble. That's what they were," said Tib.

"They were perfect Galahads," said Tacy.

"I have a good effect on people. Me and the

Blessed Damozel," said Betsy, fastening the last Waver and beginning on the cream. She applied it with strokes suggested in the women's magazines, upward and outward, smoothing out wrinkles which had not yet appeared, and giving brisk pats with the back of her hand underneath her chin.

"What are you doing that for?" Tacy wanted to know.

"It takes off double chins."

"But you haven't got a double chin. You're as thin as a rail."

"Well, I don't want to get one," said Betsy, and continued to slap vigorously.

"She wouldn't have two boys quarreling about her if she had a double chin," said Tib, beating a tattoo on her own flawless underjaw.

"They didn't quarrel. They were models. That's what we were saying," said Tacy. "I heard lots of compliments about you and Ralph Maddox, too, Tib."

"So did I," said Betsy. "Everyone was watching you."

"We did look nice," Tib acknowledged. "He's certainly handsome. But I'm more interested in his football."

Maddox's honors in that sphere didn't pile up so rapidly as Tib would have wished. Football games dotted the calendar, but Deep Valley just couldn't seem to win. The team was admittedly weak, and at first nobody blamed Maddox. But soon disappointment in him began to find expression.

He played right half. He was a magnificent broken field runner and in every game made at least one spectacular touchdown. He was beautiful cutting trickily down field, dodging this tackle, stiff-arming that. But the tricky runs never added up to enough first downs to beat the enemy, and the spectacular touchdowns never added up to enough points to win the game.

And then suddenly, all in a day, the school was talking about the amazing fact that Maddox never got banged up. Dave's nose was knocked south-by-west, Stan lost a tooth, and Dennie always had one black eye when he hadn't two. But Maddox came out of every battle his handsome, perfect self.

Perhaps Stewie had started the talk with that remark which others besides Betsy had overheard. "He took pretty good care of that classic nose at the Red Feather game."

Stewie had followed this up with another cryptic comment to Maddox himself one afternoon during football practice.

"The great mystery, Maddox," he had said, "is that a marvelous runner like you ever is tackled." Maddox had colored in gratification, but he colored deeper with some other emotion when Stewie said, "Mystery is right! Because you have a genius for ending every run out of bounds."

He had said in almost so many words that Maddox shied away from the bruising body contacts which the other men in the backfield accepted with a grin, sometimes twisted with pain, but a grin nevertheless.

Betsy talked the scandal over with Joe.

"Don't make any mistake," Joe cautioned her. "Maddox isn't yellow. But he just plain doesn't want to spoil that classic phiz. So he doesn't like to hit that line. He doesn't like to block. And he doesn't like to tackle. Above all, of course, he doesn't like to be tackled. My guess is that at St. John his team didn't have much competition and he could win with tricky, fast running and never risk his beauty."

"We simply can't go on losing games like this."

"No, we can't." Joe's eyes darkened, and Betsy knew he longed to be on the team. Over the autumn she had realized more and more plainly what it had meant to him not to play football.

Since he couldn't play, he was throwing his heart into his newspaper stories. If rhetoric had been able to win, Deep Valley would have had a championship team. But none of Joe's fighting descriptions stirred Maddox. As October progressed, Deep Valley continued to lose.

When the maples rose like flames along High Street and the hills were russet and gold, the Rays drove out to Murmuring Lake. They went every year at this season to celebrate Mr. and Mrs. Ray's wedding anniversary. It was a little hard to make the familiar excursion with Julia so far away. But they went, and when they had started they enjoyed it heartily.

Betsy told Joe all about it that evening after their return. They were making fudge, or rather, Joe was making it. He scorned Betsy's cooking and fancied his own, so he took charge of the bubbling pan while Betsy watched from the kitchen table.

Joe smiled as he stirred.

"You go every year? Your father and mother must be glad they got married."

"They certainly are," Betsy said. "They always show us where they got engaged. Papa was camping with some other young men on the lake shore and he came up to the house to borrow a cup of salt. Mamma says he didn't need the salt at all. Papa says they needed it desperately. Anyhow, they sat down under an oak tree in the moonlight and got engaged. They always show us the tree."

"Did he get the salt?"

"He went off and forgot it."

"What else do they show you?" asked Joe.

"They show us the bay window where they were

married," Betsy answered dreamily. "It looks down a long avenue of evergreens to the big front gate. Mamma's room was just above it and she says that on her wedding day she sat in an upper window and looked down that avenue, waiting for Papa to come. She was wearing a tea gown, she says. At last she saw a pair of dappled gray horses and a surrey with Papa driving. He had hired a livery rig, a very stylish one."

"He wasn't so rich as your mother's stepfather," Joe suggested, "if he had to hire a livery rig."

"He certainly wasn't," Betsy replied. "He came from an Iowa farm, one of eleven children, and his mother died when he was a boy. She asked him to look out for his sisters and he did.

"He came up to Deep Valley to work and sent money home so his sisters could go to school. Papa wanted to be a lawyer. He would have made a good one, too, but he couldn't afford to go to college himself."

Joe listened thoughtfully, still stirring.

"By and by, though," Betsy said, "his sisters all got educated, and he started his shoe store, and he met this red-haired Julia Warrington, and they fell in love and got married."

"Did your grandfather object?" Joe asked.

Betsy laughed out loud. "Heavens, no!" she said. "How could anyone object to Papa? Grandpa Newton knew that character is more important than money."

"Character's all we've ever had in our family," Joe replied.

It occurred to Betsy that there was a similarity between her father and Joe Willard. Both of them had been forced to be independent when they were very young, and it had given them strength beyond their youth. Both of them, without money, had made themselves persons of quality. Bob Ray had married Julia Warrington. And any girl in school would have been proud to go with Joe Willard. The rich and fashionable Phyllis Brandish had considered him a catch.

"Tell me about your father and mother, Joe," Betsy said.

But again she found herself facing the stone wall of his reticence. He smiled off her request.

"I've read about families like yours," he remarked. "I've learned about all sorts of people from books. Did I ever tell you about the time I resolved to read every book in the library?"

"No. Do," Betsy replied.

She knew that during the years he had been going to high school he had rented a room from a widow in the north end of town. Mrs. Blair had been kind to him, but his real home had been the library. Miss Sparrow, the librarian, was one of his closest friends. He had learned about the world, he had molded his ideals, he had even acquired his manners from the dozens and hundreds of books, books without number, he had read day in and day out, week in and week out, in the Deep Valley Library.

"I was about fourteen," he said, dropping a spoonful of fudge into cold water. "I started with the A's, progressed to the B's, and read straight along the shelves. I bogged down about the time I reached the M's."

"Mrs. Muhlbach was too much for you," Betsy joked.

"Not a bit of it. I liked the old girl. It was George Barr McCutcheon who stopped me."

The fudge had formed a ball in the cold water, so Joe poured it into a pan which Betsy had already buttered. They left it on the back porch and went into the dining room and sat down before the fire.

"While we're waiting for that fudge to harden," said Joe, "tell me some more about your family." He liked to hear about the traditions, the holidays, the family jokes, and the simple everyday doings of the Rays.

There were evenings by the fire with Joe and evenings by the piano with Tony. It wasn't bad, Betsy decided, having two boys crazy about you. She wondered why the idea had distressed her so much at first.

Beverly of Graustark came to the Opera House

and Joe took her to see it. Tony asked her, too, but he was philosophical about it when she said she was already engaged.

"That Willard and his passes!" he said. "Oh, well! I'll sit in the peanut gallery and throw shells at the two of you."

The Red Mill came and this time Tony got ahead of Joe. Betsy was almost glad he had. The music wove a tender, glowing tapestry of all the happy hours she and Tony had shared. They had sung these songs together around the Ray piano and out on Murmuring Lake.

> "Not *that you are fair, dear,*
> Not *that you are true,*
> Not *your golden hair, dear,*
> Not *your eyes of blue....*"

Tony leaned toward her to whisper, "I don't think they can come up to us. What do you think, Ray of Sunshine?" That was the nickname he had given her when they were freshmen.

"They can't come up to *you*," Betsy replied.

She meant it. When the Governor sang, "Every day is ladies' day with me," he didn't make it half so dashing as Tony had always made it. Even the two comedians, although she laughed at them until she wept, were no funnier than Tony could be when he tried.

The mill wheel, turning awesomely, carried the Burgomeister's daughter to her lover.

Betsy and Tony had a wonderful time and they sang the duet with nostalgic fervor all the way up the Plum Street hill.

> *"When you ask the reason,*
> *Words are all too few. . . ."*

No, it wasn't half bad, having two beaus.

9

"Tonight Will Never Come Again"

MADDOX DID not improve.

Deep Valley played Wells, it played Faribault, it played Blue Earth, and the scores didn't get better. They got worse. The seniors were desperate.

"We simply have to win a few games," said Betsy, as a subdued Crowd marched toward Lloyd's automobile after the Blue Earth game. "Just think! This is the last year we'll be coming out to this old field."

"We've been coming for four long years!" Tacy sighed.

"And Betsy still doesn't know a touchdown from a field goal," said Tib, at which Betsy began to chase her, and their gray and violet skull caps fell off.

The Crowd gathered at the Rays' after the Blue Earth game, Dave, Stan, and Dennie bruised and battered, Maddox unimpaired. Joe dropped in late, followed by Cab, who took as much interest in the team as though he were still in school. They drank cocoa and talked football, but no one any longer tried to think up loyal excuses for the defeat. Everyone knew that as soon as Maddox took himself off, the storm of gossip would break. And it did.

"What's the matter with Maddox, anyway?"

"I thought he was supposed to be such a miracle man."

"He's afraid of getting his hair mussed, if you ask me," said Dennie.

Tib said nothing, but she was frowning. Perhaps, thought Betsy, she was getting a little soured on manly beauty unaccompanied by manly achievements. Or perhaps she really liked him and was worried.

At school the pep meetings no longer rang with cries of, "What's the matter with Maddox? He's all right!" He still made most of the touchdowns, but he didn't, all agreed, "pitch in and fight." Someone even hazarded that he had come over from St. John just to injure the Deep Valley team. It was a plot.

"Do you believe that?" Betsy asked Joe.

"Of course not," Joe replied. "He wants Deep Valley to win, but his school spirit isn't strong enough to make him risk that profile."

Joe was depressed. Even his vigorous pen was running out of hopeful excuses and bright prospects for the Deep Valley eleven.

Fortunately, there were school activities other than football, and Betsy was persistently urging Joe to enter them. "The president of the senior class," she said, "should really go out for debating . . . he ought to sing in the chorus . . . he ought to write a paper for rhetoricals. . . ."

"Look," Joe would interrupt, "I'm earning my living. Remember?"

But because school was important to Betsy it became more and more important to Joe. Busy as he was, he found time not only for school activities but also for the aimless, carefree loafing of normal high school students.

On Halloween, he telephoned Betsy in high spirits. "Say, I hear that the juniors are having a dance. Strictly for juniors. Seniors are urged to keep out."

"If you mean what I think you mean," said Betsy, "Tib and Dennie have the same idea."

"All right," answered Joe, "we'll make it a quartet. I'll be up about nine."

It was raining then, but with evening it cleared. Mr. Ray had made Margaret a jack-o'-lantern, and they started out, her eyes shining in a delicious ecstasy of boldness and fear.

Jack-o'-lanterns began to pop up in windows. The doorbell began to ring, but when it was answered the threshold was empty. By the time Tib and Dennie, Betsy and Joe left the house, the dark wet world was filled with the muffled laughter, the rattling and tapping and running feet of Halloween.

The four trouped downtown, and standing outside Schiller Hall, looked up at the lighted windows. They could hear a faint sound of music.

"Here goes!" said Joe, squaring his shoulders with extravagant valor.

As they tiptoed up the stairs, the music became clearer. Mamie was playing a wistful waltz.

"Tonight will never come again,
To you . . . and me. . . ."

They reached the fourth floor and peeked into the lighted ballroom. Jack-o'-lanterns, black cats, and orange streamers made a festive picture. The junior girls looked pretty in their long floating party dresses. Betsy and Tib were wearing tams and coats.

Mamie's music sang on.

> "*Tonight will never come again,*
> *To you . . . and me. . . .*"

The two couples danced boldly into the ballroom. Before they had half circled the room the storm broke. Mamie stopped playing, and jumped up from the piano stool, laughing, to watch. Every junior boy in the room had made a rush for Joe and Dennie, who were heading for the door sheltering the senior girls.

Biff! Boom! Bang! Presently the music began again, but only juniors were dancing now. Down at the foot of the stairs in the moonlight, the discomfited seniors were disentangling themselves, trying to make out what had happened and whose foot was whose. As they limped toward Heinz's, they heard Mamie playing.

> "*Tonight will never come again,*
> *To you . . . and me. . . .*"

"Let us hope not!" groaned Tib.

At Heinz's they had the sort of fun that Betsy had

grown up with but which was still unfamiliar to Joe. Heinz's had invented an enormous sundae, The Imperial, which cost fifty cents. The two couples ordered one Imperial with four spoons and raced to see who would consume the biggest share.

"I win!" cried Tib, spooning the last cherry.

"What do you mean, you win?" asked Joe, beating off Dennie to scrape the dish.

"What ho, minion! Another!" shouted Dennie. "At least I've got a quarter. Have you, Joe?"

The waiter brought another, calling out good-naturedly, "Take it easy, kids! Take it easy!"

The four walked up the long hill to the Ray house. The Halloween excitement was subsiding now. There were reminders only in the soap marks on doors and windows and the noise of a distant party.

In spite of the Imperials, they went straight to Anna's kitchen and found half a cake. They sat on the kitchen table to eat it, talking and fooling. After Tib and Dennie left, Joe stayed on. Mrs. Ray had to cough several times at the top of the stairs before he went home.

Rain now had taken down the last of the withered leaves. Except for a few oaks, the trees showed bare against the sky. Slowly the world grew browner, the weather colder and more wintry.

Snow started falling. A filmy white blanket on the

ground startled the eye with its half-forgotten, half-familiar beauty.

"It always makes me feel queer to smell the first heat in the registers and see the first snow," Betsy said.

Mr. Ray put on the storm windows. Children got out sleds and everyone got out overshoes. Duck hunters were undeterred by snow, and Deep Valley kitchens were filled with savory odors. Betsy began to hint for invitations to dinner at the Mullers'. No one could bake wild duck as Matilda could, stuffed with apples and served with dumplings and gravy.

Football players slipped and slid on a snowy field, and Deep Valley lost to Faribault. This was the last home game, and it had been preceded by elaborate goings on. There was a big rooters' meeting, and the school marched to the field in a body with the band at the head of the procession. But all to no avail! The score was forty to nothing.

There was only one game left now, the St. John game. It would be a slaughter, everyone agreed. St. John had an undefeated team. Moreover, it was Maddox's old home town.

"We're lucky if he doesn't throw the game," said Lloyd when the Crowd was gathered in the Social Room and neither Tib nor Maddox happened to be present.

"Certainly it's the last team he can be expected to fight," Tony replied.

"He doesn't know the meaning of the word fight," said Dennie. "All he knows is how to comb those curly locks."

"Somebody ought to wake him up," said Stan. "He'd be darned good if he'd only get going."

"All he cares about is combing his hair," repeated Dennie, and suddenly his eyes brightened. He ran his hands through his own curly thatch and dimples flashed out in his cheeks. He looked maliciously cherubic.

"Hey, listen to this!" he said. The four boys fell into a whispered confab.

"What are you kids talking about?" Winona asked.

"Never mind," they replied, walking away.

"Where are you going?"

"To find Stewie. Say, you can come along if you like."

"Can all of us come?" asked Betsy.

"No," said Dennie. "Just Winona. She can be Florence Nightingale." The boys guffawed with laughter, and hooking arms with Winona, they hurried away.

Betsy, Tacy, Irma, and Alice looked at one another. "What can they be up to?" Alice asked.

On the day before the St. John game, Miss Bangeter called another pep rally. The students filed in dejectedly, sure that no matter how loudly they sang and cheered, Deep Valley would lose again. The team sat on the platform looking uncomfortable, with Maddox, as ravishingly handsome as ever, in the center of the front row. Stewie kept running his finger around the inside of his collar.

Miss Bangeter made a speech. The St. John game, she said, was the last one of the season, and the school must remain loyal to the end. Whether or not the team would win wasn't half so important as how the school would support them. She hoped that a large delegation of students would go to St. John for the game.

It was a fine speech, a noble speech. Miss Bangeter made everyone want to support the team. But she didn't convince anyone that the team could possibly win.

Stewie, too, failed, although he perspired and grew red in the face and talked long and hard. Various boys and girls made stump speeches. They praised the team, making everyone squirm, including the heroes themselves.

Joe didn't get up, although Betsy urged and poked him. He just sat and looked blue. But at last Miss Bangeter beckoned him to the platform.

"The president of the senior class," she said, "must always have a word."

Joe stood up and grinned. "I remember one time when the president of the senior class didn't have a word, and that was at the junior dance," he said.

This was uproariously received, and Joe's speech was snappy. But it didn't inspire the audience with confidence. The gloom in the Assembly Room could have been cut with a knife.

"Gangway!"

"Clear the track ahead!"

"Is there a doctor in the house?"

A jumble of cries caused all heads to turn. Everyone started up in excitement as four shouting boys came down the middle aisle carrying a stretcher on which reposed a recumbent form in football uniform.

"It's a dummy."

"He's wearing a St. John sweater."

"It must be a skit. Thank heaven!" Betsy remarked. "This deadly meeting!" Then she grasped Tacy's arm. "Why, there's Winona."

Winona was, indeed, swinging along behind the stretcher, looking taller, thinner, more debonaire even than usual in a nurse's uniform. A chic white cap was perched on her black hair. Her eyes glittered with fun.

She raced to keep alongside the patient, fanning him, applying sticking plaster, and dousing him from a big bottle marked ARNICA. The Assembly Room roared.

"Is there a doctor in the house?" Dennie kept shouting as he and his companion stretcher bearers rushed up the steps at the left of the platform. Up the right-hand steps strolled a figure in a long white coat. He wore wire spectacles and brandished a carving knife.

"Dr. Carver at your service," he said in Tony's deep voice. "And who is the patient, lad?"

Dennie put down his corner of the stretcher and shook sweat from his brow with his forefinger, bringing another laugh.

"A player from the St. John team, doc. I fear he's at death's door."

"Tell me what happened, lad, before I start to carve him up," said Tony, flashing the knife.

"Yes, doc. Yes, doc." Dennie could not quite hold back a grin.

"This poor John Doe here was carrying the ball," he said. "He was slamming down field for a touchdown with ten of the Deep Valley eleven on his heels. The score was tied. A score meant a St. John victory. The crowd on the sidelines was going crazy.

"This poor John Doe has slammed to within ten yards of the goal line. But who bars his way? It is Deep Valley's safety man! It is our famous, our invincible, our fearless hell-for-leather hero! It is Maddox!" Dennie roared the name like a sideshow barker. The audience applauded half-heartedly. Maddox shifted in his seat, and a line of puzzlement marred his perfect brow.

"Maddox, it is!" Dennie went on after a brief pause to fill his lungs. "And John Doe halts. He pales. He trembles. He freezes. He is duck soup. All the Deep Valley rooters know he is and yell in relief. Maddox is going to save the game. But . . ."

And with that "But" Dennie paused while the puzzlement deepened on Maddox's brow and spread to the upturned faces of the pep rally. "But what is this? Maddox ain't making the tackle. He has John Doe cold, but he is giving John time to warm up. Instead of tackling, he speaks!"

Dennie's mobile face, his staring eyes, his wide-open mouth all registered consternation.

"He speaks!" Dennie repeated. "And what is this he is saying? No!" Dennie's voice rose to a hoarse shout. "No! No! It cannot be. But . . ." And now Dennie's stricken eyes swept his audience. "But it is. He is saying . . . ! Yes, he really is saying . . ."

Again a pause. But now the consternation faded from Dennie's face. He smiled sweetly. His hand rockered over his head to suggest curls. Then he spoke, in a stage whisper that swept the auditorium, "'PARDON ME, SIR, BUT MAY I BORROW YOUR COMB?'"

For one instant the school sat stunned. Then it

went wild. It shrieked with laughter. It shouted, clapped, and pounded with unholy glee. The team laughed, too, unwillingly, but a deep flush crept into Maddox's face. He looked around with a bewildered expression and forced himself to smile.

"How mean!" Betsy whispered indignantly to Tacy.

"He had it coming," said Hazel Smith, wiping her eyes.

"I think it was terrible," said Tacy. She and Betsy were not only suffering for Maddox but also for Tib, and as soon as the meeting broke up they rushed to find her.

But Tib was rushing away.

"Where are you going?"

"To catch Ralph. He's got to get out and play at that St. John game. He'll never live this down if he doesn't." There were round red circles on Tib's cheeks. "I'm going to talk to him," she declared. "I'm going to say, 'If you don't win this game, my fine curly-headed friend, I won't go with you any more! Not ever again.'"

"But he can't possibly win it," said Betsy. "St. John has an undefeated team."

"He has to," said Tib, and started running again.

10

The St. John Game

MISS BANGETER'S REQUEST for a loyal attendance at
the St. John game was heeded far beyond her ex-
pectations. The depot platform, next morning, was
crowded with boys and girls. It was a cold day with a
driving north wind. The seniors had abandoned their
gray and violet caps. Boys wore heavy woolen caps
with ear muffs. Girls wore stocking caps, or tams, or
hats tied down with automobile veils. All wore neck
scarfs, galoshes, woolen mittens, heavy winter coats.

Maroon and gold rosettes, or maroon and gold bows with long flying ends, graced every coat. There were dozens of Deep Valley banners, a few horns. But in spite of these brave trappings, hopes were low. The team huddled about Stewie, down at the end of the platform. Joe, as a *Sun* reporter, stayed with the team. Maddox stood close to the coach, speaking to no one. There were bitter creases on either side of his beautiful, unblemished mouth.

Rooters asked one another how yesterday's joke had affected Maddox. Most people thought it was deserved, but some considered it ill-advised. It might have made him so mad that he would throw the game.

"I doubt that," said Alice mildly.

"It must have taken all the heart out of him, though," Betsy insisted, and Tacy agreed. Tib didn't speak. She still looked grim.

On the train, spirits lifted a little. The car was warm; no one minded smoke or cinders. Rooters ate Cracker Jack and drank at the water cooler. Lolling in the red plush seats, they practised cheers. Someone had brought a banjo and Winona started a song. Only the team remained gloomy, still huddled around Stewie at one end of the car. Maddox's mouth was still enclosed by bitter parentheses, and he kept his gaze fixed on the window.

Betsy, too, looked out of the window as the train sped along beside the river. Muskrats had built houses at the water's edge. Willows touched the pale landscape with yellow.

She stole these glances guiltily, aware that she should be thinking only of the game. She knew that her interest in football would always be pretended, not real and burning, like Joe's or Winona's. She wanted to win, and she liked the excitement, but she liked the flying landscape more.

St. John was only the second station up the line. Shortly the train was running past small houses and snow-covered gardens. The brakeman looked into the car to bawl, "St. John the next stop!" and with a shriek of brakes, the train jerked to a halt.

As the crowd spilled out of the train, Tacy took Betsy's arm and Tib's. "Just think how often we've planned about traveling together, and now we're doing it!" she said.

Everyone thought it was exciting to be in another town. They walked up and down the Main Street which was so like and yet so unlike Deep Valley's Front Street. There were the same rows of store fronts; banks, big and impressive on the corners; a hotel and the brand new Motion Picture Palace, and a livery stable down the street. The kinds of stores and shops were just the same, but there wasn't a familiar name or face until Winona caught sight of a cousin.

"Poor old St. John! Poor old St. John!" she began to chant.

"You've got your nerve!" he said. "St. John hasn't lost a game this year and your team isn't worth peanuts."

The Crowd roared defiance, "Poor old St. John! Poor old St. John!" The cousin laughed and turned away, and the Crowd went into a bakery and bought cakes and cookies, cream puffs and jelly roll to take out to the field.

This was swept by a biting wind filled with small sharp flakes. The ground was frozen and looked cruel. Betsy saw Joe moving efficiently about, bareheaded, copy paper handy as usual, his windblown face set.

She ran over to him. "How's Maddox?"

"He doesn't talk. I guess it cut him pretty deep."

"Tib lectured him, too."

"Well," said Joe, "he had it coming, but I can't help feeling sorry for the guy."

The St. John players looked very big and confident. The Deep Valley players looked unhappy and cold. While the teams warmed up, the Deep Valley rooters cheered, but the cheering was half-hearted.

Deep Valley kicked off, and the St. John receiver

jockeyed from his own ten to his own forty-five yard line before Dennie brought him down. Deep Valley cheered again, but still half-heartedly.

"Thirty-five yards on the kick-off!" Winona groaned. "The final score will be a million to nothing."

On the next play, St. John drove through tackle, made only a couple of yards. On the next, trying left end, St. John got exactly a foot. Then St. John was stopped in its tracks.

And now, Deep Valley's cheers had a new note— a spontaneous, excited note. Not because, with the fourth down coming up, St. John must kick. Not because St. John, that invincible, that unstoppable eleven, had been held. But because one Deep Valley player had been in on all three plays, had jammed ruggedly into each St. John ball carrier, hauling him up short as much as to say, "Where do you think you're going, Bub?" And that player was Maddox.

"Maddox! Maddox! Maddox! Maddox!" The frenzied repetition lifted into the cold air, rolled across the frozen field, and Maddox waved a hand as though to signal, "Wait till you see what comes next!" Nor did he try to conceal the fact that his lovely underlip, unmarred through all the season, was now as fat as a slab of liver from rude contact with some St. John knee, or hip or shoulder, or maybe even knuckles.

Betsy, quick with a quotation which would have delighted Miss Bangeter, flung exultant arms about Tib, "Richard is himself again!" And Tib, hugging Betsy in return, shrieked "An eye for an eye!" and thought that she, too, was quoting Shakespeare.

Well, if it wasn't an eye for an eye, it was almost exactly Richard, himself, again. Led by a brand new, or perhaps the original, Maddox, as opposed to the one previously on display, Deep Valley did what no other team had been able to do all season. It held St. John's giants, that irresistible force, to one touchdown and a field goal in the first half.

The score, according to the point system used in those days, was 8 to 0.

During the intermission, Deep Valley rooters made the gray sky ring. They talked feverishly, rushed to get information.

"What's happened?" Betsy asked Joe. "What's got into Maddox?"

He beamed into her face, although she felt sure he hardly saw her.

"Plenty!" he cried. "Plenty!"

She couldn't keep him by her side. He would pause for a moment and then he was gone, shouting, cheering, groaning.

Lloyd returned from a visit to the team.

"That lip of Ralph's is bad."

"What's he going to do? Go out of the game?"

"Not a bit of it," he answered, as though the question were absurd. "You couldn't get Maddox out of this game with a corkscrew."

The second half began in an atmosphere of tingling excitement. But in spite of Deep Valley's furious resistance, St. John made another touchdown. They kicked goal and the score stood 14 to 0. Despite furious struggle it was still 14 to 0, with ten minutes of the final half to play.

Oddly enough, Deep Valley wasn't discouraged. It had expected to lose, and it found consolation in the magnificent, unbelievable performance of Maddox. He hadn't stopped St. John. But no one could stop St. John. Defeat was inevitable. Therefore, the sensible course was to find joy in Maddox and let the score go Gallagher.

And Maddox was magnificent! No longer was he protecting his profile. He thought nothing today of his ravishing nose. He did not care a hang for his beautiful mouth, his beguiling eyes. The profile was a smear, part red, part mud. The nose was a blob. His mouth had been banged, swatted, slugged, and probably jumped on until it was less mouth than pucker. His left eye was closed tighter than a drum.

But the right eye of Maddox, the once-again great Maddox, was wide open and full of fire and fight. With the score 14 to 0 and ten minutes to play, it surveyed the battle field with heroic confidence.

St. John had just scored its second touchdown, and Deep Valley was waiting for the kickoff. Close to his own goal line, Maddox balanced lightly, and his voice charged through his fellow players like an electric shock.

"Come on, guys! Three touchdowns in ten minutes. Don't tell me we can't do it!"

St. John kicked and Maddox received. And he ran. He ran like a veteran fox. He sliced left from the fifteen-yard line until he was almost out of bounds but twenty yards forward. Thereafter nobody, not even the watchful Joe, could have told how he went. But everybody knew that in a riot of cheers from Deep Valley and groans from St. John he went this way and that, stiff-arming half a dozen tacklers for a touchdown. A moment later he kicked goal.

Deep Valley called time out. The smear on Maddox's face was more crimson than ever. Somewhere in his eighty-five-yard run Maddox had hit something with his face. Something almost beyond belief had happened to that underlip. Stewie trotted onto the field and Joe ran after him. The crowd watched the conference, saw Dennie swing a fond hand across Maddox's muddy shoulder.

Joe came back for a breathless moment later to report the conversation.

"Better come out, son," Stewie had said.

Maddox had laughed. If there was a touch of histrionics in the laugh he was entitled to it.

"Tape me up," he said. "I'll hold together. But," he added, grinning at Dennie, "don't bother to bring any comb."

That was when Dennie had hugged him.

Dennie kicked off. It was a beautiful kick, high and deep into a corner. A St. John player took it on the four-yard line, ran into destruction, and the ball exploded out of his arms and bobbled sidewise, free and more inviting than a star sapphire.

It was Maddox who had made the tackle, and it was Maddox, scrambling like a frog, who recovered the fumble. It was Maddox who carried the ball on the next play, with head lowered, like a frantic bull, to plough over for a second touchdown. This time he missed the kick and the score stood St. John 14, Deep Valley 11.

Once again he refused to go out of the game when Stewie came trotting onto the field to worry over that lip.

"How much more time have we got?" Maddox asked (and Joe repeated).

"Six minutes."

"I can do it," Maddox said, and although earlier that season the whole team would have resented the first person singular, now everyone conceded his right to it.

"He said it as calmly as he might have said, 'Give me a malted milk,'" Joe reported, and the whole Deep Valley rooting section was sure he would make another touchdown.

But not calmly sure. The Deep Valley rooting section now was made up entirely of maniacs. These banged one another on the head, beat one another on the shoulders, stamped, waved arms and blankets, even tossed overshoes in the air, although any rooter with any sense must have realized that in a little while overshoeless feet would turn to five-toed icicles.

"Maddox! Maddox! Maddox!" The urgent yell—mingled treble and bass—soared up and up.

Deep Valley kicked off again. This time Dennie did less well. A St. John player took the kick behind nice interference on the twenty-yard line and moved to the thirty. And on three plays, the big, bold St. John backfield, aided by the big, bold St. John line, moved twelve yards more. On the next three plays, the same combination made a second first down. On the next three, a third, then a fourth.

Now with the ball on Deep Valley's twenty-two, St. John struck again, off tackle; but this time Deep Valley gave only a yard. Rather, Maddox gave. He was in on the runner like a heavy, tired battering ram. Nor did St. John gain much on the next play or the next; only a yard each time. So it was Deep Valley's ball, on Deep Valley's nineteen-yard line. It was eighty-one yards to go for a touchdown. And once again Maddox asked his same question.

"How much time?"

"Four minutes."

Joe came back with the story.

"I can't run with the ball any more," Maddox said. "Not a long run. My legs are giving out. But look! We'll do it this way. Listen!"

They listened, and agreed, and to the confusion of St. John's followers and the delight of the Deep Valley rooters, hoarse now, but still able to rasp out some sort of roar, they did it Maddox's way.

Maddox smashed six yards through center, his lip crimson, bare of tape because he would not stop to patch it. Stan made three off tackle, because St. John was set to stop not him, but Maddox. Dennie made a first down, loping wide around left end for the same reason. That brought Deep Valley to its own thirty-five-yard line.

Maddox smashed through center, and lost his helmet but would not bother to pick it up. Dave, long, light, and swift, duplicated Dennie's earlier lope. It was first down again on Deep Valley's forty-seven. And so, with Maddox smashing just often enough to make St. John watch him, while Stan, Dennie, or Dave loped the needed distance, Deep Valley got to St. John's forty-yard line, to the twenty-five, and the twelve, and finally the two.

Off on the side line, Betsy and Tacy were screaming, but Tib was standing as stiffly silent as a triumphant little blond school teacher who had succeeded in larruping her class's biggest boy. Joe was watching coolly on the flank, his penciled notes accurate and precise, but his eyes flashing. And all around, Deep Valley rooters even in advance of victory were taunting the sons and daughters of St. John, dejected now even in advance of defeat.

There was a pause, and once more Joe brought back the story.

"You take it over, Ralph," said Stan.

"That's right," said Dave. "You take it, Ralph. We'll open a hole." And the breathless line, gathered around, echoed him. "We'll open a hole."

Maddox looked at them with affection, but his

smeared face, with its incredible lip, set decisively.

"Nope," he said. "I'll open the hole, with some help from the rest of you. Dennie will go for the touchdown."

"No!" cried Dennie. "Say! I've just been going along for the ride."

"You rode me, kid," Maddox said. "But I had it coming and now you're going to get what you wanted."

They couldn't talk him down. That was the way it was. Dennie took the ball, Maddox ran interference, shouldered one tackler out of the way, rammed another full, and, falling, had his nose almost ripped by Dennie's cleats as Dennie's feet flashed through the hole Maddox had made to victory. Dave kicked goal. The final score was Deep Valley 17, St. John 14.

On the St. John side of the field, loyal rooters tried to cheer and didn't do badly. In the Deep Valley section, the cheers were better than good. Everyone was jumping up and down and screaming. Tib wasn't only screaming; she was crying. She kept wiping her eyes and blowing her nose but she didn't seem to know that she was doing it. She kept right on cheering through it all.

Maddox tried to walk off the field but found himself seized by strong, affectionate, and perhaps apologetic hands. Then he was up on the shoulders of Stan and Dave and three or four more. That was the way he went off the field.

The Deep Valley rooters cake-walked off behind him. They cake-walked up Main Street and all who could crowd in had supper in a restaurant which was only slightly less noisy than the football field had been. Winona started a game of drop the handkerchief under an arc light, and they waited for their train at the depot in the midst of bedlam, while chaperoning teachers looked on with sympathetic mirth.

On the return trip, Maddox sat with Tib. His left eye was green, blue, and black, and an enormous bandage covered his lip. Tib's hand was slipped through his arm. She was preening her yellow head.

The other girls hung over him. Even Irma came.

"How did you ever do it?" she asked, her large eyes soft and adoring.

Tib nudged her and clapped her hands lightly.

"Shoo!" she whispered. "Shoo!"

Maddox turned his battered head stiffly to look down at Tib and smile.

11

"Cheer Up"

IT WAS FORTUNATE THAT November was cold, with
snow on the ground and an icy bite in the air, for the
Rays had to create some early Christmas spirit. Julia's
box must be mailed by the first of December. And it
must be crammed with love and fun and the feeling of
home, for Julia was homesick.

In spite of the luxury at the Von Hetternichs', in

spite of her joy at studying in Germany, she was homesick, as she had been at the State University. It was torturing, she said, to be homesick all the time and yet not want to come home.

She definitely didn't want to come home. She was studying the role of Susanna in Mozart's *The Marriage of Figaro*, and loved it. But Deep Valley, the green house on High Street, held her more firmly than she had dreamed they would when she went out into the Great World.

"Oh, dear!" she wrote. "I dread Christmas Day both for you and for me. I'm sorrier for myself, though. You have only me to be lonesome for, but I have each separate one of you to long for and be sorry I was ever bad to."

"As though she was ever bad to any of us!" said Mrs. Ray.

Betsy, feeling weepy, said briskly, "She certainly needs that motto, Margaret."

Margaret was embroidering a motto for Julia. "Cheer Up," it said. Betsy was embroidering one for her father that said, "Don't Worry," in black thread tricked out with red French knots. No one ever worried less than Mr. Ray, and Betsy was very poor at sewing. But all the girls were making mottos, and so Betsy was making one. Whether it would be finished in time for Christmas was problematical. She lost her needle, tangled her thread, pricked her finger, and dripped blood.

"You don't need to bother with French knots. Just keep on pricking your finger," Tacy joked.

Margaret's motto was a model of neatness. Every day when she came in from school, after she had practised her piano lesson and petted the dog and cat, she sat down in her rocker and embroidered.

Mrs. Ray was making Julia a waist, silk, of a violet-blue which matched her eyes. Betsy had bought her a set of collar pins. Anna was stuffing dates and making nougat.

Mr. Ray was sending an extra check. It was what Julia had asked for. She had not realized until she went to Europe how many different kinds of lessons were necessary if you were going to be an opera singer.

By the time the box had gone, Thanksgiving was upon them. This year it was the Slades' turn to entertain. The Rays alternated Thanksgiving dinner with their friends, the Slades.

Betsy liked the arrangement, for Tom was just her age. He always came back from Cox Military full of the latest slang. This year he said, "Curses, Jack Dalton! Give me the child!"

Tom was a large boy, with rough dark hair and thick glasses. In his uniform he was meticulously neat; he had to be. But he didn't like being neat, and in "civvies" he was always rumpled. He liked to read and play the violin.

He was a very old friend. He had sat behind Betsy and Tacy in kindergarten. He liked Tacy.

"Let's go up to the Kellys'," he said off-handedly, after Thanksgiving dinner was over.

The Kelly house was crowded with brothers and sisters home for the holidays. Tom and Betsy were warmly welcomed and offered nuts, chocolates, apples, and spare pieces of pie. But Tacy paid more attention to Betsy than she did to Tom.

"I don't seem to get anywhere with Tacy," Tom burst out, as he and Betsy started home through the gray November dusk.

"Oh, Tacy's like that. She doesn't make a fuss over anybody."

"She makes a fuss over you."

"With boys, I mean. She likes you a lot, Tom."

"Well, she certainly doesn't act it," growled Tom. "Not that it matters! The world is full of girls."

Betsy couldn't permit that. "Not redheaded ones with big Irish eyes," she said.

Tom burst out laughing. "Curses, Jack Dalton!" he said.

The next day Betsy was going to have coffee with Tib, but she went to the Kelly house first. She maneuvered to get Tacy alone and with what she considered great tact brought the conversation around to Tom.

"Dearest Chuck," she said, "if you don't mind a suggestion, you ought to be nicer to Tom."

"Why, Sweet My Coz?" Tacy inquired.

"Well, he's a nice boy. And he likes you. And everybody's going with somebody."

"I don't want to go with anybody."

"You like him, don't you?"

"No more than I do anybody else," said Tacy honestly. "I like Cab and Dennie and Tony and Tom . . . all those boys I know well."

Betsy grew earnest. "You'd better look out. Tom is too desirable a boy to keep running after a girl who treats him like a stick of wood."

"I don't treat him like a stick of wood," said Tacy. "But I certainly don't feel mushy about him."

"He'll start rushing somebody else."

"Let him!"

"But, Tacy, who would take you to the holiday parties?"

"Nobody, probably, and I don't give a hoot," said Tacy serenely.

The puzzle was that this was true. Tacy liked the Crowd, she liked fun, but she just didn't like boys, not in the way the other girls did.

Betsy and Tib talked it over later at coffee. The Mullers had coffee every afternoon. Betsy had acquired the delicious vice in Milwaukee. There were usually cakes—apple cake or coffee cake sprinkled with sugar and cinnamon. At the very least, there were delectable cookies.

Betsy, who had a sweet tooth, dropped in often, and her visits were mirth-filled occasions, for the Mullers, who took a great interest in her study of German, would allow her to speak no English. She must ask for cream, sugar, cakes, say "please" and "thank you," tell her news only in German. Fred and Hobbie, choking down laughter at her mistakes, would point to objects on the table and shout their German names. Matilda came in from the kitchen to join the fun.

But today Betsy and Tib took their coffee upstairs.

Tib was cutting out a dress. She was making some of her own clothes this year.

"I was so fussy that Mamma told me I'd better make them myself, and I told her all right I would," said Tib, running daring scissors through a length of pink silk spread out on the bed.

"Oh, Tib, how smart you are!" Betsy said. "Is that for the Christmas parties? I'm going to have a white wool, trimmed with gold."

"It sounds lovely. I hope there'll be millions of dances. I hear there's going to be one at the Melborn Hotel."

"Really? How marvelous!"

"You'll go with Joe or Tony. I wonder who Tacy will go with?"

"She could just as well go to all the dances with

Tom," Betsy answered, and told about the conversations with Tom and with Tacy.

Tib shook her head. "I hate to say it, but I believe that Tacy is going to be an old maid."

"Oh, Tib!" cried Betsy.

"You don't get married without lifting your finger."

"I know it," said Betsy in an agonized tone. "But she can't be an old maid! She just can't! If all the rest of us get to work, we ought to be able to marry her off. She's so beautiful, with that gorgeous hair and those big blue eyes."

"But she doesn't do anything with them," Tib protested. "I wish I had them for about five minutes."

"You do all right being little and blonde," Betsy said.

"Ralph likes blondes. I'm glad of that," said Tib. She had felt romantic about Ralph Maddox ever since the St. John game. "Lloyd and Dennie are both having fits," she went on, holding a piece of pink silk shoulder to shoulder and looking in the mirror. "I hope Ralph asks me first for that dance at the Hotel . . . if they give it. Who do you want to go with, Betsy? Which one do you like best, Tony or Joe?"

"I've loved Tony for years," said Betsy, lightly.

"You're not answering my question, and you know it."

No one knew which one Betsy liked best, but the rivalry began to attract attention, and the general opinion was that Joe was edging ahead. Word got around school that Betsy and Joe Willard were practically going together.

Miss Clarke, the Zetamathian faculty advisor who had seen Betsy through the Essay Contests, beamed upon them; and Miss O'Rourke, the Philomathian faculty advisor who had sponsored Joe, looked mischievous. Miss Fowler, the little English teacher who had given them both so much encouragement and praise, smiled when she saw them together.

In Miss Bangeter's Shakespeare class they sat side by side at the back of the room. Miss Bangeter, with her dark magnetic eyes and sonorous voice, had almost transformed that roomful of desks and blackboards into the Forest of Arden. Trees with love songs hung and carved upon them seemed to rise between the desks. The sun slanted down through leafy aisles upon gallants and fair ladies, shepherds, shepherdesses, clowns, and courtiers. The Forest of Arden always made Betsy think of the Big Hill.

She underlined a sentence and passed it across to Joe. "Fleet the time carelessly, as they did in the golden world."

"That's what I'd like to do," she whispered.

"That's what we'll do next spring," Joe whispered back, while even Miss Bangeter looked pleased.

12

"Don't Worry"

BURSTING IN TO CALL FOR Betsy one morning in mid-December, Tib and Tacy cried, "Say, what about our Christmas shopping trip?"

This was an annual event, as heavily weighted with tradition as a Christmas pudding with plums. As children they had gone with just ten cents apiece to spend. They had visited every store in town, priced everything from diamonds to gum drops, and bought, each one, a Christmas tree ornament. The last few years, they had been less carefree; they had had real shopping to do. But they had never failed to make the trip, savoring Christmas together all up and down Front Street.

"Of course," said Betsy. "Let's go after school tonight."

There had been repeated falls of snow, and Deep Valley was bedded down in drifts. But bright sun and jingling sleighbells made the cold seem festive. Front Street masqueraded in evergreen and holly. The store windows were full of gifts, and the stores were full of merry harassed crowds and the smell of damp clothing.

The girls bought presents for their parents, for their brothers and sisters, and for other members of the Crowd. Tacy bought beauty pins for Mrs. Poppy, with whom she studied singing. Betsy bought a Deep Valley pennant for Leonard. At last, for old times' sake, they bought the Christmas tree ornaments, each selecting just one after prolonged debate.

As they paid their dimes, they were laughing at themselves, but Betsy admitted silently that she had never ceased to be thrilled by the sight of a Christmas tree ornament, so fragile, so glittery, so full of the promise of Christmas. When they were drinking coffee at Heinz's, she took her silver ball out of its wrappings.

"Just think!" she began—Betsy was always saying

"Just think!" this year. "Just think! This may be our last Christmas shopping trip!"

"What do you mean by that?" asked Tib, startled.

"Well, next year I'll be at the U. You'll be going to Browner College in Milwaukee, probably . . . or maybe on the stage; it wouldn't surprise me . . . and Tacy will be going to the College on the hill, studying Public School Music. We may very well not get downtown together."

"Heavens!" said Tacy. She looked aghast.

"We can't go on doing the same things forever," said Tib. But she looked sober, too.

"Maybe we ought to have more cakes," suggested Betsy, by way of consolation. So they ordered another round of cakes.

They went home laden with bundles, but Betsy had not yet bought her most important gift. She had not even mentioned it to Tacy and Tib. This was for Joe.

He had already bought her present.

"It doesn't amount to much. Just something I thought you might like," he had said with shining carelessness one Sunday night at lunch.

He almost always came for Sunday night lunch now. Tony was often there and the relationship between them had grown a little stiff. Joe was aware that although Betsy's feeling for Tony might be sisterly, Tony's feeling for her was more than brotherly.

And Tony had heard the general rumors about Betsy and Joe.

Tony had the inside track at the Ray house Sunday nights. But Joe was winning a special place, too. Margaret actually permitted him to tease her. He pelted Mrs. Ray with compliments, and when Mr. Ray was making the famous sandwiches, Joe always kept him company. He got Mr. Ray to talk about the shoe store, about his youth, about Deep Valley history. Mr. Ray loved to talk and Joe to listen.

"I think your father is the finest person I ever met in my life," Joe said one night. "He has the finest character and philosophy, he is the happiest. I've been trying to decide what makes him so happy. I believe it's because he never thinks of himself. He is always thinking about doing something for somebody else . . . you, or Margaret, or your mother . . . or Anna, or the shoemaker who works for him, or some poor widow across the slough with a house full of kids."

Mr. Ray, for his part, was highly gratified with his attentive listener. Now when he brought home especially good anecdotes he was eager to share them with the Willard boy. Betsy was occasionally almost annoyed by this. She and Joe didn't have much time together. Sometimes when they were sitting by the fire, happily alone for once, Mr. Ray would join them, sit down, and begin to talk.

"A remarkable fellow came into the store today. Name of Kerr. And guess what he did. I'm always selling the other fellow a bill of goods. But this fellow Kerr sold me. I didn't want to put in a line of knitwear. Never thought of doing it. Perfectly content with shoes. But, by golly, I did!"

Joe was delighted. "How did he manage it?" he asked.

"He was so darned positive," Mr. Ray replied. "He knows exactly what he wants and what you ought to want, whether you do or not."

At this point, Mrs. Ray, to whom Betsy had been lifting eyebrows in appeal, called Mr. Ray away. She asked him to fix a squeaking door.

"Shucks!" said Mr. Ray. "That door has been squeaking for weeks. Why do I have to fix it right now when I want to talk to Joe?"

There could certainly be no doubt about Mr. Ray's liking for Joe, and even Anna, although she adored Tony, allowed that Joe was "puny."

"There was a boy something like that who used to call on the McCloskey girl," she remarked to Betsy. The McCloskeys were a legendary family for whom Anna had worked in a legendary past. When Anna quoted the McCloskeys, it was important.

She quoted them, as Christmas drew near, about cookies. They had always made three kinds, she said, and so she was making three kinds now.

The December issue of the *Ladies' Home Journal* had an impressive page entitled "Twenty Christmas Cookies from One Batter." Betsy showed it to Anna, who sniffed.

"*Ja*, and I'll bet they all taste alike. Mrs. McCloskey's recipes are good enough for me."

Mrs. Ray was rapturously shopping. Betsy was worrying darkly over her "Don't Worry" motto. Margaret was working on something—it looked like a blotter—which she whisked out of sight whenever Betsy came near.

Mr. Ray brought home holly wreaths, which were put up in the windows. He brought home mistletoe, and candy canes. A Christmas tree waited on the chill back porch, sending out whiff of aromatic fragrance whenever the door was opened.

Mr. Ray called the girls aside. "You could never guess what my present for Jule is, not if you tried a hundred years."

"What is it, Papa?" Betsy urged.

"Never mind. You'll find out."

Margaret protested. "You never kept Mamma's present a secret from us before."

Mr. Ray only chuckled.

Margaret, who sang in the seventh-grade chorus, was practising Christmas carols.

"It came upon the midnight clear. . . ."

Betsy and Tacy were practising for the high school Christmas program.

> *"The first Noel, the angel did say,*
> *Was to certain poor shepherds,*
> *In fields as they lay. . . ."*

Betsy was busy with choir practise, too. And there seemed to be a sound of carols in the air even when she wasn't in chorus or choir. She thought sometimes that in spite of the void caused by Julia's absence, this was going to be a wonderful Christmas.

It was getting difficult, though, to divide her time between Joe and Tony. Balancing their claims, she felt sometimes like an acrobat on a tight rope. She consoled herself by thinking of Tony. He wasn't any longer stealing rides on freight cars. He wasn't going with that wild crowd. And soon, certainly, he would get a crush on some other girl.

But Tony, she admitted reluctantly, hadn't had very many crushes during the years she had known him. Moreover, in an offhand nonchalant way, he was letting her know that he liked her . . . too much.

Walking downtown with Joe after school, she asked where he was spending Christmas

"Butternut Center," he replied. "My uncle and

aunt sort of like to have me around."

"Do you suppose you'll get in town during the day?"

"Does your father make turkey sandwiches at night?"

"He certainly does." Betsy smiled. "They're the most famous of the year. He puts cold dressing in them."

"When do you get your presents?"

"Christmas morning, in our stockings. We hang them the night before and then after we've decorated the tree and sung carols, we turn out the lights and fill them. It's lots of fun."

"You Rays know how to do things," Joe answered. "Well," he added, "the last day of school is Christmas Eve. I'll give you your present then and you can put it into your own stocking."

They parted at the usual corner and Joe went on to the *Sun*, but Betsy didn't go to the library. She went to Front Street, and she came nearer to duplicating the traditional Christmas shopping trip than she and Tacy and Tib had done. She traversed Front Street from end to end, looking into every store.

It was proper for a boy to give a girl only books, flowers, or candy. It would be proper for Betsy to give Joe nothing more. A box of home made candy might be the best thing, but she did want to give him something he could keep. She ended at Cook's Book Store, her favorite store in town, and browsing about, she found a small, red, limp-leather edition of Shakespeare. The Avon edition, it was called. She purchased *As You Like It*.

Hurrying to her father's store in order to get a ride home in the sleigh, she passed Alquist's. She remembered that she hadn't bought a present for Tony and went in and bought a red tie. It wouldn't be proper to give a tie to the average boy, but Tony was so much more than just a beau. So much more, and also . . . so much less.

On the evening before the last day of school, the Crowd went to the high school to decorate. They stopped by for Cab and made him go, too. Decorating the school for Christmas was a senior prerogative and a very hilarious occasion.

A few industrious persons really worked, hanging popcorn and cranberry strings and loops of silver paper on a tall evergreen tree set up on the platform. The others drew pictures and scrawled slams on the blackboards, tacked mistletoe in strategic places. Clutching mistletoe, Dennie pursued Winona over the tops of the desks.

Tib ran up to Betsy. "Remember what I told you about a dance at the Melborn Hotel? Well, it's going to be on New Year's Eve. Ralph just asked me."

Betsy had a tightrope walker's shiver. She didn't

want to go to this all-important dance with Tony.

During the rest of the evening she stayed so close to Joe that he asked, "What's the matter? Scared of something?"

"Scared to go home in the dark."

"Gosh!" said Joe. "That's too bad. I have to get down to the roller rink to cover an exhibition of skating. You don't want to come along, do you?"

"I mustn't," said Betsy. "There's too much to do at home."

She thought of bringing up the subject of the dance. After all, she and Joe were almost going together. But Betsy wasn't sure she had the poise. Besides, she didn't want to. It would take away something of the thrill to ask him instead of having him ask her.

She thought she could manage. "If Tony asks me," she planned, "I'll say I'm engaged. It would be just a white lie. Or I'll tell him frankly I'd prefer to go with Joe. He has to know sometime."

Probably, she thought, he wouldn't get the chance to ask her. She had come with Tacy and Tib and would go home with them.

At the time for departure, however, Tony came up.

"I'll walk you home," he said, taking her arm.

"I came over with the girls, Tony, and I think I'd better . . ."

"I think you'd better go home with me," he interrupted, insouciant as ever.

Dennie, Cab, and Lloyd had joined Tacy, Tib, and Winona. They sauntered along High Street together. In desperation, when they reached her home, Betsy asked them all in.

It was the worst thing she could have done. Everyone began to talk about the dance.

"What's this? What's this?" cried Tony. "A dance on New Year's Eve? Mar-vo-lous!"

He turned to Betsy, and his manner was unconcerned, but not the look in his black eyes.

"How about it, Ray of Sunshine? Will you go with me?" he asked.

Betsy felt the room listening and panic overwhelmed her. She couldn't, in this company, say she was engaged. Julia with her cold confidence could have done it, but Betsy lacked the poise, and she certainly couldn't be frank. She had to protect Tony.

"Why, thanks," she said. She noticed that some of the boys were looking at her keenly and tried to act careless, as though it didn't matter with whom one went to the New Year's Eve dance.

But it did matter, she felt with foreboding.

Joe was so proud. She had watched him and thought about him a great deal over the autumn, and she had never seen him make a frankly friendly overture. She knew the reason: he felt he had nothing to offer. Other boys and girls had homes to entertain in, parents to give treats. He had nothing. He could never say, "Come on over to my house," and bring a friend in for an apple or a cookie. He didn't want to accept favors he couldn't return. So he never made advances.

Betsy had made the advances. She had been generous with her friendship, with her admiration, with her praise. It was her nature to be that way and it had drawn Joe to her. Some boys might be spurred to greater devotion by a rival, but not Joe.

Betsy went to sleep worrying and she woke up still worrying.

Morning brought a diversion. Before breakfast was over, the doorbell rang, and she found no one less than Carney on the porch, Carney, dimple flickering!

They flew into each other's arms. "Why, you haven't changed at all!"

"Why should I have changed?" asked Carney. Tacy, Tib, and Alice came shouting up the steps. Carney was conveyed with a guard of honor to the high school.

She wasn't the only Old Grad back that day. Al and Pin and Squirrelly were back. Tom was there, quite markedly avoiding Tacy, telling Carney that he would be at West Point next year.

"Maybe," he said, "you'll come over to some dances."

The Christmas exercises went off merrily, with Mr. Gaston a sardonic Santa Claus as usual. There was so much excitement that Betsy wasn't surprised that she didn't encounter Joe. But after the exercises it came to her that he was deliberately avoiding her. He was talking and joking with other groups and didn't even look in her direction.

At last she went over to him with the little package she had brought.

"Merry Christmas!" she said, extending it. "I hope I'm going to see you Christmas night."

"Not a chance," he answered rudely. He didn't take the package and Betsy put it down uncertainly on a desk.

"Why? What's the matter?"

He turned on her fiercely.

"You certainly didn't lose any time in getting Tony to take you to the New Year's Eve dance."

"Why, Joe!" faltered Betsy. "Who told you. . . ." It was, she realized, a stupid answer. It made her sound guilty, as though she had done something wrong. She blushed scarlet.

"The whole school told me," Joe answered hotly. "They've been laying bets, I hear, on which one of us you would go with. I can't take it, and I won't. Either you're my girl or you're not."

Betsy felt sick with misery. "But we've talked that

all over. I thought you understood."

"I understand. I understand that you're not my girl."

"Why, Joe!" But he didn't hear her. He strode off, and the little package she had wrapped with such care in tissue and bright ribbons still lay on the desk. Betsy picked it up, feeling cold inside.

Not ten minutes later, catastrophic news floated across the Assembly Room.

"Joe is taking Irma to the New Year's Eve dance."

"Oh, well!" Tacy was saying. "He couldn't take Betsy. Tony asked her first."

"How under the sun did Irma happen not to have been asked?"

"She was going with Dave. And he has . . . of all things . . . the measles."

Joe was taking Irma. He was mad at her and he was taking Irma. Betsy felt a lump like a clump of burrs in her throat, but she tried to laugh and enter into the fun echoing around the room.

When she was leaving the building, in a group of boys and girls, Joe came up and called her aside. He looked very poised and stiff. He was smiling, and his eyes were bright.

"I want to apologize, Betsy," he said. "Gosh, I made a fool of myself! You have fun New Year's Eve with Tony, and from now on all bets are off."

"All bets are off!" What did he mean by that? Betsy still felt cold inside.

"I'll play the field," said Joe. "I'll really play the field. By the way," he added, reaching into his pocket, "here's something for that Christmas stocking."

Mustering a smile, holding back tears, Betsy took the package and offered her own.

"Merry Christmas," she said. The words were a mockery with Joe looking like that.

Not until she got home and began to unwrap the package did Betsy realize that it was just the same size as the one she had given Joe. Unwrapping it, the lump in her throat got bigger as comprehension grew. It was the same volume, a red, limp-leather, Avon edition of *As You Like It*. Inside he had written "We'll fleet the time carelessly as they did in the golden world."

But Betsy knew he had written that before he knew that she was going to the dance with Tony. She put her face into her hands and began to cry.

13

Christmas without Julia

BETSY DIDN'T ALLOW HERSELF to cry very long.

Downstairs, Margaret was laboriously but fervently pounding out on the piano:

"It came . . . upon the midnight clear. . . ."

Mrs. Ray was laughing. Mr. Ray was demanding tissue paper. The smell of oyster stew was rising from the kitchen.

Betsy got up and went to the window. The gas in her room was not yet lighted, so she could see clearly into the out-of-doors. Snowflakes were whirling against the arc light, and the drifts which covered the lawn had already received a fresh, soft, unblemished blanketing.

It was Christmas Eve, and she was seventeen. Julia was across the ocean, and so there devolved on her the subtle responsibilities of oldest daughter. All the careful planning in the world, the nicest presents, wreaths in the windows, and candy canes in the doorways would not make Christmas Eve a happy time in any house unless the people in that house were happy. If Betsy's eyes were red, no forced gaiety would make the hearts of the others light.

"I couldn't be so mean," Betsy said fiercely. "Please, God, help me to take Julia's place, tonight."

She went into the bathroom to splash cold water on her face, and the music downstairs ended abruptly. Margaret called, "Betsy! Betsy! Come help with the joke presents!" The Rays always wrapped up onions and lumps of coal and other choice articles to put in the stockings along with oranges and candies and small gifts.

"Coming!" Betsy called.

When her cheeks were pink from cold water, she powdered carefully, combed her hair, and put a sprig of holly behind her pompadour. Then she ran down-stairs into the Christmas Eve bustle.

"What do you suppose Papa's getting for Mamma that is such a secret?" Margaret asked, tying a knot firmly over a turnip that was going to Mrs. Ray, "From an Old Beau."

"I can't imagine, except that it's something for the house and sort of for all of us. I wonder what I'm going to get. Nothing big, I'm sure, with Julia having such an expensive year."

Margaret choked, then coughed concealingly.

"That's right," she said with elaborate carelessness. "You couldn't possibly be getting anything big."

"Shall we open Julia's box tonight or in the morning?" Mr. Ray called out.

"I say tonight," said Mrs. Ray. "There's always so much in the morning."

"I say tonight, too," said Betsy. "It will make it seem more as though Julia were here."

"I don't believe in opening anything on Christmas Eve," said Margaret. "But that's a good reason, Betsy. I'll give in."

Anna banged on the gong to summon them to oyster stew. She was wearing a white apron and her hair was curled. The dining room table was set with the company dishes, but the room was littered with tissues and ribbons, and packages, large and small.

After supper was cleared away, Mr. Ray brought in the tree. Cold and a delicious forest smell came with it. It was set up in the dining room, and Betsy and Margaret brought the cardboard boxes of decorations down from the garret.

"Trimming the tree is a messy job," Anna always said. But Betsy, unwrapping the baubles, red, green, blue, and gold, many of which she had bought with Tacy and Tib on their Christmas shopping trips, insisted that it was almost the nicest part of Christmas.

"No," said Margaret. "Coming downstairs Christmas morning in the dark is the nicest." But she, too, loved fastening stars and angels on the fresh, good-smelling branches.

The tree was a beauty.

"We say every year that our Christmas tree is the nicest we ever had, but this one really is," said Betsy, gazing at the tall balsam, which carried its glittering load with proud ease.

When the candles were lighted, she went to the piano. She couldn't play the carols as well as Julia, but she could play them. She was thankful for her piano lessons as the family gathered around her singing, "O, Little Town of Bethlehem," "Hark! The Herald Angels Sing," and the tender "Silent Night."

"Now for the ritual," said Betsy, jumping up. "Silent Night" had made everyone think too hard of Julia.

Margaret recited *'Twas the Night Before Christmas,* as usual. But tonight Mrs. Ray read what Betsy usually read, the story of the Cratchits' Christmas dinner, and Betsy read what Julia usually read, the story of the first Christmas, from the book of Luke. She tried to read it as Julia did, gravely and reverently.

"'And there were in the same country shepherds abiding in the field, keeping watch over their flock by night. . . .'"

Outside, the snow was coming down and down and down. She wondered whether it was snowing in Berlin.

After the reading, they opened Julia's box and it did, indeed, seem to bring her nearer. There were gifts for everyone, even Abie and Washington, festively wrapped. Betsy received some popular music by the composer of *The Merry Widow.* It was *"Kind, Du Kannst Tanzen."* She was proud to be able to translate it—"Child, You Can Dance." The presents all looked foreign—gold-embroidered collars, prints of famous pictures, strange little painted boxes.

Before anyone had a chance to start missing Julia again, Betsy proposed filling the stockings. This rite, performed in a dim light, was a sure source of excitement.

"I can't put Jule's present in her stocking until tomorrow, can I, Anna?" Mr. Ray asked.

"In her . . ." Anna began to sway with laughter. "Stars in the sky, Mr. Ray! Sure, we're going to put it in her stocking, if she has a good big one. Ha! Ha! Ha!"

After the stockings were filled, they had cider and Christmas cookies.

Betsy had tried so hard to be like Julia that she had almost forgotten the ache in her heart. Margaret came in to sleep with her and they had fun talking, as they undressed, about Christmases up on Hill Street, across the street from Tacy's, Christmases which now seemed almost like a dream to Margaret.

"I remember that I used to hear the reindeer on that roof," she said.

"So did I," answered Betsy. "And I could hear Santa Claus sliding down the chimney. We didn't have a fireplace, you remember, and the stovepipe leading from the coal stove downstairs ran through our bedroom. It was only about as big as my two hands. But I could imagine Santa Claus sort of thinning out as he slid down and getting round and fat again as soon as he landed on the back parlor floor."

Margaret laughed as she snuggled into Betsy's bed. "I wonder what Julia's doing."

"She'll have a wonderful Christmas with the Von Hetternichs," said Betsy. "It will be like my Christmas in Milwaukee." And she told Margaret stories about that fabulous holiday until Margaret grew sleepy.

After Margaret had fallen asleep, Betsy's thoughts went back to Joe. The Christmas Eve proceedings had cheered her up so much that she began to believe things couldn't be so bad as she had feared. Perhaps, when he opened her gift, he would be affected just as she had been by the fact that they had both bought *As You Like It*. Perhaps he would telephone tomorrow. Perhaps he would even come for turkey sandwiches.

She woke to the sound of her father shaking down the furnace. She had wakened before Margaret, which was a miracle on Christmas morning. Last night's optimism was still with her, and she jumped up and ran to the window.

"Merry Christmas," she whispered into the ghostly world and turned to pounce on Margaret, shouting "Merry Christmas!"

Heat began to come up through the register. The smell of coffee rose. Betsy and Margaret were dressing hurriedly when Mrs. Ray came in.

"Papa says we have to stay here till he calls us."

"Why? What's it all about?"

"I can't imagine," said Mrs. Ray. "I usually catch on, but I have no idea what this secret is. Bob, are you ready?" she called.

"You hold your horses," Mr. Ray replied.

"We're coming!" she threatened.

"You stay there till you're invited down."

There was a hammering. There was a wrenching sound. There was a thud, and another, and Anna's giggle, and a long pause in which Mrs. Ray, Betsy, and Margaret clutched hands. Then Mr. Ray shouted, "Now!"

As they took the first step down the stairs, chimes sounded, wonderfully sweet. Betsy recognized the song. It was the one played every hour by the chimes of Big Ben in London, the one of which Julia had written.

> *"Oh, Lord our God,*
> *Be thou our guide,*
> *That by thy help,*
> *No foot may slide."*

Just as she and her mother and Margaret reached the landing, they heard a deep-toned resonant striking.

"One," they counted, "two, three, four, five, six, seven, eight, nine, ten, eleven, twelve."

"Bob Ray!" cried Mrs. Ray, running down the stairs. "It's a chime clock!"

Mr. Ray was laughing so that his stomach shook.

"Where is it?" asked Betsy, looking around.

"And why did it strike twelve?" asked Margaret. "It isn't twelve o'clock."

"He set it at twelve, to make it exciting," cried Anna. "Stars in the sky! The trouble we took getting that thing unpacked."

The tall grandfather clock stood against a wall of the music room, looking as benevolent and yet as dignified as Mr. Ray himself. The girls danced about it while Mrs. Ray hugged her husband.

"I've wanted a chime clock for ages. Ever since Julia was in London. How did you know?" she cried.

After this magnificent gift, which was really for everyone, of course, Betsy didn't expect very much for herself. She didn't mind. What made Christmas morning so glorious wasn't actually the presents, but the mystery, the thrusting of one's hand into a crammed stocking, the unwrapping of mysterious-looking parcels under the tree.

This began now beside a crackling fire, while Mr. Ray urged everyone to help themselves to coffee, sausages, and toast set out on the dining room table.

It was exciting not only to unwrap your own gifts but to watch others unwrap what you had planned for them. Margaret's eyes sparkled while Betsy exclaimed over the homemade blotter. Betsy waited eagerly as her father examined the "Don't Worry" motto. Anna had pressed it and Betsy had pasted it on cardboard and framed it. The glass hid the deficiencies in her embroidery.

"That's mighty nice, Betsy. I'm glad you're learning to sew. It expresses my sentiments exactly, too."

Margaret had a doll, of course. A beautiful, jointed, bisque doll, with blond curls, a pink dress, openwork stockings, and patent leather slippers.

"How awful it will be, Bob, the first Christmas Margaret doesn't want a doll!"

"I'll always want a doll," Margaret promised, looking sober.

"Either she will or our grandchildren will," said Mr. Ray. "We'll be having grandchildren around in a few years, don't forget."

There was one big box left to be opened. Mr. Ray brought it to Betsy.

"It's almost like the box I got my furs in last year, but I can't be getting furs again. It's probably a joke," she thought.

Mrs. Ray was beaming. Anna leaned forward with delighted eyes. Margaret hugged her father's arm to restrain excited giggles.

Betsy untied the ribbons, pulled off the tissues, lifted the box cover.

"An opera cape!" she squealed. Jumping up, she shook it out. It was pale blue broadcloth lined with white satin, trimmed with silk braid and gold and blue buttons.

"Papa! Mamma! It's a perfect dream!"

"It's time you had an opera cape, now you're a senior," Mr. Ray said.

"It just matches that blue dress Julia sent you," Margaret cried.

"You'll look tony in it, lovey," Anna exclaimed.

Mrs. Ray was talking excitedly. "You would have to have one in the spring anyway. So Papa and I thought you might as well have it now. The New Year's Eve dance is going to be so elegant this year, down at the Melborn Hotel."

Betsy's heart sank. What fun would an opera cape be when Joe was going with Irma? But maybe, she thought hopefully, they would have made up by then? Probably he would telephone today. Certainly he would. She put the opera cape on over her morning dress and paraded up and down.

The day was quite like other Christmas days. Julia was so much on their lips that she seemed to be actually there.

Tony went to church with Betsy. Soft mountains of snow covered the lawns and shrubs. Soft clumps of it lay on the evergreens; soft strips showed white along black boughs. Mr. Ray had already shoveled his walk, but many householders had slept later, so Betsy and Tony had to take to the road.

In the small crowded church, smelling of evergreens and radiant with candles, Betsy sang with all her heart:

"O come, all ye faithful,
Joyful and triumphant. . . ."

She actually felt joyful and triumphant.

Dinner followed with four kinds of dessert—caramel ice cream, mince pie, fruit cake, and plum pudding. The afternoon was filled with grown-up naps and company, Christmas books and games, and the chiming of the clock.

It made one conscious of the passing of time, that clock.

"Oh, Lord our God," and then in no time at all, "Oh, Lord our God, Be thou our guide"; and in what couldn't possibly have been fifteen minutes more, "Oh, Lord our God, Be thou our guide, That by thy help . . ." After that there was nothing to do but wait for the completed verse.

At first Betsy loved it, but that was because she was still happy. She was still sure Joe would telephone. As the afternoon wore away, twilight dulling the snow until it was gray, her hopes dwindled.

The telephone rang, and it was Carney saying that she was involved with family doings and would not be up for supper. It rang again, and it was Anna's Charlie. It rang again, and it was Cab.

Inexorably the clock pulled the afternoon into evening. The Christmas tree was lighted. Mr. Ray was out in the kitchen making sandwiches. Winona was at the piano and Tony was urging Betsy to come and sing.

Joe hadn't come. He wasn't coming. He was still mad at her, Betsy thought, with that swelling back in her throat.

> "Oh, Lord our God,
> Be thou our guide,
> That by thy help,
> No foot may slide."

sang the chime clock and struck eight . . . and nine . . . and ten.

14

The New Year's Eve Dance

THE NEW CHIME CLOCK tolled off the days of the holiday week. As usual in Deep Valley, there was a parade of parties. On the day after Christmas came the church Christmas tree. That was followed by the Crowd Christmas tree. Hazel acted as Santa Claus and made a very funny one. The presents caused laughter, too, for everyone received at least one boudoir cap. The coquettish little mobcaps, trimmed with lace, flowers, or bows of ribbon, were the rage.

"Ye Gods! When do I wear the thing?" asked Tacy, adjusting the delicate confection she had received from Tib.

"For breakfast, silly!"

"But I have to have my hair combed for breakfast," grumbled Alice.

"So do I," said Carney. "Neat as a pin."

"These will be fine for covering up my Magic Wavers," said Betsy, putting the two caps she had received on her head together.

She was acting nonsensical. She acted nonsensical all that week, wilder and more absurd as party followed party. Joe didn't come to any of them; he stayed at Butternut Center. But the chime clock kept reminding Betsy that the New Year's Eve dance was approaching.

There were several parties for Carney—evening parties with the boys, and afternoon parties where she told the girls all about Vassar. To one of these Betsy brought her Christmas letter from Herbert. She called Carney aside and gleefully pointed out a paragraph.

"What kind of a dame has Carney turned out to be? Larry is still mooning about her."

Carney looked serious.

"Well, how *have* I turned out?" she asked, fixing her forthright gaze on Betsy.

Betsy looked at her, pink-cheeked, bright-eyed, in a snowy shirtwaist, a well pressed skirt, and polished shoes. She no longer wore the hair ribbon she had clung to until her graduation from high school. Like the other girls, she now wore a band around her hair with a big bow on the side. But she still had her fresh, woodsy, honest look.

"You haven't changed," said Betsy.

"Are you going to tell Herbert that?"

"Don't you want me to?"

"I suppose so," said Carney. "But maybe Larry has changed awfully. Maybe he's sophisticated now."

Betsy threw up her hands. "I should think you'd go crazy with that Mystery in your life," she said. "Is Larry going to like you or isn't he? Are you or aren't you going to like Larry?"

Carney chuckled.

The Crowd of girls repeated last year's progressive dinner. As before, each course was served in a different home. But this year small programs showed with whom one took the dark icy walk from house to house.

Betsy went with Carney to Irma's for grapefruit with brandied cherries in it. The table was in red.

She walked with Alice over to Hazel's for bouillon

with place cards and favors.

She walked with Katie to her own house for the fish course. Her table was in pink.

She walked with Hazel to Carney's for the meat course. It was, however, chicken, and there was cranberry ice.

She walked with Tacy to Tib's for delectable salad.

With Tib she took the long walk up Hill Street to the Kellys'. They loitered, having an important matter to discuss. Tom had asked Carney to the New Year's Eve dance. Who, then, was going to take Tacy?

They arrived late and half frozen for the Kellys' hot mince pies. Betsy clowned with Winona. She laughed and quipped in the giddiest spirits, for she dreaded the walk to Alice's. Irma was her partner for that.

But Irma didn't mention Joe or the dance. Slipping her arm sociably through Betsy's, as they started down the frozen path, she suggested that they sing. She had a sweet soprano voice, and Betsy sang alto. They sang Christmas carols all the way to Alice's house, throwing the music at the cold bright stars. Betsy felt ashamed, and squeezed Irma's arm when they parted. Alice served after-dinner coffee and her decorations were in the holiday colors.

They went last to Winona's. Betsy walked down with Winona. She wrote in her diary:

"That Winona is a scream. She had fixed up their

dining room to look like a beer garden. And we drank grape juice and smoked cubebs. They're just for asthma, of course, but the boys who were looking in the windows thought they were real cigarettes. We gave 'Florabelle.'"

Betsy had composed "Florabelle" or "She Loved But Left Him" during the holidays. It was supposed to be a takeoff on a melodrama but it was definitely influenced by Shakespeare. The frenzied lovers lapsed frequently into atrocious blank verse. There were grave diggers and a balcony scene.

The shades were closely drawn, for Betsy and Winona had borrowed Winona's father's wardrobe. Winona and Tib were the lovers; Betsy, the villain. The audience, on pillows on the floor, collapsed in laughter.

At the end, there were cries of "Author! Author!" Betsy took her bows, flame-cheeked and mirthful, her thumbs in Winona's father's suspenders, which were holding up Winona's father's trousers.

But when she reached home, the chime clock was striking twelve. And from twelve to one and one to two it wrapped the quarter hours and half hours and hours into neat packages and stowed them away. Betsy stuffed her fingers into her ears. Hot tears dripped into her pillow.

She tried to see the quarrel from Joe's point of

view. That was simple. He was proud. He thought he had been made ridiculous and he was determined not to compete with Tony any longer. But she was proud, too. If he hadn't gotten mad and asked Irma so quickly, she would have tried to explain. But now it was too late. There was nothing she could do.

At last the chime clock brought the New Year's Eve dance.

Tacy wasn't going. She had been given a second chance; Cab had asked her. But she had decided that she would prefer going to her uncle's with the family.

"Her *uncle's*!" said Tib, throwing complete incomprehension into her voice.

"I can't make her out," said Betsy.

"She's sure to be an old maid unless we take steps."

Tib had come as usual to dress for the party with Betsy—and to do Betsy's multiplicity of puffs. The pompadour was rolled over a big sausagelike mat and each puff was rolled over a small one.

"The rat and all the little mice, Tony calls them," said Betsy, acting lighthearted.

The new white wool dress was a dream. Below the tucked, form-fitting bodice, the skirt fell into pleats. It was trimmed with gold and she wore a gold band, of course, around her hair.

Tib's self-made pink silk was a triumph. She wore

pink shoes and stockings and a wide pink band around her head.

"You both look lovely," said Mrs. Ray, dashing in, in her taffeta petticoat. She, too, was dressing for the ball.

Margaret, who was going to stay up for the first time to see the old year out, with Anna, making fudge, leaned over the rail as Betsy and Tib went lightly, proudly down the stairs.

Ralph and Tony waited, pressed and immaculate. Tony held the pale blue opera cape.

"Pretty skippy!" he said admiringly, putting it around Betsy's shoulders.

Betsy didn't like the new opera cape. She felt as though it were a hoo-doo.

The boys had engaged a hack. This unheard-of gesture was a tribute to the elegance of the Melborn Hotel. Betsy felt unbelievably worldly as the hack, on its winter runners, slid along the snowy streets and halted at the illuminated entrance to the Melborn.

They went through the swinging door into the lobby. It smelled of cigars and the fat red leather chairs. They crossed the room and ascended the grand staircase which rose at the far end.

The ballroom was two stories high and over-looked the river. Here Deep Valley gave its most fash-ionable parties. Mamie Dodd didn't play for this dance. Lamm's Orchestra, behind a screen of potted palms, was tuning up provocatively. The ballroom was decorated with poinsettia and holly. There were red shades on the chandeliers.

"Supper is going to be served in the Ladies' Ordinary," Carney told Betsy and Tib. She looked very pretty in the store-bought party dress, and Tom looked distinguished in his uniform.

The high school crowd seemed stimulated by this entrance into the world of fashion. All the girls looked pretty and the boys were kindled to unusual politeness, gallantry, and wit.

Betsy was excited, almost joyful, in spite of that doom in her breast, but her spirits died like a quenched fire at her first glimpse of Joe. She and Tony were dancing the opening waltz, "I Wonder Who's Kissing Her Now." She was happily floating in his arms—no one could waltz like Tony, no one!—when she saw a light pompadour and stalwart shoulders. Joe's lower lip was outthrust in a look Betsy knew. He was gazing at Irma, whose irresistible face, framed in natural (not Magically Waved) curls, was lifted to his.

"If he isn't crazy about her now, he soon will be," Betsy thought, and suddenly felt completely wretched. But she didn't show it. She smiled glowingly at Tony.

Joe didn't ask Betsy for a dance. The program ran on through "Howdy Cy" and "Ciri Biri Bin" and "Tonight Will Never Come Again." Betsy grew gayer and gayer, but none of her vivacity came from within. Inside, she ached. She ached all over, as you do when you have the grippe.

Laughing and flushed, she barn-danced, waltzed, and two-stepped. She chattered with the other girls about the marvelous party. She rushed up to her mother to exclaim. Tony went with her, to ask Mrs. Ray for a dance. He nodded his head negligently at Betsy.

"That daughter of yours! She's like a balloon on a string."

"Not a balloon! Oh, Tony! No! I only weigh a hundred pounds."

Mrs. Ray smiled at them. Loving parties, she was as happy as Betsy seemed to be. She whirled off with Tony, while Betsy, more sedately, circled with her father, who danced, as he did everything else, with benevolent dignity.

When the New Year came in, the orchestra played *Auld Lang Syne*. Everyone joined hands in a giant circle which revolved, singing:

> *"Should auld acquaintance be forgot*
> *And never brought to mind. . . ."*

Tony's dark eyes were bright with joy. He looked at Betsy as they swung hands and sang. Then the circle broke and people threw confetti and blew horns. Everyone called, "Happy New Year!" "Happy 1910!"

Nineteen-ten! That was the year they would graduate in, the year they had been looking forward to so long. How could it possibly start off so badly, so horribly! In the crowded, clamorous room, filled with laughing voices and the bright rain of confetti, Betsy felt forlorn.

She looked around and found Joe across the room. He was looking at her. But as soon as their glances crossed, he looked away.

And presently she saw him dancing with Irma to "Yip-i-addy-i-ay!"

15
Tacy's Eighteenth Birthday

WHEN BETSY WOKE UP on New Year's morning, she lay in bed looking at the window as it slowly changed from black to gray. She was more seriously unhappy than she had ever been in her life, but she was filled with a new determination.

She wanted to deal with her unhappiness in a manner worthy of her years.

"Like an adult," she said out loud.

She remembered that day last spring when she had found out that Cab was going to leave school and take over his father's business. She had realized then that she, too, was growing up.

She had been slow doing it, she reflected. One reason was that Tacy and Tib both loved her so much. They thought she was just about perfect, which had always made it easy for her to believe herself that she was pretty nice. You don't grow up, she reasoned now, until you begin to evaluate yourself, to recognize your good traits and acknowledge that you have a few faults.

"To begin with," she thought, "I'm too much of a baby."

That came partly from having an older sister. Julia had always taken the brunt of things.

"We used to expect Julia to be perfect," Betsy had often heard her mother say regretfully, speaking of the early years.

Julia had taught her father and mother not to expect perfection from a child. And she had done other kinds of pioneering. She had persuaded her parents that when you reach a certain age you are old enough to do certain things. She had thrashed out such matters as where one was allowed to go, how late one could stay out, the subject of boys.

And in school, as Betsy went from grade to grade and up into high school, she had always had a ready-made place, because she was Julia Ray's sister.

To be sure, Betsy acknowledged, in justice to herself, she had to make good. The teachers had soon discovered that she had none of Julia's talents. She had had to carve out a place for herself with her own abilities. But she had always been given a chance. And meanwhile Julia had sheltered and protected her.

"It's a wonder I braced up for Christmas Eve," Betsy thought. "I'm glad I did."

She knew she had helped the family, and as a matter of fact, she had been happy. That, she realized, was because she had stopped thinking about herself.

"I've heard all my life that that's the way it works. Papa is always thinking about other people and he's always happy. I've got to stop thinking about myself so much—about how I look, how I'm impressing someone, whether I'm popular or not. I've got to start thinking about other people, all the people I meet."

At the moment she didn't want to meet anybody, not even her mother, who would want to talk over the party. She wished she could stay in bed. In the past when she had had blows of one sort or another she had sometimes pretended to be sick. The family had always fallen in with these deceptions, and she had been able to take her time in gathering her forces for recovery.

"Well," she thought, "I won't do that today. I'll go down to the Y and serve punch the way I'm supposed to."

With this resolution, she jumped out of bed. The room was frigid, but it suited her mood. She shut the slot in the storm window with a bang and scratched a little hole in the frost to look out at the world. It was cold, snowy, and desolate. So much the better!

It seemed a little ironic that her companion today was to be Irma. She and Irma had been invited days before to preside behind the punch bowls at the Y.M.C.A. New Year Reception.

"But nothing that has happened to me is Irma's fault," thought Betsy, pulling on her clothes. "She didn't try to get Joe to ask her. He asked her because she's the belle of the school. I might as well start right now being fair to Irma. All of us girls, except Tacy, have had it in for her just because she's so popular with boys."

Smiling a little fixedly, but smiling, she went through the holiday breakfast, the holiday dinner. She dressed in her white wool dress again and went to the reception. The Y.M.C.A. was having an open house for men and women, boys and girls. Tea was served in the parlors, fruit punch in the big gymnasium.

She answered Irma's smile resolutely, and it was diverting to be serving punch to the boys and girls who flocked about their table. In a quiet moment, she and

Irma served some to themselves.

"Wasn't it a wonderful party last night?" Irma asked, sipping.

"Beautiful," said Betsy.

"It was lucky for me," said Irma, "that Tony asked you ahead of Joe. I don't know what I'd have done, Betsy, when Dave got those terrible measles, if Joe hadn't happened to be free."

That was a gallant remark, and Betsy matched it.

"Half the boys in school would have broken their dates to take you, Irma. You know that," she said.

A new wave of guests surged up to the table. Betsy was as busy as Irma; she wasn't envious or jealous. But listening to Irma's sweet laugh, observing her confiding manner, her fascinating way of gazing starry-eyed into people's faces, Betsy felt a pressure about her heart. Joe was free to go with Irma if he cared to. All bets were off, he had said.

She waited with dread for him to appear at the reception, but he didn't come. She didn't see him until the following Monday when school reopened. By that time, Carney had gone back to Vassar; Tom had returned to Cox; Al, Pin, and Squirrelly, to the U. The Rays' Christmas tree had been cast out into the snowy world. Wreaths had been burned and presents put away.

This ended the holidays, and Betsy returned to

school wearing a clean, starched shirt waist and even more stiffly starched resolves.

More snow had fallen. The thermometer had sunk to ten degrees below zero and with regrettable bravado was still descending. Tib, who loved the winter sports, was exultant, but Betsy and Tacy were glum.

"'Blow, blow, thou winter wind,'" Tacy murmured, as, rigid with extra wraps and underpinnings, they hurried through tunnel-like channels in the drifts.

"'Freeze, freeze, thou bitter sky,'" Betsy chanted in return. She might well have added:

> *"Thy sting is not so sharp,*
> *As friend remembered not. . . ."*

For Joe plainly had forgotten the warmth and sweetness of their old companionship. They didn't speak to each other now except for casual hellos in the hall. He stared at a book when she recited in Miss Bangeter's English class. They had changed seats at the new term and didn't sit together any more.

But at least he didn't seem to have fallen a victim to Irma's charms. It appeared that he intended to do what he had told Betsy he would do—play the field.

January brought its usual diversions—sleighing parties, skating parties, debates, and basketball games.

Joe went to everything, and he always took a girl. But it was seldom the same girl twice, although he lavished each one with flattering attentions.

By the time examinations put a stop to such activities, the high school had almost forgotten that the names of Betsy and Joe had ever been linked. It began to think of Joe as a single man again, to wonder when and with whom he was going to settle down.

Mr. Ray inquired for him several times. He wanted to tell Joe when Mr. Kerr came back to town and persuaded him to make a display of knit goods in the window.

"That Kerr! Joe ought to hear how he wangled me this time."

But Mrs. Ray told her husband privately to stop asking for Joe. Betsy knew she had, for Mr. Ray avoided the subject with clumsy finesse. He began to joke about Tony, something he had never done before—the Rays had long since taken Tony for granted.

Tony was happy these days. He was really working at school. And although his manner was always scornfully reckless, he was behaving very well indeed.

"He's trying to live up to me," Betsy thought, with a little twinge of guilt.

He still didn't act lover-like. He wasn't mushy. But he had come quite rigidly to claim the prerogatives of a "steady beau." He called for her at choir practice, took her to all the school activities, and never failed to come for Sunday night lunch.

Betsy tried to make the best of it. Her trait of dogged stubbornness stood her in good stead now. She was surprised at how much it helped unhappiness not to give in to it.

"Last year at this time I'd have been just wallowing in misery," she thought.

She did grow a little thin and tense, and her father kept heaping her plate and saying that she ought to get more sleep. But she protested that she would be all right as soon as exams were over.

As usual, she was cramming for mid-term exams. She and Tib brought their physics notebooks up to date together, and Tib tried to explain the subject, which was easy for her but an occult mystery to Betsy. She helped Betsy in German, too, and Betsy tried to help her and Tacy in English.

No one worried about Civics.

"What would we do without Miss Clarke?" Tacy asked one day. "Each graduating class ought to give her a medal."

They joked and toiled and burned the midnight gas, and examinations were all successfully disposed of in time to celebrate Tacy's eighteenth birthday.

Of the three girls, Tacy got to be eighteen first. She

always had the honor of ushering in each new age. Betsy and Tib were invited to her house for supper, and they walked up to Hill Street gladly in spite of the sub-zero weather.

Winter seemed closer at the Kellys' house. From the bay window, one looked out at the hills submerged in snow with regiments of bare, black trees. When the curtains were drawn, the glowing windows of the Kellys' coal stove expressed winter's cheer as a register never could.

The big family gathered for supper in the dining room, but Betsy, Tacy, and Tib ate alone at a table set up in the parlor. Over creamed chicken, fruit salad, and hot rolls, they talked about past birthdays. The fifth birthday when Betsy had met Tacy. The tenth one when all three had been so eager to get two numbers in their age.

"You had told us, Betsy," said Tib, "that we were going to be grown up when we got two numbers in our age. It was the beginning of growing up, you said."

Tacy laughed. "I got to be ten first, of course. I didn't look any different or feel any different. But I knew why that was. You and Tib weren't ten yet."

"Then *I* got to be ten," Tib continued. "And I didn't look any different or feel any different. But, of course, I didn't expect to until Betsy got to be ten, too, and her birthday didn't come until April."

"Well," Betsy said. "I was right. Wasn't I? After I got to be ten, things did start happening. We all fell in love with the King of Spain."

In the midst of their laughter, Katie came into the room and blew out the lamp. Everyone knew what that meant. She went back to the kitchen and returned bearing a birthday cake covered with eighteen flickering candles. Betsy and Tib started to sing:

> *"Happy birthday to you,*
> *Happy birthday to you,*
> *Happy birthday, dear Tacy. . . ."*

Tacy made a wish and blew out her candles. She blew them all out in one puff.

"Now," said Tacy, pounding her chest grandly, "I'm officially eighteen years old."

"You're of age," said Betsy.

"You're old enough to get married," said Tib.

Tacy looked alarmed. "Oh, no," she said. "I'm eighteen, but it doesn't count yet. It doesn't count until you and Betsy are eighteen. Remember?"

But Tacy was wrong. She was definitely eighteen.

16

Mr. Kerr

"THAT KERR!" SAID MR. RAY, chuckling. "What do you suppose he's made me do now?"

The family, and Tacy, who had come to supper, looked up expectantly. For months they had been hearing anecdotes about Mr. Kerr, the super sales-man. He had talked Mr. Ray into putting a line of knit goods into the shoe store. "Although I didn't want it," Mr. Ray always said, "any more than a cat wants nine tails." He had achieved the virtual miracle of getting his knit goods into the shoe store's display window.

"What has he done now?" Betsy asked.

"Now, by George, he's wangled an invitation to come here for Sunday night lunch. He's coming next Sunday if that's all right with you, my dear," Mr. Ray ended, addressing his wife.

"Of course," said Mrs. Ray. "I'm dying to meet him. Is he married?"

"No. A bachelor."

"How old is he? I ought to find him a girl."

"Oh, twenty-seven or twenty-eight."

Betsy groaned. "Heavens! How ancient! Why do your interesting friends all have to be gray-beards, Papa?"

Tacy looked up innocently. "Why," she said, "I don't think twenty-seven is so old."

Everybody laughed and Tacy blushed, as only she could blush, to the roots of her auburn hair.

"All right, honey," Mrs. Ray said. "You can look after Mr. Kerr."

"I'm not even coming for Sunday night lunch this week," Tacy said hastily.

"Oh, yes, you are!" answered Betsy. "Don't you re-member? We're invited to Mrs. Poppy's that afternoon, you and Tib and Tony and Dennie and I. She has some plan she wants to talk over. Then we're all coming back here for lunch."

On Sunday, Tib had a cold, but the others went down to the Melborn Hotel, and Mrs. Poppy's plan proved to be engrossing. Her brother, who was an actor, was coming to visit her and put on a home-talent play. Mrs. Poppy wanted Tacy and Tony both to sing solos, and Tib to do a dance. The prospect was so exciting that it drove gray-beards of twenty-seven completely out of mind.

When they neared the Ray house, a stream of music told them that Winona had arrived. The quartet burst in and found that Cab and Lloyd were there, too. Then they saw Mr. Kerr, who was sitting in the parlor with Mr. and Mrs. Ray, somewhat removed by age, as well as by the archway, from the noisy music-room group.

Mr. Kerr was a fine-looking young man, very well groomed. He was moderately tall, with broad shoulders and a frank open face, lively blue eyes, fresh color, strong white teeth. He looked very good-humored, but something in the set of his jaw showed the determination Mr. Ray had described. He looked predominately likable.

He and Mr. Ray had been talking business, Mrs. Ray said.

"We'll never get any sandwiches made at this rate," she remarked briskly. "Tacy, Mr. Kerr is your responsibility now."

Tacy blushed again as only Tacy could. Mr. Kerr surveyed her with his bright appraising eyes.

"And is Tacy my responsibility?"

"She certainly is."

"I agree, if Tacy does," he said.

Mr. Ray went out to make the sandwiches, and Tony strolled negligently after him. Tony, although he acted so lazy, knew how to be useful, mixing an egg with the coffee, filling the pot with cold water, and setting it to boil. Betsy put Anna's cocoanut cake on the dining room table, along with pickles and olives, cream and sugar, cups and saucers. Winona was playing the piano and the Crowd was singing, when they weren't joking, teasing, scuffling, and yelling. Mr. Kerr took everything in with a lively, observant twinkle.

Mr. Ray spoke in an undertone to Tony and Betsy.

"You're seeing," he said, "a smart young man in action. That Kerr is in command of a difficult situation. He doesn't hold himself aloof from those kids, but he doesn't mix too much either. He mixes just enough to make everyone at ease, but not enough to lose his dignity."

Betsy watched and saw that what her father had said was true. Mr. Kerr was completely poised with the pretty girls, the clamoring boys. He didn't make himself one of them. They all called him Mr. Kerr. But he wasn't a wet blanket.

"Smart," Mr. Ray said, as he applied a different sort of skill to buttering bread, slicing ham, adding mustard, salt, and pepper, and cutting the double sandwiches in two halves, slantwise, until a large platter was heaped.

Betsy noticed something else as the evening progressed. Mr. Kerr had been told to take charge of Tacy, and he was certainly doing it. Tacy was habitually shy, and sometimes in a crowd she went off by herself. Tonight, Mr. Kerr followed. Tacy was plied with sandwiches. Her coffee cup was never allowed to be empty. She had the choicest piece of cocoanut cake.

Tacy and Mr. Kerr ate supper together and he talked all the time. He was, Betsy observed, a great talker. Tacy didn't act shy. She was listening attentively, and now and then she laughed or asked a question.

"It's because he's so old," Betsy thought. "She feels as though she were with her own father."

When everyone was carrying out the dishes after supper, Betsy went up to Tacy.

"Do you like him?" she asked.

"Who? Harry? Yes, he's very nice."

Harry! Betsy could hardly believe her ears. Harry!

Then Mr. Kerr *didn't* seem to Tacy like her father.

After a while, when the music gave way to general conversation, Mr. Kerr brought up the subject of cameras.

"Anybody interested in photography?" he asked. "I just bought a new Eastman."

Lloyd had received an Eastman for Christmas, and he and Mr. Kerr plunged into a technical discussion. Betsy said she used a square box Brownie.

"I'm so dumb I can't take pictures with any other kind."

"Why, you take good pictures, Betsy," Tacy said.

Mr. Kerr turned away from Lloyd abruptly.

"I'll *bet* you take mighty good ones," he said, smiling persuasively at Betsy. "Won't you show me some?"

Betsy brought out her bulging Kodak book, filled with pictures of the Rays, of the Crowd, of winter and summer excursions.

"Someone will have to explain this to me," Mr. Kerr said, and presently he and Tacy were sitting on the couch while she told him who was who, laughing as she turned the pages.

"Betsy says this is me at my silliest," Betsy heard her remark, and remembered the picnic up on the Big Hill when she had snapped Tacy acting like an Irish Colleen.

Mr. Kerr and Tacy looked at the Kodak book until the doorbell rang. One of Tacy's brothers had come to call for her.

That was the signal for everyone to go. There was a scramble for wraps and overshoes, a burst of good-nights, shouted plans to meet in school.

Mr. Kerr waited, leafing through the Kodak book until all the young people had gone. Then he closed the book and said he, too, must leave, and Mr. Ray gave him his overcoat. The young man shook hands heartily with Mrs. Ray and Betsy and said to Mr. Ray, "Would you show me which direction I start off in?"

When Mr. Ray accompanied him to the porch, Mrs. Ray turned to Betsy.

"What a delightful young man!"

"Isn't he!" said Betsy. She looked puzzled. "And wasn't he nice to Tacy?"

"They got along beautifully," Mrs. Ray replied. "I was pleased because Tacy is usually so shy."

"She wasn't shy with him," Betsy said. She couldn't quite make it out.

Mr. Ray returned from the porch. He closed the door behind him slowly, and came into the parlor with a strange look on his face. He sat down, rubbing his hands over his forehead, and then put them firmly on his knees.

"Well, I don't know what to think! That Kerr just

said the most amazing thing."

"What was it?" Mrs. Ray and Betsy cried together.

"First, Betsy, he apologized to you for having stolen one of your Kodak pictures. He said you're going to get a box of chocolates in return."

Betsy ran to her Kodak book and riffled the pages quickly. She knew which snapshot would be missing.

"The Colleen from Hill Street!" she breathed.

That was, indeed, gone. Tacy, laughing, her braids loose, her hair blown into curls, was no longer in Betsy's Kodak book.

Mrs. Ray and Betsy stared at each other. Her mother, Betsy thought, looked actually pale.

"But that isn't all," Mr. Ray went on. "In fact, it's only the beginning. Do you know what else he said?"

"Tell us, for heaven's sake!"

"He said," answered Mr. Ray, "that Tacy was the girl he was going to marry. He said he didn't care how long he would have to wait. She was the girl he was going to marry." After a pause in which no one seemed even to breathe, Mr. Ray added, "Tacy had better watch out. If Harry Kerr can talk me into putting in a line of knit goods, he can talk her into marrying him."

"Well!" said Mrs. Ray, color coming back into her cheeks, and her eyes beginning to sparkle. "I never heard the like."

Betsy was stunned. She was dazed and confounded. Marriage was something infinitely remote. It had never occurred to her that it could touch her circle yet. And to touch, of all people, Tacy!

She could hardly wait to tell Tacy, who would be thrilled. Or would she? You never could tell about Tacy. But she would think it was ridiculous, of course. She would laugh long and heartily and remind Betsy of how they were going to see Paris and New York and London and the Taj Mahal by moonlight.

Somehow, Betsy was anxious to hear that laughter. It was thrilling, but it was painful, too, to have Mr. Kerr in love with Tacy. She went up to bed still dazed, and early the next morning telephoned Tacy that she would walk to meet her.

"And see that you're alone! Don't be with Alice, or Tib, or anyone!"

Betsy hurried through breakfast and hurried into her winter coat, tam, and furs. She ran out of the house, in the direction opposite the school house, down the hill to the corner where a watering trough, now frozen and rimmed with icicles, marked the junction with Cemetery Road.

When she saw Tacy coming, she ran to meet her.

"Stand still! This can't be told walking."

She repeated dramatically what her father had said

when he came in from the porch the night before.

"He said he was going to marry you! TO MARRY YOU!" Betsy repeated.

Of course, Tacy blushed. Betsy had expected that, but she hadn't expected Tacy's eyes to light with such a mischievous glimmer. Betsy had expected her to be flabbergasted, dumbfounded, but she didn't seem very surprised.

When she spoke, it was in the Irish brogue she affected when she felt especially merry.

"Well, and sure now, did he?" she said, hooking her arm into Betsy's. The next moment she asked Betsy about a physics formula. Then she brought up the subject of the home-talent play.

Betsy's head was spinning. It felt actually light. Childhood seemed to be receding like a rapidly moving railway train.

"And Tib and I thought she was going to be an old maid . . . if we didn't help her!" Betsy marveled.

17

Up and Down Broadway

THERE WAS NO DENYING that Mr. Kerr's astounding
announcement and Tacy's calm reaction to it made
Betsy feel blue. She was proud of Tacy's conquest; she
was stirred by it. But it made her feel lonely, too.

It was strange to be excluded from something
which concerned Tacy. She and Tacy had always
shared everything. Tacy had shared Betsy's love affairs.

She had rejoiced with her when things went well and grieved when they went badly. Betsy would gladly have rejoiced with Tacy now, but Tacy didn't need her. She wasn't half so excited about Mr. Kerr as everyone else was. She liked him, she said; and her aura of serene radiance showed that she did. But she had no confidences to impart.

It was fortunate for Betsy that the new home-talent play came along just then. Not only did she feel blue, but school had reached its February dullness. Winter had reached its February dreariness. She needed the tinsel world of make-believe.

All Deep Valley needed it. Tired of snow and more snow, of deceptively fair days followed by rain that turned to snow and sometimes blizzards, of shoveling walks and shoveling coal, Deep Valley yielded itself joyously to *Up and Down Broadway.*

That was the name of Mr. Maxwell's production.

"I'm calling it *Up and Down Broadway* because I'm going to take a cast of amateurs and whip up a revue fit for Broadway," he told Betsy. Broadway was Mr. Maxwell's Paradise; he talked about it all the time.

He almost overflowed Mrs. Poppy's doll-like apartment, for he was fat, like his sister. Like his sister, too, he was a figure of elegance. Blond, with side whiskers, he wore a plaid vest, a satin tie with a diamond stickpin in it, a long coat, and striped trousers.

He wanted Betsy to choose a chorus from among the high school girls. *Up and Down Broadway* wasn't just a high school affair. It was a Deep Valley affair, a benefit for the Elks Lodge. Attractive young matrons, business men with a flair for theatricals, the town's child wonders were all taking part. Most of the singers were from Mrs. Poppy's class.

"*How* I wish Julia were here!" she kept interjecting now.

Choosing the chorus, Mr. Maxwell explained to Betsy earnestly, was important.

"On Broadway," he said, fixing her with a gleaming eye, "the chorus is more important than the principals. You have to have cute snappy broilers, Georgie Cohan always says. Can you find me thirty cute, snappy girls in Deep Valley High School, Miss Ray? They must be able to sing and dance, of course."

"Certainly," said Betsy. She felt that the honor of Deep Valley was at stake.

Fortunately, the high school had plenty of pulchritude. The girls in the Crowd were secured first; then the junior, sophomore, and freshman classes were searched for talent. When the thirty assembled, glowing and smiling, on the bare dusty stage of the Opera House, Mr. Maxwell surveyed them with satisfaction and said that they would be a credit to Broadway.

His pleasure in them was short-lived. His good humor, they were to find, was spasmodic. When coats were doffed and the girls began singing timidly, dancing self-consciously in response to his suggestions, Mr. Maxwell changed completely. His rosy face grew purple. He shrieked and pounded the piano. He told them they were nitwits and dunces, clodhoppers, gawky as a bunch of milkmaids. He made Irma cry. Some of the girls told Betsy that they wouldn't be in *Up and Down Broadway*, after all.

But while they were huffily putting on their wraps, Mr. Maxwell changed again. He moved about jovially, making jokes, beaming. He told them that they mustn't mind him. That was the way Broadway producers always yelled at the broilers. He said they were so cute that he wished Flo Ziegfeld could see them.

After a while, the girls grew accustomed to his rapid changes of mood. It was nervous work, though, singing and dancing to please Mr. Maxwell.

Usually, after they had rehearsed, the broilers sat on boxes or folding chairs around the stage to watch the principals perform . . . especially those from the high school.

Tib's Dutch Girl number was good from the start. She could not sing, but she could talk a song with airy coquetry, and her dancing was light, feathery, and bewitching. Mr. Maxwell wasn't cross with her long, for she was always able to do exactly what she was told. He would stand at the edge of the stage to watch her practise and say to Mrs. Poppy, "That girl has talent. Broadway needs that girl."

When Tacy first heard Mr. Maxwell rave and rant, she withdrew hastily from her scheduled solo. But Mr. Maxwell and Mrs. Poppy pleaded with her to reconsider, and she did. After that, Mr. Maxwell was gentle with Tacy.

> *"I'm awfully lonesome tonight,*
> *Somehow there's nothing just right,*
> *Honey, you know why. . . ."*

She was to sing that all alone on the stage, looking at an artificial moon.

Dennie was to be a ballet dancer. Tony was singing an old Joe Howard success:

> *"What's the use of dreaming,*
> *Dreams of rosy hue,*
> *What's the use of dreaming, dreaming,*
> *Dreams that never could come true. . . ."*

He had sung it for years at the Ray piano; it was a favorite song of Mr. Ray's, and Mrs. Poppy had transposed the music to suit Tony's deep bass voice. Betsy liked to hear him rehearse it, but Tony almost drove Mr. Maxwell to distraction. Mr. Maxwell liked him, of course. Everyone liked Tony. But he was late at rehearsals. He didn't learn his lines. He was always clowning.

At the back of the stage among dusty piles of scenery, Tony would take off Lillian Russell, or he would borrow spectacles to imitate the church choir tenor, whose solo was one of the classical highlights of the show. When there was music, he and Betsy waltzed in the wings. Sometimes they wandered through the empty Opera House, which always reminded Betsy of Uncle Keith.

When she came there to plays, it seemed elegant beyond description—the glittering crystal chandelier, seats upholstered in red velvet, boxes hung with red velvet draperies tied back with golden cords. Now it was dark and chilly and the curtain (which showed a sedan chair and ladies in hoop skirts) was half way up, revealing the barnlike stage. But Betsy was still enchanted by it.

"I even like the smell," she said to Tony, sniffing.

"I feel at home here myself," he replied thoughtfully, gazing around.

Rehearsals were glamorous. They made many new matches—and revived some old ones. Take Dennie and Tib! Maddox was the star of the basketball team now, but such was the influence of Thespis that Dennie was crowding Maddox out of Tib's life.

All the girls were thinking that perhaps they should go on the stage, that their talents were better suited to Broadway than to Deep Valley High School.

Of course, everyone was getting behind in school, and Betsy was dimly worried because she wanted to make the Honor Roll. She knew that she ought to be practising, too, "A Night in Venice" for Miss Cobb's recital. And Joe grew stiffer and stiffer in the class-room, and she heard that he had bought two tickets for the show. But none of this seemed as real as it would after *Up and Down Broadway* was over. What was real now was the big, bare Opera House filled with staccato excitement.

The dress rehearsal was terrible. Mr. Maxwell shouted at the top of his voice. The girls wept and the boys stormed, but nobody could possibly have been persuaded to leave.

On the day of the performance, it snowed, as heavily, as persistently, as though there hadn't been a flake all winter. But nobody minded. The house had been sold out for weeks, from the first row in the parquet all the way to the rafters.

After Betsy was dressed for the opening number in her glow worm costume, she visited Tacy and Tib in their dressing room. Tib was cool and poised, arranging her yellow curls under a winged cap. Tacy was so pale that the paint on her cheeks looked grotesque, and her hands were as cold as ice.

Betsy kissed her on the top of her head.

"Cheer up!" she said. "It will all be the same a hundred years from now."

But Tacy was too wretched to joke. She was stiff with wretchedness.

On the stairs which lead up to the stage, Betsy met Tony. He was wearing a plain dark suit, but his face was painted, and charcoal made his black eyes look even wickeder than usual.

"Come on!" he said, catching her hand. "Let's take a look at the audience."

Sets were being run into place on the stage, and they made their way cautiously to the curtain, found two peep holes, and looked out.

The audience was streaming in. Betsy saw her father and mother and Margaret. Where the dress circle met the parquet, in the very center of the house, were two wide, well-padded seats. These had been built especially for the excessively stout Mr. and Mrs. Poppy, who were seated in them now, Mr. Poppy in a dress suit, Mrs. Poppy in a low-cut gown, with plumes in her yellow hair.

Joe was coming in with a girl Betsy didn't know.

She was very, very pretty. They talked all the way down the aisle, and she kept turning around to smile into his face while he was helping her off with her coat and laying it over the chair.

Betsy felt that pressure about her heart. She turned and smiled meaningfully into Tony's black-rimmed eyes. This was unfair to Tony, and she knew it, but she didn't seem to care.

"Take a look at Margaret," she said. "She looks so serious. I know she's praying for you."

"You praying for me, too, Ray of Sunshine?"

"You don't need anybody's prayers. You're wonderful."

"Say that again."

But the orchestra was tuning up now, and Mr. Maxwell, suave and smiling in a dress suit, called everyone out on the stage. He told them he knew the performance was going to be fine, because it was good luck to have a dress rehearsal go badly.

"On Broadway we're scared to death if the dress rehearsal goes well. I've known Belasco to call off a performance just because the dress rehearsal clicked."

Betsy thought this sounded a little excessive, but she had to admit that in spite of last night's mistakes and wearisome confusion, *Up and Down Broadway* went off to perfection.

The high school chorus opened the show:

"Shine, little glow worm, glimmer,
Shine, little glow worm, glimmer. . . ."

The stage was dark at first, and the girls carried phosphorescent wands. Then the lights went on, and the girls in their black and orange costumes were themselves the glow worms. The audience stamped and whistled. It seemed that Deep Valley thought broilers important, just as Broadway did.

The leading lights of the town did their numbers, and the high school celebrities did theirs. Dennie, with his cherubic face, made a fetching ballet dancer. He wore a short-skirted tulle dress, a feather head-dress, ropes of pearls, earrings, and long white gloves with bracelets and rings outside. A big spangly orna-ment on one black-stockinged leg almost brought the house down.

Tacy came out on the stage like a sleep-walker. Her dress was of old blue Liberty silk, covered with gauze of changing coppery colors. Mr. Maxwell had wanted her to wear a picture hat, but Tacy had unexpectedly objected. People didn't go out singing to the moon in picture hats, she said. She hadn't even dressed her hair in the fashionable puffs, but wore her familiar coronet braids. And although she looked beautiful, she looked just like Tacy when the curtain rose and the spotlight found her gazing at a tinsel moon.

"I'm awfully lonesome tonight,
Somehow there's nothing just right,
Honey, you know why. . . ."

The house was very quiet listening to Tacy's harp-like voice. At the end there was a burst of applause, and after Tacy reached the wings where Betsy and Tib were listening tensely, there was another burst so loud that she had to go back. She was slow returning this time.

"What can it be?" asked Betsy, peeking.

"Flowers, probably," said Tib.

Every girl performer received a bouquet. Their families sent them if no one else did. But Tacy came into the wings with a bouquet no father would have sent. It was the biggest bouquet anyone had received that evening. Her arms could hardly hold the dozens of long-stemmed yellow roses.

Betsy and Tib spoke together, the same words, "Mr. Kerr?"

Tacy nodded happily. "He came all the way from St. Paul just to see the show."

The most professional number on the program was undoubtedly the Dutch Girl's song and dance. The quaint costume with its many petticoats emphasized Tib's tiny waist, and she didn't forget one of the winning smiles or dainty gestures Mr. Maxwell had taught her. The chorus came out and danced behind her for many, many encores, and she had flowers galore.

Yet Tib wasn't the hit of the show. To everyone's surprise, especially Mr. Maxwell's, that honor went to Tony.

When the music for his song began, he strolled carelessly out on the stage and straddled a chair. He got out his pipe and filled it, tamping down the tobacco as thoughtfully as though he were sitting in the Rays' parlor, with all the time in the world. The orchestra kept on playing. Then, holding the pipe in his hand, his arms folded on top of the chair, he began to sing:

> "*What's the use of dreaming,*
> *Dreams of rosy hue,*
> *What's the use of dreaming, dreaming,*
> *Dreams that never could come true. . . .*"

His lazy charm, his rich deep voice won the audience completely. He was called before the curtain again and again. He sauntered out, at ease and smiling, saluted nonchalantly, retreated. He couldn't sing an encore, for he had none prepared. At last Mr. Maxwell signified to the orchestra that Tony could repeat the chorus, and he did.

"You are worth a million,
There is not a doubt,

.. ..

.. ..
Then your pipe goes out."

Betsy and Tony, Dennie and Tib went to the Moor-
ish Cafe after the show. Betsy and Tib kept a little of
their make-up on their cheeks and felt like actresses.
Joe and the pretty girl were there, but Betsy ignored
them. She flirted gaily with Tony.

She started a game which had just reached popu-
larity, writing down dashes which, properly decoded,
spelled out words and messages.

Her "---- ----- ---- -- --- ----?" was translated at last:
"What color eyes do you like?"

Tony pulled his curly thatch and wrote, "---- ---- ---
---- -- - ----." "They have the name of a girl."

"Hazel!" Tib shrieked, and Betsy wrote (in code, of
course), "I like curly hair."

Tony's eyes sought hers with laughing boldness. He
set down dashes firmly. "I like unnaturally curly hair."

Dennie seized the pencil then, and Tib peeped over
his shoulder. Their table resounded with mirth.

Tib came to stay all night at the Rays'.

"You were darling," Betsy told her as they undressed. "You really ought to go on the stage, Tib."

"Maybe I will," Tib said. "But there are lots of things I like to do. I like to draw, I like to cook, I like to keep house. . . ."

"If I were making up a plot," said Betsy, "I'd have Mr. Maxwell getting back to New York and telegraphing for you to come and go into the Follies."

"You can make up all the plots you like," said Tib, matter-of-factly. "But I'm going to go through high school and graduate along with you and Tacy."

"Betsy," she added after a moment. "You're getting to like Tony pretty well, aren't you?"

"What makes you think so?" Betsy asked.

"You acted that way tonight. Joe didn't like it, either. I could tell, the way he stuck his lip out."

"That . . . go-to-the-deuce . . . look, you mean," said Betsy flippantly.

But she didn't answer Tib's question.

18

"Toil and Trouble"

BETSY SAT AT THE PIANO, practising Nevins' "A Night
in Venice," which she was going to play at Miss
Cobb's recital. She played badly, for she felt cross. She
had been feeling cross for some time, although she
tried not to show it . . . ever since *Up and Down
Broadway*, in fact.

She had been having difficulties with Tony. En-
couraged by her coquetry that night, he had changed.

All winter, in spite of the fact that he had been going with no one but her, he had not acted lover-like.

"He was never spoony," she thought. "And not because he doesn't like me, either!"

He liked her—too much. She had known for some time that he did. She had seen it in his touchingly good behavior, his mock-serious gallantries, the adoring look his black eyes held sometimes. But he had tried not to show it. He would have kept on trying—because he thought she didn't share his feeling—if she hadn't given him false hopes.

She had brought it all on herself. Just because she had seen Joe with that girl at the show! And after all, he hadn't taken her out again. She was just a girl who had been visiting in town. Of no consequence at all! Betsy brought her hands down bitterly on the keys.

In the Crowd, she had been snappish. She had quarreled violently with Winona and Irma—Betsy, who never quarreled! They didn't speak for three days until Irma apologized for something she hadn't even done. She had quarreled with Cab about whether he had broken some casual date. It was something that really shouldn't have mattered a fig.

"I don't know what ails me," Betsy thought. "Of course," she added defensively, "I'm working pretty hard."

She was. Everything that had been pushed away and put aside while *Up and Down Broadway* was in preparation now had to be faced. In Miss Bangeter's Shakespeare class they had finished the comedies, *As You Like It* and *The Merchant of Venice,* and were deep in the grim tragedies of *Hamlet* and *Macbeth.*

"Bubble, bubble,
Toil and trouble. . . ."

Toil and trouble expressed exactly what she was going through, Betsy decided. In physics she was facing an examination on "Light."

"Why does anyone have to do anything about light except enjoy it?" she demanded, running a scale.

In German, she was struggling with adjectives. It seemed so unreasonable of the Germans to change their adjectives, for gender, number, case.

"Why can't they just say *klein* for 'small'? Why does it have to be *kleiner, kleines, kleine,* and goodness knows what else! If one adjective is good enough for English, it ought to be for German," stormed Betsy, banging.

The Honor Roll would be announced soon. And Betsy wanted to be on it. She wanted to be on the program commencement night, to give an oration as Carney had done.

"I should have thought about that earlier in the year, or last year, or the year before that, or the year before that," she told herself, making a discord.

She wasn't properly prepared even for Miss Cobb's recital, although Miss Cobb had been planning it happily for months. Well, Betsy thought, she would stick to her practising for an hour this morning if it killed her.

But she wasn't too sorry when the telephone rang.

It was Alice, who was also to play at Miss Cobb's recital.

"Betsy! Have you heard? Miss Cobb has left for Colorado. Leonard died last night."

"Leonard . . . died?"

She could hardly take it in.

Then Leonard had lost his fight! He would never compose that music which had been running in his head. He would never hear the operas, the great orchestras he had longed to hear.

"There won't be any recital, of course," Alice said.

After she shut down the telephone, Betsy stared at it through a blur of tears. She was sorry she hadn't written Leonard that long funny letter about *Up and Down Broadway* which had been rolling around in her head. She would never write it now, and he would never read it. It would have made him laugh.

She thought about Miss Cobb. Dear, brave Miss Cobb! This was the third child to die, of the four she had taken to raise. And she had been so cheerful all winter, although the news from Leonard had been bad.

Betsy dashed the tears out of her eyes and went upstairs to her mother's bedroom, where Mrs. Ray and Miss Mix were busy with the Easter sewing.

"Oh, I'm so sorry!" Mrs. Ray said, when Betsy had told her the news. "It's a very good thing she has Bobby."

Bobby, the one remaining nephew, was a youthful, masculine counterpart of his sturdy aunt. The family enemy wouldn't get him, at least.

"Let's ask Bobby up to supper while his aunt is gone," said Mrs. Ray. "Ask Margaret to telephone him."

Betsy went reluctantly to tell the news to Margaret. Margaret had taken Miss Cobb into the small circle of her affections along with Washington and Lincoln, Mrs. Wheat and Tony. And Margaret had deep feelings, although she could never express them. She could never find an outlet for her emotions in small ejaculations of pity or sympathy as other people did.

She said nothing at all now, just stared with dark, troubled eyes. When Betsy asked her to telephone Bobby, she marched away, her back very straight. But she went into the coat closet and stayed there a while before she telephoned.

Betsy closed "A Night in Venice" and put it away. She never wanted to hear it again.

But she did. Bobby came to supper. And after a few days Miss Cobb returned from Colorado with Leonard. Half the high school went to the funeral, and Miss Cobb's pupils sent a big wreath. Then lessons began again. Miss Cobb looked pale, but she was as calmly cheerful as ever. She didn't mention the recital, though. There was no recital that year.

Sadness weighed Betsy down for several days, although there was good news at school. When the civics class was leaving the classroom, Miss Clarke beckoned to her.

"Will you drop in to see me after school?" she whispered.

That meant, Betsy knew, that she had been chosen for the Essay Contest. She ought to be glad, but she didn't feel anything. She just felt tired out.

In English class, she did what she rarely did these days, glanced across the room at Joe. He was leafing through *Macbeth*, but just as she looked at him he looked at her. He didn't smile. He only looked at her and turned back to his book. But Betsy felt sure that he, too, had been asked to write in the Essay Contest. He was thinking what she was thinking: they would be competing again this year!

Entering Miss Clarke's room, she tried to muster a

smile which would match Miss Clarke's kind excitement.

"I've some good news for you, Betsy. The Zetamathians have chosen you again for the Essay Contest. The Philomathians have chosen Joe, of course."

"Of course," said Betsy, smiling.

"And . . . I want you to know . . . there was no dissenting voice about you this year. Miss Bangeter, Miss Fowler, and I all think you are the one to represent the senior Zetamathians."

Betsy tried to look as happy as she knew Miss Clarke expected her to look.

"What is the subject?" she asked with forced eagerness.

"It is 'Conservation of Our Natural Resources.'"

"'Conservation of Our . . . Natural Resources'?" Betsy repeated blankly.

"You know," Miss Clarke said helpfully. "Keeping up our forests and things. You like the out-of-doors, Betsy. I think you can write a good essay on that subject."

Betsy felt dubious, but she tried to act assured.

"I'll get right to work," she said.

As a matter of fact, she put off going to the library. She dreaded meeting Joe at the little table in the stalls where contestants for the Essay Contest worked. She didn't feel up to seeing him across the table, his bent head shutting her out.

More good news followed. The Honor Roll was announced, and she was on it! She would give an oration at Commencement and Tacy would be singing a solo. Tib had the leading role in the class play.

"Oh, bliss! Joy! Rapture!" they cried.

Rejoicing, they went to Mr. Snow's Photographic Studio to sit for their class pictures. Betsy had one taken in her shirt waist, wearing her class pin; another, in her Class Day dress, the pale blue embroidered batiste Julia had sent from Switzerland. They got the proofs, and Betsy saw that in the shirt waist picture she looked just as she really looked. But the Class Day picture was dreamily flattering.

Miss Mix was making her beautiful clothes, because she was a senior. They included a new tan suit with a frilly white waist for Easter. Betsy bought her Easter hat—a big rough straw, turned up at one side, covered with red poppies. It was glamorously becoming.

Easter came early. And as though nature understood, spring came early, too. Long since, there had been pussy willows in the slough and blackbirds, with red patches on their wings, calling in raucous voices. Now the sun had melted the snow to gray slush. Patches of soggy exuberant grass appeared.

On the day before Easter, when Betsy and Margaret were coloring eggs in the kitchen, Mrs. Ray rushed in.

"Mail from Julia!" she called, waving a letter.

Every letter from Julia was an event, but this one brought especially dramatic news. Julia was going to spend Easter at the Von Hetternichs' castle in Poland.

"Only a hundred rooms are open," Julia wrote, underlining the "only."

Mrs. Ray telephoned Mr. Ray, and when he came home Betsy read the letter aloud to him. After they had eaten supper and Margaret, as usual, had made a nest for the Easter bunny out on the lawn, Betsy read the letter again.

Her father looked at her thoughtfully after she had finished.

"Julia doing all this traveling," he said, "puts an idea into my head."

"What is it?" the others wanted to know.

"I think that Betsy ought to do a little traveling—to the farm."

"To the farm?" asked Betsy. She added jokingly, "Why not Chicago or New York?"

"You don't need Chicago or New York," said Mr. Ray. "You're tired out."

"Are you thinking of the Taggarts?" asked Mrs. Ray, mentioning the farmers Betsy had visited the summer before she went into high school.

"No," said Mr. Ray. "I was thinking of the Beidwinkles, German customers of mine. They were in the store today and asked if one of you girls wouldn't like to come out. Why wouldn't Easter vacation be a good time?"

"Oh, not Easter vacation, Papa!" cried Betsy. "There's a party planned for almost every day."

"That's the trouble," said Mr. Ray. "That's just what I'm getting at. You don't need parties. You need a rest. Don't you think so, Jule?"

"Yes," said Mrs. Ray. "I hate to have her miss the parties." (Mrs. Ray loved parties.) "But you do seem tired, Betsy. You have all spring."

Betsy wanted to cry. She wanted to cry if anyone looked at her these days. But she certainly didn't want to go to a lonesome old farm away from all the fun and excitement of Deep Valley. She winked her eyes rapidly.

"I'll go to your Beidwinkles sometime, Papa. I'd love to. But not in Easter vacation. Please!"

"All right," said Mr. Ray, but he looked dissatisfied.

The telephone broke in on the conversation. It was Winona, suggesting that since the night was so warm, with a moon, it would be fun to go out serenading. Betsy agreed, and soon Tony called for her. A group of eight boys and girls wandered down the street in the mild air seeking the houses they would favor with song.

Tacy didn't come. Mr. Kerr was in town, Alice said.

But Irma was there to lead the sopranos, and the Crowd sang with full throated joy "My Wild Irish Rose," "On Moonlight Bay," "Rose of Mexico."

Betsy loved singing, especially in parts. And Tony wasn't acting mushy tonight. He held her arm in comradely fashion, while his deep voice plunged downward in the bass, inventing impudent harmonies. When they walked he was full of tomfoolery, making everyone laugh.

"Wouldn't I be foolish to go to the country and miss fun like this?" Betsy thought.

After an hour, the serenaders broke into smaller groups. Tony and Betsy called good night and started up Plum Street Hill.

"Say," said Tony, "this is a swell night."

"Just like summer," Betsy answered, looking up at the moon.

"Summer!" said Tony, turning her about. "That calls for ice cream!"

"Heinz's?" she asked.

"Heinz's! But let's not eat it there. Let's make them give us a sack and two spoons."

Mr. Heinz, of course, complied. He was used to the vagaries of the young. Betsy and Tony took a quart of ice cream to Lincoln Park, that pie-shaped wedge of land with an elm tree and a fountain on it which stood where Hill Street began. They sat down on the bench and consumed ice cream with relish, making absurd conversation.

When they had finished, they fell silent. Moonlight flooded everything and made a cloudy shadow of the big elm tree. Tony had been cheerfully unromantic all evening. Betsy was astonished, and taken unprepared, when suddenly he put his arm around her and kissed her.

She jumped up.

"Tony Markham! What are you doing?"

Tony got up, too, but only to kiss her again.

"There's nothing so strange about it, is there?" he asked. "We're going together, aren't we?"

"No . . . not exactly."

"We certainly are."

"We certainly aren't!" cried Betsy. "Not if it means acting spoony like this. I hate this."

"You're acting stupid," said Tony, roughly. "If you don't like me . . ."

"I do like you . . . but not in that way."

She started toward home, Tony walking beside her in silence. He was angry. She could tell it by the swift pace of his walk, usually so slow. She wasn't angry with him; she was angry with herself, angry and confused.

They reached her house. By the arc light on the corner she saw the little nest Margaret had put out.

Since their departure, the bunny had visited it. It contained a fluffy hen and a flock of yellow chicks.

Betsy pointed to it, trying to speak naturally.

"Isn't that cute?"

But Tony didn't answer. They paused awkwardly.

"Come in?" she asked.

"No, thanks," he answered. He brought his hand up to his cap in a reluctant concession to manners, walked rapidly away.

When Betsy went in the house, she dropped down on the sofa and started to cry. The house was dark and she didn't want the lights. "Oh, dear! Oh, dear! Oh, dear!" she wept. She felt forlorn and ashamed of herself.

Tony had not meant any disrespect when he kissed her. He respected her; he looked up to her. She knew it. He understood, too, that you didn't let boys kiss you unless you were in love with them. She had let him think she *was* in love . . . or falling.

And he was really in love with her. She knew it as well as though he had told her. He probably would have told her, if she had been different tonight. He might even have said that he wanted them to be engaged. But maybe not. Tony, although so bold, was inarticulate. It would have been hard for him to find words for that. He would have meant it, though.

Still crying, she jumped up and tiptoed down to the

basement. She went to the small room where luggage was kept, brought out her satchel, and tiptoed upstairs. She started throwing piles of clothing into the satchel.

Tomorrow, after Margaret had found her nest, after Easter church and dinner, she was going away. She was going to ask her father to take her to the Beidwinkles' after all.

19

Beidwinkles'

BETSY WOKE EARLY on the morning after Easter, flooded by a sense of peace. She had slept dreamlessly on a puffy feather bed beneath Mrs. Beidwinkle's fresh-smelling sheets, her patchwork quilts and downy comforter, and she lay staring at a framed motto which said "Grüss Gott" in cross stitch, unable for a moment to remember where she was.

The window was a square of gray, but through the slot in the storm sash, she could hear a delicious jumble of bird voices. She recognized the killdeer shouting his own name and the robin going joyously up and down.

She felt happy. It came to her that she had not been happy for a very long time. Now the things which had been making her unhappy . . . the quarrel with Joe, the worry about Tony, the nervous, strained anxiety about school affairs—all these had faded away. She lay in bed smiling.

Presently she jumped up, closed the window, and poured water from the pitcher into the bowl. She gave herself a vigorous cold sponge, despite the fact that the room was chilly. She dressed warmly, putting on a red flannel waist and a plaid skirt. Not bothering with puffs, she braided her hair and turned it up with a ribbon. She realized suddenly that she had forgotten last night to put it up on Magic Wavers. When, she thought, bursting into a laugh, had she ever forgotten that before?

She and her father had arrived late, after supper. She had not even unpacked her suitcase, except for her dresses. She saw them on hangers in the closet, her Peter Thompson suit, the white and gold wool dress. Why on earth had she brought that? she wondered. She must have been crazy when she packed, thinking that parties pursued one everywhere.

Briskly, she laid her underwear and shirt waists in neat piles in the bureau drawers which stuck when she tried to open them, but were immaculately papered inside. She arranged her toilet articles on top of the bureau and set her family photographs around. She laid out her comb and brush and mirror.

There was a little table in one corner which would be perfect for her writing. She brought it up flush to the window, which looked out into a bare box elder tree and across the Beidwinkles' front lawn, a sheet of gray snow in the gray light.

She took the starched white spread off the table, folded it, and put it away. Then she set out her tablets, notebooks, and pencils, her pencil sharpener and her eraser and the ruler she had brought . . . goodness knew why! She added the Bible, her prayer book, and the dictionary. There!

"I'm going to start a story this morning," she decided. "I think it will be about a girl who goes away somewhere, to Newport, maybe. I'll bet it will sell, too," she added. (None of last summer's stories had sold, although she had kept them continuously on the go.)

Last night's impression of the house returned as she literally skipped down the narrow stairs. It was the cleanest house she had ever been in, and it looked very old-fashioned, with rag carpets and crocheted tidies on the chairs.

There was an organ in the parlor, she noticed, peeking into that formidable room. The horsehair chairs sat about in prickly splendor. On a square table there was a gigantic family Bible with a velvet-covered photograph album on the ledge beneath. On a round table were wax flowers under glass, with a stereopticon set on the ledge.

Betsy and her father had sat in the kitchen, which was, she soon found out, the most used and the pleasantest room in the house. It was large, with blue and white curtains, red geraniums in the windows, and a wood-burning cook stove, its nickel trim polished to the gleam of solid silver.

Fire was roaring in the stove this morning, and beside it Mrs. Beidwinkle leaned over a crate which held a flock of chirping yellow chicks. She was a large, big-busted woman with a childlike face. Her graying hair was parted and brushed smoothly down over her ears, in which tiny earrings were set. Graying braids were twisted round and round to make a bun in the back.

Betsy stooped to admire the chicks.

"The sweet little things! May I help you get breakfast?" she asked, feeling rather proud of being down so early.

Mrs. Beidwinkle laughed gleefully. "Breakfast!" she ejaculated. "Mein Mann milked the cows two hours ago. We had breakfast then. I have my wash on the line and was just going to have a little coffee."

"Do you get up so early every day?"

"Earlier in the summertime. But you are to sleep as late as you can. I always have second breakfasts. My second can be your first."

On a red-cloth-covered table Mrs. Beidwinkle set out coffee cake and a plateful of cookies, thickly sliced homemade bread, and a bowl of milk. She poured a cup of coffee for herself and offered one to Betsy, but Betsy didn't want it. It had obviously been reheated and looked as black as ink. The bread and milk, coffee cake, and cookies were delicious.

Betsy enjoyed talking with Mrs. Beidwinkle, who plainly enjoyed talking with her. All her children— four sons and five daughters—were married and gone.

"But Amelia lives near. She is the youngest one."

Mrs. Beidwinkle was full of legends of her children, their illnesses, their love affairs, their triumphs and disappointments, the death of one. When she got up at last, saying that she must bring in her wash, Betsy put on her cravenette and went out to explore.

It was cold. The wind almost blew her off her feet, and the windmill was whirling. Big clouds, some dark, some pearly white, sailed in a gray sky.

She went to the barn, where she made friends with

a sheep dog and saw a litter of kittens. Big, bearded Mr. Beidwinkle, less impressive than he had seemed last night, called out to her from a shed where he was tinkering with a plough. He introduced her to small, grizzled Bill, the hired man.

They weren't so busy as they would be later, Mr. Beidwinkle said. He couldn't start ploughing until the frost was out of the ground. Meanwhile he was repairing and oiling farm machinery; he and Bill were building a new chicken house; he was hauling wood from the wood lot.

Betsy returned to the house, cold and blown, went up to her room, and started her story.

After dinner, which was eaten in the kitchen, she helped with the dishes, then went up to her room, undressed, and took a nap. She slept from two to four, got up and dressed again, put on her cravenette and overshoes, and took another walk.

It was colder than ever; she couldn't face north. But the smell of spring was in the air. A crow flew out of an oak tree, flapping his big wings and croaking, "Caw! Caw! Caw!" She saw the green spears of tulips on the south side of the house.

She ate voraciously at supper, which was like a second dinner, with beer for the men. Mr. Beidwinkle addressed his wife in German and Betsy volunteered the information that she was studying it. They were delighted.

"*Sie sprechen Deutsch, ja?*" Mr. Beidwinkle asked.

"*Ein wenig,*" Betsy replied. "I'd love to try to talk it with you sometimes while I'm here."

Bill began to point out articles on the table, giving their German names. But Betsy had played this game with the Mullers. She cried out the names before he had a chance to utter them and soon everyone was laughing. She was so expert that they had to point to the cupboards, to the stove, to find words she didn't know.

After supper, the Beidwinkles went into the back parlor, where a ruddy-windowed coal stove reminded Betsy of Hill Street. Mr. Beidwinkle and Bill buried themselves in German newspapers, Mrs. Beidwinkle went to work on her embroidery. Betsy started *Little Dorrit*, which she had brought from home, but her thoughts kept going to the organ locked away in the front parlor.

At last she mentioned it hesitantly. "Would you mind if I went in sometimes and played your organ? Not tonight when Mr. Beidwinkle is reading, but to-morrow maybe."

"What?" cried Mr. Beidwinkle. "You play the organ? Mamma! She plays the organ. We can make music."

Mrs. Beidwinkle was as excited as her husband, and Bill, too, eased himself to his feet.

"That organ is never played since our last daughter

married and went away. Ach, we would be happy to hear some music again!"

Mrs. Beidwinkle bustled into the front parlor and lit the lamp. Mr. Beidwinkle and Bill came in and took chairs, and Betsy began to feel stage fright.

"I don't play very well, you know. Not like my sister, Julia. I just thought maybe I could practise . . ."

"You practise, and we listen," Mr. Beidwinkle said. "You are used to an organ? *Ja?*"

"No. But I don't think it's very different from a piano."

Mrs. Beidwinkle unlocked it proudly. She pointed out the eleven stops, the knee swells, the pedals covered with Brussels carpet. Betsy sat down timidly, and tried them out. She started her simple repertoire.

"Can't you sing?" Mr. Beidwinkle demanded.

Betsy was nonplused. Of course she could sing; she had been singing all her life. But she didn't sing for people all alone, as Julia and Tacy did. She just sang.

She discovered now that she could sing if she had to for other people, all alone. Mr. and Mrs. Beidwinkle and Bill were looking so radiantly expectant that she couldn't disappoint them. Finding the proper chords, she sang "Juanita" and "Annie Laurie" and some of the other old songs her father loved. Then she began on the popular songs: "Tonight Will Never Come Again" (at which Mrs. Beidwinkle wiped her eyes), "I Wonder Who's Kissing Her Now," "The Rose of Mexico," "Yip-i-addy-i-ay." Bill liked that one.

At last she began the new song Julia had sent her at Christmas. Just for fun she sang it in German— "*Kind, Du Kannst Tanzen.* . . ."

Mr. Beidwinkle laughed and slapped his knee. "Gollee, gollee," he said over and over.

After that, every evening Betsy sang "Tonight Will Never Come Again" for Mrs. Beidwinkle, who always wiped her eyes, "Yip-i-addy-i-ay" for Bill, and "*Kind, Du Kannst Tanzen*" for Mr. Beidwinkle, who chuckled and said, "Gollee."

Betsy went upstairs and into her little room smiling. It was cold, but she didn't mind. Without lighting the lamp, she sat down by the window and looked out at the ghostly landscape.

She was glad she had studied German. There had been such satisfaction in being able to talk a little with the Beidwinkles. And she was glad that when Julia went away, she had learned to play the piano! She would never play well, she knew. She could never sing like Julia. She didn't even want to; she wanted to write stories. But how pleasant it was to be able to play enough to give pleasure to people!

"I'm going to write Miss Cobb and tell her. She'll be glad to hear."

Her thoughts turned to Leonard. She had thought

about him when she was out walking today. She felt a little better about Leonard out here in the country. It was just being close to nature, she supposed. In the country you felt as you never could in town the return of spring after winter. You felt a sort of pulse in the earth, which proved that nothing dies, that everything comes back in beauty.

Leonard was coming back . . . in some place beautiful enough to pay him for leaving the world. God knew all about his music, too. He would use that music someplace.

"I should have known that in church Easter morning. I'm surprised that I didn't. But I was awfully mixed up."

She was thankful to her father for having sent her out here. The trip had already given her perspective. The problems about Tony didn't seem so difficult now. There would be some way to get back to the old loving friendship.

The days fell into a pattern similar to the pattern of the first day. Betsy had her first breakfast with Mrs. Beidwinkle's second. She took a walk every morning and every afternoon, going farther and farther afield. The weather warmed up, melting the snow, so that there was a terrible mixture of ice, slush, and water underfoot. But there were compensations.

There was the vivid spring sky. There was the

spring taste in the air. There were buds swelling on the trees in the wood lot, and white bloodroots, pink and lavender hepaticas under wet mats of last year's leaves. There were meadow larks rising with a flash of yellow to sing in a rapture that made one catch one's breath.

She finished her first story and began a second one. She finished the second and began a third. She and the Beidwinkles talked in German every night at supper. Mrs. Beidwinkle taught her a poem in German which she recited to uproarious applause. Every evening she went into the parlor and played the organ and sang.

She wasn't homesick. She remembered how homesick she had been at the Taggarts' farm four years ago. That farm had been just as nice; the Taggarts had been just as kind as Mr. and Mrs. Beidwinkle. But she had suffered so much with homesickness that for months the mere memory of it had filled her with desolation. Now she was happy from morning until night.

"You do grow up," she thought.

It was pleasant to talk with her mother, who telephoned sometimes in the evening. And she had letters from Tacy and Tib. But the letters seemed to come from a great distance. She had forgotten the woes which had weighed her down at home.

"Betsy," Mrs. Beidwinkle said on Friday at dinner. "We would like to have a little party before you go home."

"A party?" asked Betsy, startled. The word surprised her. She associated parties with the Crowd and Deep Valley, not this peaceful haven.

She saw that Mr. Beidwinkle and Bill were watching her eagerly. Mrs. Beidwinkle looked as pleased as a child.

"*Ja*," she said. "We would like to invite Amelia and her husband to come and hear you sing."

"To hear me *sing*?"

"*Ja*," said Mrs. Beidwinkle. "On Saturday night. We'll have refreshments. It will be a regular party."

Betsy knew then why she had brought the white wool dress!

That evening Mr. Beidwinkle remarked, "Tomorrow's Saturday. Mamma usually goes to town with me on Saturday. Would you like to go along?"

"To town?" asked Betsy, startled.

"To Butternut Center. We buy at Willard's Emporium, there."

Somewhat to the Beidwinkles' mystification, Betsy blushed. Her heart began to pound inside her shirt waist. Willard's Emporium! She might see Joe! She wanted to see him, but she didn't want to seem to be running after him. He knew she knew that he spent his vacations with his uncle and aunt in Butternut Center.

That was where she had seen him first, four years ago, when she was taking the train home after her visit with the Taggarts. It was a very little village, just a depot and a grain elevator, a white church, a sprinkling of houses, and a general store. The store was Willard's Emporium, where she had gone to buy presents for her family.

Joe had waited on her. She had been struck by the way he walked, with a slight challenging swing. She remembered his very light hair brushed back in a pompadour, his blue eyes under thick light brows, his lower lip pushed out as though seeming to dare the world to knock the chip off his shoulder.

He had been reading *The Three Musketeers*, she remembered, but he had put it aside when she said that she was going to buy presents. He had been amused at her statement that no Ray ever came home from a trip without bringing presents for the rest.

No Ray . . . ever came home from a trip . . . without bringing presents! Suddenly Betsy's heart raced faster. Why, she was away on a trip! She would have to buy presents. She simply had to go to Willard's Emporium.

Looking up, her cheeks still flushed, her eyes dancing, she replied, "Of course. I'd love to go. How early do we start?"

20

Butternut Center

IT WAS VERY EARLY, still dark and cold, when Mrs. Beidwinkle knocked at Betsy's door. That morning springtime concert of the birds, to which Betsy had become accustomed during her week at the farm, was more uproarious even than usual. It sounded like a contest, but a contest without rules or regulations. Each bird was trying to sing down every other bird, caroling, warbling, whistling, some humble anonymous performers chirping wildly, while others executed elaborate arias.

Lighting the lamp, she dressed quickly. She put on the plaid skirt and the red blouse, of course, braided her hair, looped it up with the red ribbon. It hadn't been put up in Wavers all week. She had forgotten about Magic Wavers.

Still sleepy, she stumbled downstairs into the kitchen. The coffee, freshly made, was stimulating and delicious. She put on her red tam and cravenette and high buckled overshoes and went out into the barnyard.

The world was still gray, but the east was a river of crimson. It seemed strange to see the windmill whirling against that lurid sky. A team of horses was pawing the ground in front of a wagon full of milk cans. Mrs. Beidwinkle was critically directing the addition of a case full of eggs. The egg money went to Mrs. Beidwinkle; she didn't want any eggs broken.

Mr. Beidwinkle helped Betsy to a box covered with a rug, which was placed just behind the high seat. "I'll bet you never rode to town with milk cans before," he said.

He and Mrs. Beidwinkle climbed into the seat, he clucked to the horses, and they were off.

It hadn't frozen the night before, Mr. Beidwinkle

pointed out. Yesterday's pools and puddles were pools and puddles still. The road was very muddy. Down and up, down and up went the heavy wheels, making a sucking sound, and Betsy would have bounced on her box if she hadn't held fast to the seat in front of her. Slowly the sky paled and light spread over the prairie.

Mile after gray-white mile slipped past: frozen fields which would soon be ready for the sowing; planted groves of trees which would soon be green; orchards which would soon be fragrant bowers of pink and white. Farm houses were flanked with big red barns, granaries, and silos. At last they saw an elevator sticking up over the prairie ahead.

In Butternut Center, Mr. Beidwinkle went first to the depot and unloaded the milk cans. Then he drove down the street to Willard's Emporium, and with Mrs. Beidwinkle watching, unloaded the eggs.

Betsy scrambled down from her box and went into the store. Excitement fluttered inside her as she went, but Joe wasn't there. Probably he hadn't come out this week. Probably he was working at the *Sun*. She realized with a pang of disappointment how much she had counted on seeing him.

Mr. Beidwinkle had disappeared. Mrs. Beidwinkle was now supervising the counting of her eggs by a tall, square-faced man, Joe's Uncle Alvin, probably. Well,

Betsy thought, she must buy the presents whether Joe was there or not, and she started browsing along the overflowing counters.

Willard's Emporium seemed to have everything under the sun for sale. Kitchen stoves, straw hats, clocks, calico, buggy whips. She remembered how Joe had helped her buy cheese for her father, a butter dish for her mother, side combs for Julia, doll dishes for Margaret, a mouth organ for Tacy.

She paused before a case full of china and looked at a little speckled vase. That would be nice for the wild flowers Margaret would soon start bringing home from the hills.

She felt someone looking at her and turned to see Joe.

His blue eyes, under those heavy brows, were boring into her. His lower lip looked defiant, and so did the swinging walk with which he came toward her. She blushed.

"What are you doing here?" Joe asked. His tone was almost rough.

"Don't act as though you were going to put me out," she said. "I'm buying presents to take home to my family."

"Oh." He seemed nonplused.

"The Rays always take presents home when they've been away on a visit."

"Oh."

"It's an old family custom," Betsy said, and smiled.

Joe looked odd. Something in his face seemed to melt. He didn't smile, though.

Betsy kept on talking. "I've picked out this little vase for Mamma. Don't you think it's nice? But what do you suppose Papa would like? Now don't say cheese again!"

Joe smiled. And when he smiled there were the most attractive, warming crinkles in his face. One of them looked almost like a dimple, but you didn't associate dimples with Joe Willard. His eyes began to shine.

"How about tobacco? Pipe tobacco? Willard's Emporium will throw in some pipe cleaners in honor of . . . in honor of . . . well, to be brief, we'll throw in some pipe cleaners."

"That's fine," said Betsy. "Now, Margaret likes things for her room."

"How about a calendar? Here's one full of dogs and cats. This ought to suit her."

"Yes. This will do." Betsy kept her eyes lowered longer than she needed to, the expression in his eyes was so disturbing.

"When you were here before, you bought something for Tacy, too."

"Of course. I want something for Tacy and Tib."

"Lollipops. A pink one and a yellow one."

She looked up to laugh. Joe's face was alight and glowing.

"You staying with the Taggarts?" he asked, coming nearer.

"No. The Beidwinkles." She nodded to Mrs. Beidwinkle, who had disposed of her eggs and was buying groceries now. Her purchases bulked so large on the counter that it looked as though she were going to start a store herself.

"I adore the Beidwinkles," said Betsy.

"I adore Mrs. Beidwinkle myself. What's more, she adores me."

He went swinging toward her, and Betsy followed.

Mrs. Beidwinkle's face did indeed wreathe itself in smiles when Joe spoke. "How do you do, Mrs. Beidwinkle. How are you today?"

"Hello, Joe," she said. "Do you know Betsy?"

"We're classmates," Betsy put in.

"She's terrible in school," Joe said. "How does she behave at your house, Mrs. Beidwinkle?"

Mrs. Beidwinkle frowned at him. "She behaves like a nice little girl. She wipes the dishes and sings for us every night. We wish she stayed with us all the time."

Joe turned to Betsy. "A good report! I never expected it."

"Mrs. Beidwinkle," he said, turning back to her, "won't you let me see Betsy home? There are some places around here I'd like to show her. Maybe my uncle would loan me the phaeton."

Mrs. Beidwinkle beamed. "Why, of course," she said. "I don't mind at all. In fact, I'd just as soon have Betsy out of the way today."

"Aha!" cried Joe. "I knew that report was too good to be true. What does she do? Bite her nails? Track in on your floor?"

Mrs. Beidwinkle pushed him, laughing. "*Dummkopf!* Nothing like that. Betsy knows, or she can guess."

Betsy raced after Joe, while he searched out a youth named Homer. Homer, looking at Betsy curiously, promised to take Joe's place at the store.

They raced back to the square-faced man who had been waiting on Mrs. Beidwinkle. He *was* Uncle Alvin, but he didn't look at all like Joe. Joe introduced Betsy and then nudged her to retreat. He returned to her, smiling.

"Uncle Alvin says I may drive you home."

They raced up some stairs which ran from the street to the second floor. There was a small parlor, as crowded as the store beneath, but with fat chairs and sofas covered with tidies, and embroidered sofa cushions. Betsy met Aunt Ruth, who was spare, sad, and kind. They clattered down the stairs again.

"I have an idea," said Joe.

"What is it?"

"Haven't I heard you say you like picnics?"

"Joe!"

"Then we'll take along some crackers and cheese."

"And olives and cookies . . . Nabisco wafers, maybe, and that kind with marshmallows on top."

"Why, you little glutton! I'll slice some bologna, too. What else shall we take?"

"A bottle of milk," said Betsy. "If you can borrow some cups."

"Of course I can," said Joe, and went clattering back upstairs.

He left Betsy again to hitch up the horse. She went happily around the store until he returned with a stocky cream-colored animal hitched to a buggy with a fringed adjustable top.

"Rocinante," said Joe, helping her in. "Ever read *Don Quixote*? Do you get these literary allusions?"

They put the top down. They wanted the whole width of the sky from end to end, the whole width of the flat prairie landscape.

With their basket and Betsy's presents at their feet, they drove down the single street, which was all of Butternut Center. The muddy road was very muddy, so that the buggy lurched in and out of holes. But Joe and Betsy didn't mind.

They didn't mind anything. They didn't mention Tony or their quarrel. Their happiness overflowed the phaeton and ran like spilled water to the edge of the horizon on both sides.

"Joe," Betsy said, "you don't look like your uncle."

"No. I look like my mother's people. He's my father's brother. My father," Joe went on, "died when I was a baby. He was a lumberman, yanked down trees in the north woods. I've always been strong as a horse, and I guess it's because of him."

"How did your mother look?" asked Betsy.

Joe paused before he answered.

"She was beautiful," he said slowly, at last. "People toss that word around a lot, but my mother really was. She had dark golden hair and blue, blue eyes and the reddest, sweetest lips I ever saw.

"She was a dressmaker . . . after Father died, that is. She worked hard; too hard. I can still hear that sewing machine. I tried to help when I got old enough, but I couldn't do much."

"What did you do?" Betsy asked.

"Sold papers at first." He paused as his thoughts went back. "Once, when I was about nine, I lost my route list. I borrowed a bike from another boy to go back and find it. When I returned the bike and thanked him, I offered to shake hands. I thought, from the books I had read, that that was the proper thing to do. But all the boys hooted. I'll never forget it."

He looked at her suddenly. "I never told that to anyone before."

Betsy didn't answer.

"Mother was a great one for books, too," Joe continued. "She's the one I get my love of writing from. I found poems and unfinished stories and bits of description among her things after she died."

"How old were you then?"

"I was twelve. Uncle Alvin is the only relative I have on either side. He and Aunt Ruth gave me a home and I helped them in the store until I was fourteen and finished country school. I had to come to Deep Valley then, to high school."

"I'm glad you did," said Betsy.

They drove on and on. No matter how far they drove, there was no variety in the landscape. It was just prairie, poles, and wires! Prairie, poles, and wires! But there were song sparrows trilling on the wires. There was heavenly warmth in the air.

It grew so warm that Betsy took off her cravenette, her tam.

Joe turned and looked at her. His eyes studied the red hair ribbon.

"You look different," he said.

"That's right," Betsy replied.

"Your hair isn't curled. Do you know," he continued, studying her critically, "I like your hair straight."

He liked her hair straight! If he had looked through all the poetry books in the world he couldn't have found a better compliment to pay her.

Joe wanted to know when they ate, and they

stopped Rocinante at a point where a brook, just un-frozen, babbled with frantic joy over brown leaves. He unfastened the horse's checkrein and gave him some oats. He took out their basket and they found a large rock which provided a seat a little above the soggy ground. There they ate their bread and cheese and bologna and olives and cookies, smiling at each other.

"Do you know," Betsy said, "this is the first picnic I've ever been on with you? That seems strange, for picnics are so important and . . ." She blushed.

"Go on," said Joe, "finish it."

Betsy didn't answer.

"Why are picnics so important? I know why I am, of course."

"They just are. There's nothing so nice as eating out of doors. And I've discovered since I've been visit-ing the Beidwinkles that I like to live in the country. I shouldn't like to be a farmer's wife. I'd be no good at it. But to have a house in the country and write would be nice."

"Very nice," said Joe.

They started riding again, and Betsy realized sud-denly that the sun was getting low. She remarked that she liked sunsets almost as well as she liked picnics.

"We'll ride until the sun sets, then. What else do you like?"

"Sunrises. But I don't see very many of them."

"What else?"

"Oh, dancing, and writing stories, and reading. I've been reading *Little Dorrit*. Have you read it?"

"You haven't said the right thing yet."

They stopped Rocinante to watch the sunset. Rows of clouds made a pearly accordion, the creases touched with gold.

Mrs. Beidwinkle met them at the kitchen door.

"Well!" she said. "I thought you were lost, for sure. I was just going to send Bill out looking for you."

"All my fault, Mrs. Beidwinkle," Joe replied.

"I'm sure it was your fault. Betsy, come here!"

Betsy came there and Mrs. Beidwinkle whispered in her ear.

"Maybe," she said, "Joe would like to come to the party?"

Betsy smiled and gave the invitation. Joe accepted.

It was a wonderful party. Betsy had never been to a party quite like it. They had supper first—Joe stayed for supper—and Rocinante had supper in Mr. Beidwinkle's barn. After supper, Betsy washed the dishes, then went upstairs to put on her white wool dress.

Mrs. Beidwinkle wore her Sunday black silk dress with a brooch at the neck. Mr. Beidwinkle wore his Sunday black. Bill put on a paper collar and loaned a tie to Joe.

In the back parlor, a table was spread with a hand-embroidered cloth. Mrs. Beidwinkle set out bottles of beer and soda pop, rye bread with caraway seeds, thin slices of sausage, Dutch cheese, egg salad, and cake, cookies, and a jelly roll she had baked the previous day. She had made ice cream, too, she said, but she wouldn't bring that out until they were ready to eat.

The Beidwinkles' daughter and her husband arrived. Amelia, in a flower-sprigged dress, her husband, red-faced and suspicious, in a high choker collar. Betsy, in the white wool dress, feeling like a visiting countess, sat and talked with them.

They went into the parlor and looked at the photograph album. Betsy showed Joe all the bearded men, the anxious ladies, the stiff boys and girls in the album. They looked through the stereopticon set at views of the Holy Land, Niagara Falls, Europe with Side Trips to Egypt, Algeria, and the Madeira Islands.

At last Mr. Beidwinkle said, "How about some music?"

Betsy wondered for a panicky moment whether she could play the prima donna in front of Joe, but she certainly couldn't refuse. Her singing was the whole reason for the party. So she went to the organ.

She urged Amelia and her husband and Joe to join in, which they presently did. Amelia's husband, it developed, loved to sing. He took off his stiff collar and sang with a will. They sang Betsy's repertoire of songs not once, but twice, three times, while Mr. Beidwinkle and Bill sipped their beer contentedly and listened. At the end Betsy had to sing alone: "Yip-i-addy-i-ay" for Bill, and "Tonight Will Never Come Again" for Mrs. Beidwinkle who wiped her eyes, of course, and "*Kind, Du Kannst Tanzen*" for Mr. Beidwinkle, who laughed and said, "Gollee!"

Then they went to the parlor and had ice cream and cake and cookies and jelly roll and soda pop and rye bread and egg salad and sausage and cheese.

They ate and ate until Amelia and her husband said they must go home and Joe said that he must go, too. The others looked tactfully away while he said good-by.

"Be back for school Monday?"

"Yes. I'm going back tomorrow night. Papa's driving out for me."

"See you in Deep Valley then."

"See you in Deep Valley."

He looked into her eyes very hard, with his blue eyes which looked so bright and happy. He shook hands with her hard. Then he was gone.

21

No Ivy Green

On Monday, Miss Raymond, who directed the high school chorus, announced that there would be a rehearsal after school. It was time, she said, to begin work on Commencement music. This made all the seniors look self-conscious.

"Commencement!" Tacy leaned across the aisle to groan.

"It's creeping up on us!"

Betsy welcomed the rehearsal because it would give her a chance to talk to Tony. She had come back from the Beidwinkles' determined to talk with him frankly. He realized now that she didn't care for him in a romantic way, and probably he would soon get over that feeling about her. She wanted to tell him that they must keep on being friends, good friends.

She looked for him while they were waiting for rehearsal to begin, but he was elusive. He took his place with the basses at once, instead of fooling around with the girls, as he usually did. She would see him at the end, Betsy decided, and at last Miss Raymond got the chattering group quiet.

She announced the numbers they would sing for Commencement . . . Schubert's "Hark! Hark! The Lark!" and a musical setting of Dickens' poem about the ivy.

"It has a bass solo in it and, of course, Tony Markham must sing that," said Miss Raymond, smiling. Since *Up and Down Broadway* Tony's reputation as a singer had expanded.

The words of "The Ivy Green" were grim.

> *"Oh, a dainty plant is the ivy green,*
> *That creepeth o'er ruins old!*
> *And right choice foods are his meals, I wean,*
> *In his cell so lone and cold. . . ."*

Betsy and Tacy looked at each other and shivered.

"Why the dickens did Miss Raymond choose that?" Betsy whispered. But when Tony's voice rolled out in the solo she knew why.

> "*Creeping where no life is seen,*
> *A rare old plant is the ivy green.*"

It was perfect for his deep-pitched velvety voice.

At the end of rehearsal, Betsy blocked his way into the cloakroom with a casual joking remark. But Tony was unresponsive. His big, sleepy eyes that had always looked at her so laughingly, so teasingly, were cold. They didn't look like Tony's eyes at all.

He had more poise than Betsy had. She couldn't keep acting flippant in the face of that cold gaze. She blurted out her message without preparation.

"Tony, I want to talk with you. I want to straighten things out between us."

"Nothing needs any straightening out."

"Yes, it does. Will you come up to see me tonight?"

"Sorry. I'm busy."

"Tomorrow night?"

"Tomorrow night I'm even busier."

He left her abruptly. She would have to wait for another chance, she thought, turning away.

But no other chance came. For now Betsy and Joe started going together—in earnest. Things were different from what they had been back in the autumn. Then when they were together they had spent their time mostly talking about books and school. Joe had plainly enjoyed her. He had reveled in the company of a girl whom he liked wholeheartedly and who he knew liked him. But except for gay extravagant compliments, he had never talked personalities.

Now he was crazy about Betsy and didn't care who knew it.

The whole school knew it. The school was electric with it as schools are sometimes with affairs of that sort. The truth was in Betsy's eyes and Joe's, in the way they passed notes, and met after classes, and lingered in the halls. At the library, where they were studying for the Essay Contest, Miss Sparrow regarded them fondly. They strolled back to the Ray house slowly, through the purple spring twilights.

Tony didn't telephone Betsy nor come to see her. He hadn't been at the house since she returned from the Beidwinkles'. Margaret had asked for him at first; now she only looked at Betsy with grave accusing eyes.

Betsy's eighteenth birthday came along. She received a jade ring in a silver setting from her father, engraved calling cards from her mother.

"Miss Betsy Warrington Ray," they said.

Margaret gave her a burned wood hand-mirror. She had made it herself in school.

From Joe came a dozen red roses. Betsy put them in a big vase on the parlor table. She put one in her hair when Tacy and Tib came for supper-with-birthday-cake. She put one in a bud vase beside her bed and sniffed it rapturously before she went to sleep.

At the last Zetamathian Rhetoricals, Betsy and Tacy sang their Cat Duet. They had sung it every year since they were in the fifth grade and the audience now joined in the caterwauls. But Tony didn't laugh. Looking in exasperation at his sullen face, Betsy resolved again to talk with him. She would do it Friday at the senior-faculty picnic.

"And nothing will stop me!" she declared.

Friday proved to be an ideal day for their famous annual picnic. The weather was so tantalizingly warm that even if they had been in school they couldn't have kept their minds on their books. At Page Park, the willows on the river bank were covered with tiny leaves. Birds were singing; the picnic ground was strewn with dandelions; and the seniors were wearing their gray and violet skull caps.

It was strange to be mingling, almost on an equal footing, with the teachers. The seniors paid their respects to Miss Bangeter in pairs, but they were flippant with the others.

Winona flirted openly with Stewie. Betsy tried out her broken German on Miss Erickson. She and Tacy told curly-haired Miss O'Rourke that they had memorized all their geometry propositions without understanding them. She chased them with a switch.

Betsy and Joe went up to Mr. Gaston. "Seen any apple blossoms lately?"

Betsy had quarreled with Mr. Gaston in her sophomore year about the color of apple blossoms. Tib, always daring, even mentioned the herbariums she and Betsy and Tacy had made once under strange conditions.

The seniors had provided overflowing baskets and they ate at the long wooden tables. They swung, they waded in the river and skipped stones. The senior boys challenged the men teachers to a baseball game. Joe pitched; he was good, too, Betsy noticed.

It was a notable senior-faculty picnic. But Betsy didn't speak to Tony for the reason that he wasn't there.

On Saturday he wasn't at the Inter-Society Track Meet. The Zets won. The Philos had already won the athletics cup, so the Essay Contest was of vital importance to both sides now.

Sunday evening Margaret came running upstairs and burst into Betsy's room, her eyes glowing.

"Betsy! Tony's here. He's come for lunch."

"Really?" Betsy swooped down to give Margaret a hug. Running downstairs, she remembered that Joe wasn't coming. He was covering a Christian Endeavor convention which was meeting in Deep Valley. Perhaps Tony had known that Joe wouldn't be there? But as soon as she saw him she knew that it wouldn't have mattered. He was the old Tony.

He had Washington on his shoulder and Abie followed at his heels. He greeted Betsy carelessly, annexed Margaret's hand, and strolled out to the sandwich-making. He himself made the coffee.

"You're sure of a good cup of coffee tonight," he joked with Mrs. Ray.

He was oblivious to the excitement his presence caused when the Crowd started drifting in.

Winona played the piano, and the Crowd sang. Harmonizing voices rolled out the open windows into the soft spring night: "My wild Irish rose. . . ." "I wonder who's kissing her now. . . ."

"What's the use of dreaming. . . ." Tony sang that alone, by request, straddling a chair as he had done in *Up and Down Broadway*.

> "*What's the use of dreaming,*
> *Dreams of rosy hue,*
> *What's the use of dreaming, dreaming,*
> *Dreams that never could come true. . . .*"

It was wonderful to have Tony back, and acting just like himself.

When he out-stayed the others, Betsy began to worry. Maybe that frightening ardor would return when they were alone? But it didn't. They did the dishes. Tony scraped and washed, Betsy wiped, and they talked and joked as usual.

Here was her chance, she thought, to make that speech she had planned. But she hated to break the mood of the evening with a speech. Moreover, it seemed unnecessary with Tony's attitude so matter-of-fact.

They returned to the parlor, and Tony went to the pile of photographs lying on the table, class photographs with the seal of the class in the upper left hand corner. They had been delivered the day before, and the Crowd had been busily exchanging them. Tony had not asked for one of Betsy's, but he looked them over now.

The large beautiful one, taken in the blue Class Day dress. The small Betsyish one, taken in a shirt waist.

"Do I rate one of these?" Tony asked.

"Of course," Betsy replied. "And you're going to give me one of yours."

"Heck!" said Tony. "I didn't sit for one."

"You didn't . . . sit for one! Why, Tony Markham! How can you graduate without a class picture?"

"You'd be surprised."

"Which one do you want?" Betsy asked. "The big one or the little one?"

"The little one."

"The big one is much prettier."

"But it doesn't look like you."

"Oh, thanks," mocked Betsy.

"Sorry," said Tony. "Is it my fault if you're not good-looking?"

It was the old Tony come back, and Betsy felt a weight lift from her heart. But when they said good night she discovered that it wasn't the old Tony after all.

She strolled out on the porch with him, as she had done a thousand times. The stars were low and bright over the German Catholic College. Tony was telling her that he had hopped a freight and gone up to Minneapolis with his brakeman friend on Friday. That was why he hadn't been at the picnic.

"I wish you wouldn't do that, Tony," Betsy said. "I'm like Papa. I worry for fear you'll lose a leg."

"All right," said Tony. "I can almost promise you I won't do it again."

"You can?" Betsy asked, delighted.

"Almost," said Tony. "Well, good-by, Ray of Sunshine." And to Betsy's surprise he kissed her. He didn't ask if he might kiss her. He merely kissed her. She was so startled that she couldn't find a word to say.

No words were necessary, for Tony swung off the porch and went down the walk. He didn't even look back until he reached the arc light. Then he turned and lifted his hand in a rakish salute.

"Good-by," he called again.

Betsy stood on the steps, disturbed and puzzled. Tony usually said "So long!" There had been something strange in the way he said "Good-by." It had been strange, too, that he kissed her.

The next day at school she looked around for him. He wasn't there. At chorus practise Miss Raymond was annoyed.

"Where is Tony Markham? Does anyone know where Tony is? We can't practice 'Ivy Green' without him."

Nobody knew.

The next day he was still not at school. He wasn't there the next day either. On Thursday there was chorus practise again.

Miss Raymond distributed copies of a new song. It was from Wagner's *Tannhäuser*—"Hark! Hear the cannons' thunder pealing."

She asked Tib to collect the copies of "The Ivy Green."

Someone waved a hand. "Why, Miss Raymond? Aren't we going to sing 'The Ivy Green'?"

"No," said Miss Raymond.

"Why not? We have it all learned."

"Tony Markham won't be here."

"Tony won't be here? Why, of course he will be! He's graduating."

Betsy felt color creeping into her neck and face.

"I understand he won't be here," Miss Raymond replied. "I can't give you any details."

After chorus practise, Betsy sought Miss Clarke. Miss Bangeter was the one to ask, of course, but she was too awesome. Miss Clarke could always be approached.

"Miss Clarke, do you know what's happened to Tony Markham? Miss Raymond says he won't be graduating."

"That's true," Miss Clarke answered. She took off her glasses and polished them nervously. "Tony's gone away."

"But where?"

"Nobody knows. He's gone away, that's all."

Betsy looked into her face with entreaty. "But what do they think? Has his mother told Miss Bangeter? Tony's a very, very dear friend of mine. I didn't know he was going away."

Miss Clarke hesitated. She lowered her voice.

"Yes, his mother has talked to Miss Bangeter. But she doesn't know where Tony has gone. He left a note and told her not to worry."

"Could he have graduated? Were his grades all right?"

"I think so."

"I'm so sorry. I'm so sorry," Betsy said.

She thanked Miss Clarke and went out of the room, out of the building, down to the street. Tony was gone, and nobody knew where. Betsy didn't see exactly what she had done that was wrong, but she felt to blame. She had a lump in her throat.

Two things comforted her. Tony had said he wasn't going to be stealing rides on the freight cars any more. That meant, Betsy reasoned, that he had some sort of a job.

And the kiss he had given her! It hadn't seemed angry or accusing or desperate. It had been gentle, it had been loving. But it had definitely, she realized, been good-by.

22
Surprises

IT WAS HARD telling the family about Tony.

Anna cried sadly, "Stars in the sky! We'll never see him again!" Mrs. Ray exclaimed, "Oh, his poor mother!" Mr. Ray said with stout optimism, "He'll be back! Don't worry!" But his face was sober. Margaret got up and went to her room and shut the door.

The other Rays looked at each other.

"You'd better go to her, Betsy," Mrs. Ray said. For Margaret talked more freely to Betsy than to anyone else in the family, although even Betsy didn't understand her very well.

Betsy waited a little while, then followed her upstairs, knocked on the door, and went in.

Margaret was sitting very straight in her little chair. Her eyes were red. Betsy sank to the floor and put her arms around her.

"Margaret! You know, I love Tony, too."

"I thought you *didn't* love him," said Margaret in a choked voice. "I heard Mamma say that just the other day. She said that was the reason he'd stopped coming here."

"But I do love him," Betsy insisted. "You know, Margaret, there are lots of kinds of love in the world. I love him in a different way from the way he loves me, that's all. I feel badly, too, about his going away."

Margaret was silent a moment. Then she put her hand into Betsy's. "Where do you suppose he's gone?"

"I don't know," answered Betsy. "But I know one thing, Margaret. He's not hopping freight trains."

"How do you know that?"

Betsy told her about the promise. Margaret's small tense faced smoothed out a little.

"And I'm like Papa," Betsy continued. "I think we'll hear from him."

"Do you?" asked Margaret.

"Yes, I do. We'll hear. You wait and see."

She tried to believe this and be happy as May came in with all its sweetness. Dooryards smelled entrancingly of lilacs; hillsides smelled of the wild plums in dazzling snowy bloom. Warmth came suddenly. One day the girls were wearing their spring coats; the next, they were in thin dresses.

Betsy had two new gingham dresses. One was blue, the other a gay red plaid. She wore them both with the big straw hat covered with red poppies and had never, Anna said, looked punier.

And one Saturday morning, Joe called for her to go to the high school and write the Essay Contest.

Joe didn't give a hang about the Essay Contest. He had, Betsy realized, a different attitude from hers about high school. It was more the attitude Julia had had. He was looking ahead to his own Great World, to the University, the Minneapolis *Tribune*.

High school was still important to Betsy. The Essay Contest was important. She assumed that Joe would win, but as a loyal Zetamathian she was going to try her hardest.

"I'll do my best, too," Joe said. "But how can I think about 'Conservation of Our Natural Resources' when it's so much more interesting thinking about Betsy?"

The high school was empty except for Miss Clarke and Miss O'Rourke, waiting, of course, in the upper hall.

"All notes and books must be left here," Miss Clarke said, as usual.

Betsy waved her pen and Joe jokingly pushed up his cuffs to show that he had no notes concealed. They went into the algebra classroom where two juniors, two sophomores, and two freshmen were already seated. The bell rang and they started to write.

Joe finished first, but when Betsy came out he was waiting for her.

"I did my best," he said, "for the sake of dear old Philo. But somehow I have a notion my essay isn't much good. It seemed to get all mixed up with Betsy. The color of her hair. The way she blushes. The way she sings when she dances. I just couldn't seem to get going."

"Well, I did," said Betsy. "But I don't believe a word you say. I think I'll have the unutterable chagrin of losing again to Joseph Willard."

With the Essay Contest out of the way, they had to think about Commencement orations. Betsy chose for her subject "The Heroines of Shakespeare," and began to reread Shakespeare's plays.

Joe's subject was "The Bread Basket of the World." He wasn't doing much research. He had done it in harvest fields, he said, from Texas to North Dakota. He was already writing.

Tib was practising for the class play, *A Fatal Message*; Tacy was practising her Commencement solo.

> *"Sylvia, take the lily, daffodil,*
> *Sylvia, take whate'er the garden grows,*
> *But Sylvia only shook her pretty head*
> *As she picked a simple wild red rose. . . ."*

And all of them being members of the chorus were practising madly on "Hark! Hark! The Lark!" and "Hark! Hear the cannons' thunder pealing."

"Lots of Harks!" Tacy remarked.

To make life even more exciting, graduation presents began coming in. They came by every mail and were brought by friends every day. Betsy had received a Prayer Book and Hymnal, a hand-embroidered corset cover, a blue silk party bag, beauty pins, Dutch collars, a little silver pin tray, the U. of M. Gopher.

Everyone was cramming, too, for final examinations, and these at last arrived. The seniors shuddered when they thought how awful it would be if they didn't pass.

"To think of being flunked out *now*!" they cried.

Now Betsy's oration was finished and she was learning it.

"The heroines of Shakespeare are essentially human," she chanted all day long. She asked Joe, "What's your opening line?"

"I let Walt Whitman write it," he answered, grinning. But he didn't say what it was.

Festivities opened, of course, with the junior-senior banquet.

"Remember how hard we worked last year?" Betsy, Tacy, Tib, and Hazel asked each other.

The juniors had been working feverishly for days, and on the big night the high school was turned into a street fair with booths. Frankfurters were made of red tissue paper with fortunes inside. Betsy's said she was going to live on a farm.

Following Joe's lead the year before, the menu was full of literary allusions.

> *". . . sit down; at first and last,*
> *the hearty welcome."*
> —SHAKESPEARE

And the dinner was marvelous, beginning with fruit punch, and ending with demitasse and 1910 mints. In between were prime rib roast of beef, asparagus, fruit salad, and other good things.

There were toasts. Joe, of course, spoke for the seniors. And the toasts were followed by dancing. Betsy wore the pale blue Class Day dress, Tacy wore pale green, and Tib wore lavender.

The next day was Betsy's last day of real school. She said so that night at supper.

"What did you do?" her father asked.

"Oh, finished my physics notebook, practised my oration for Miss O'Rourke, opened presents, and wept."

Mr. Ray got up abruptly and went into the parlor. He had been acting strangely for several days. He had been too cheerful, which usually meant that he was worried about something. He had gone around the house whistling, but with a little line between his brows.

"I believe Papa hates to see you graduate," Mrs. Ray said in a low tone.

"Maybe he's lonesome for Julia," whispered Betsy. "It's an awfully long time since we had a letter."

Mr. Ray suddenly reappeared in the doorway.

"Do you like surprises?" he asked, looking at the group around the table.

For a moment they were too startled to reply.

"You know I don't," Mrs. Ray said at last.

"Neither do I," said Betsy.

"I do sometimes," said Margaret. "But not after I know there is one. Then I can't bear to wait. What is it, Papa?"

The line between his brows melted away.

"Julia," he said, smiling broadly, "is on the bounding billows."

"Julia!" Mrs. Ray stared in stupefaction. Betsy jumped up and began to scream. Margaret was too ladylike for that, but she hugged Betsy.

Anna came running into the dining room. "Stars in the sky! What's going on here?"

"Anna!" gasped Mrs. Ray. "Julia . . . Julia. . . ." Then Mrs. Ray began to cry and Mr. Ray went around the table and hugged her.

"Julia's on the way home," he explained to Anna. "She wrote me at the store, and told me not to tell anyone. But Jule doesn't like surprises."

"Oh, Bob! Bob! Oh, Anna! Anna!" Mrs. Ray wept, and Anna came around the table to help hug her.

"Of course she doesn't like surprises, my poor lovey! We have to clean this house, if Julia's coming. Don't we, Mrs. Ray?" Anna wiped her eyes and blew her nose.

"I know," Mr. Ray said. "That's what Julia was afraid of. You'll even scour the coal scuttle."

"When will she be here?" Betsy asked.

"Might be any day now. I don't know just what boat she's coming on. But I know she's on the way. I wrote and told her to come. She'll be going back, of course. But I thought she ought to be here to see Betsy graduate."

"She'll be here to see me graduate!" cried Betsy. She ran to telephone Tacy, Tib, and Joe. Margaret went to the piano and started practising on her new piece, "Woodland Fancies."

"I want to have it ready for Julia," she explained.

Mrs. Ray and Anna began planning. They were going to wash the curtains and bedspreads, polish the floors, polish the brass and silver.

"We'd better start baking, too."

"That spice cake Julia likes."

"And she always liked that Perfection Salad I used to make for the McCloskeys."

"But, Bob," Mrs. Ray asked suddenly, "how will we know when she's coming, if she's planning to surprise us?"

"She's going to wire me at the store the minute her boat lands," Mr. Ray replied.

Monday was Memorial Day, but the parade was abandoned because of rain. It poured from every corner of the sky. Betsy practised her oration at the Opera House in the morning, and in the afternoon she washed her hair.

The following day was the Assembly at which the Essay Cup would be awarded. The day after that was Class Day. And the day after the day after that was June third, Commencement Day itself. If Betsy's hair was going to be soft and shiny for this great week, it must be washed, rain or no rain.

There was one advantage in the downpour. It made visitors so unlikely that Mrs. Ray and Anna decided to continue their cleaning into the afternoon.

"After all, we don't know how many days we'll have. That wire might come any time."

"I'll bathe Abie," said Margaret, "to get him ready."

Mr. Ray was at home from the store on account of the holiday. He retreated with his cigar to the bedroom. Mrs. Ray, still in a house dress, was polishing silver, Anna was washing windows, Betsy was drying her hair, and Margaret was rinsing Abie when the front doorbell rang.

"The hack's out in front," Anna said.

"Who under the sun could be coming in this rain! You'll have to answer, Bob," Mrs. Ray called, closing the door which led into the kitchen. She didn't close it entirely. She peeked around it. Anna peeked in from the parlor, and Betsy and Margaret peeked down the stairs.

Mr. Ray opened the door, and in walked Julia!

The Rays forgot all about not liking to be surprised. They smothered Julia with kisses. Mr. Ray broke away only to pay Mr. Thumbler and bring her suitcases and trunk into the hall.

Julia had changed.

"You're fat! You're fat as a roll of butter!" Mrs. Ray cried.

"The Von Hetternichs eat all the time. Besides, Fraulein wants me fat. I have to be fat to sing opera," Julia said.

"You look cute," Betsy said. She did.

"Let me see my baby sister," Julia cried.

Margaret stepped proudly forward.

"Why, she's grown tall! Bettina! Stop rubbing your hair and let me look at you."

"Did you know," joked Betsy, "that people were wearing their hair this way? Wet, I mean. It's all the rage in Paris."

"Speaking of Paris," said Julia, "open my trunk! I brought something from Paris for your graduation outfit."

Mr. Ray unlocked the trunk and as Julia hunted through it, flinging things in all directions, they all watched her. She looked very different; and not only because she was plump. She looked foreign. She looked fascinating. She wore earrings!

There were presents for everyone. Paris waists for Mrs. Ray and Betsy. Betsy's was a pleated pink silk. There was a German doll for Margaret, a musical jewel box for Anna, a Meerschaum pipe for Mr. Ray.

Mrs. Ray forgot to change her house dress. Betsy forgot to curl her hair. Abie dried himself, running about and shaking his damp little body.

Julia went from one to another, giving them hugs and kisses.

"Oh, it's so good to be home!" she kept saying. "So good, good, good to be home!"

She went to the piano and started to play.

"How's Tony?" she called suddenly.

Silence fell into the room like a stone into a lake.

"There's bad news about Tony," Betsy began. "That is, we hope it isn't bad. But Tony's gone away."

"Where?" Julia whirled about.

"Nobody knows. He left unexpectedly."

"He'll be back," said Mr. Ray. "You know Tony. He'll show up one of these days."

"Most any day," added Mrs. Ray, with such brightness that Julia sensed a sore subject, and turned back to the piano.

Betsy told her the story that night. It was wonderful to be back in Julia's room, upon which the old gay confusion had descended. Wrapped in her kimono, Betsy sat in the window seat while Julia undressed. Then she changed to the foot of the bed and they talked till long after midnight.

Julia's comment on the situation was clean-cut.

"It's a very good thing he went away. You meant to be kind, but you weren't being kind, really, when you deceived him all year. Now that he's cut loose, he'll find himself, I'm sure. I always knew you liked Joe, Bettina."

But Betsy couldn't go into that, even with Julia.

She asked about the Von Hetternichs.

"They were wonderfully kind, but I got bored with my life there. Rich people's lives are very stuffy. I grew to love the girls, of course, but what made the winter really glorious was my work."

She talked with the old contagious enthusiasm about operas and operatic roles, where and when she would make her debut.

"It can't be for a long time. I've so much to learn. You've no idea how much."

"When are we going to hear you sing?"

"Not until I've had a chance to practise. And I want you all to understand that I'm just a beginner."

The next day the sun came out and the curtains in the Ray house were hung at sparkling windows. The kitchen was fragrant with the smell of spice cake baking. Neighbors dropped in, the Poppys, the Crowd.

A boy from Windmiller's Florist Shop came with a long box for Julia. She looked at the card.

"He's absolutely dippy," she said, throwing it down.

"Who's *he*? Who's *he*?" Betsy and Tib demanded.

"Someone I met on the boat. A New York man."

She didn't even open the box, but the others did, squealing. It held a forest of American Beauty roses.

"And I thought that for once you didn't have a beau," Betsy said jokingly.

"Well," said Julia, "I didn't in Berlin. Not exactly, that is. Of course," she added, "Else had a twin brother but he was just nineteen. And I didn't give him a bit of encouragement."

"Oh, didn't you!" Betsy scoffed.

Julia was still Julia, only more so. That night she played the piano and Betsy stood beside Joe to sing. Everything was wonderful! she thought. Julia had come home to see her graduate. She and Joe were going together. If only she could know that Tony was all right . . . somewhere!

The next day, when Betsy came home from the Opera House where she had been practising her oration, she found Margaret waiting in front of the house.

Margaret was standing as straight as a tulip, and a smile spread across her small freckled face.

"Betsy!" she cried. "I thought you'd never get home. I've had a letter from Tony."

"Margaret!" Betsy pounced upon her.

"He wants to correspond with me," said Margaret, trying not to sound proud.

"Where is he?" Betsy asked eagerly.

"He's in New York. He's an actor, like Uncle Keith."

"An actor!"

"He's on the stage, and he likes show business. He says it's the life."

Betsy sat down on the steps abruptly.

"Margaret," she said, "I don't believe I was ever so happy in my life!"

Margaret sat down beside her, after dusting off a little place to sit on and spreading the skirts of her stiffly starched gingham neatly beneath her.

"I'll read you his letter if you like," she said, drawing it out of her pocket. She did not give it to Betsy, but read it slowly and carefully aloud.

"'Dear Margaret, I wonder whether you would like to correspond with me? I'd certainly like to have some news of you and the rest of the gang.

"'I'm in New York. I'm in a musical show called *Lulu's Husbands*. I'm in the chorus now but Maxie thinks I'll be doing better soon. He thinks I can sing comic bass roles.

"'That Maxie (he's Mrs. Poppy's brother) wasn't fooling when he said he knew Broadway. I wired him from Minneapolis—couldn't do it in Deep Valley for fear of someone tattling. He said he could get me a job here, and he did.

"'Tell Betsy not to worry about my not graduating. A high school diploma doesn't matter in show business. And I like show business. It's the life! I've told my folks, and everything's hunky dory.

"'Betsy will be graduating along about now. See that she uses that curling iron! Give her my love, will you? Give my love to all the Rays. They don't make cakes like Anna's in New York or sandwiches like your father's.

"'I'm depending on you, Margaret, to tell me all the news. Love, Tony.'"

"There's a postscript, too," said Margaret, as Betsy did not speak. "He's sending me a Statue of Liberty to put on my bureau."

23

"After Commencement Day, What?"

JULIA'S FINGERS HAD LOST none of their magic when it came to dressing Betsy's hair. She dressed it in a Psyche knot—all the rage in Paris—for the Assembly Tuesday night at which the Essay Cup would be awarded. Betsy was wearing the pale blue Class Day dress, for she would be sitting on the platform, and she might . . . she just might . . . have to rise and bow as a winner.

Joe was in a fever for fear she wouldn't win.

"I can't stand it, if you don't. I'll cut my throat. Of course, you know, it's not of the slightest importance. . . ."

"Then why," Betsy wanted to know, "would you cut your throat?"

"Oh, well! I know you want to win the darn thing."

"I shan't care at all if I don't. And I don't expect to. After all, I was competing against that Joseph Willard who signs his stories for the Minneapolis *Tribune*."

But she won. Standing on the platform, before a roaring assembly, decorated in orange and turquoise blue, Betsy received her class points. Miss Bangeter smiled when she announced it.

Joe, clapping vociferously, joined in the Zetamathian cry:

"What's the matter with Betsy? She's all right."

He even started to join the chant, "Poor old Philos! Poor old Philos!" but he caught himself in time.

The Zetamathians won the cup, which gave them two out of three. All the Zets were happy about that. And other Philos than Joe were pleased that Betsy had won at last. Winona looked almost as happy as

Tacy and Tib. Miss Fowler was radiant and Miss Clarke wiped her eyes.

The next night, Class Day, was Tib's night of glory. She played the lead in *A Fatal Message* with triumphant success. The play came last on a crowded program. Preceding it, various members of the Class of 1910 delivered the Class Will, the Class Prophecy. Everyone was ribbed and slammed.

Betsy Ray was supposed to will a curling iron to a straight-haired sophomore. Tib willed all the junior boys to the junior girls. It was prophesied that Tacy would demonstrate a henna rinse, that Hazel would become the first woman president.

Cab, who had come to share in the fun, enjoyed it all hugely. He was wearing a new gray tailor-made suit.

"See?" he said to Betsy. "I can have the suit if I can't have the diploma."

He joined the Crowd, which swarmed into the Ray house afterwards for one of Julia's rarebits.

Commencement Day, that never-to-be-forgotten third of June, dawned hot.

"Shades of my ancestors!" Betsy wrote in her journal. "Such a day!"

The telephone kept ringing, for all the girls in the Crowd had to confer. The doorbell kept ringing, too, as presents arrived. There was a telegram of congratulations to Betsy from Julia's man. There were red roses from Joe.

Betsy rehearsed her oration to Miss O'Rourke in the Opera House. She rehearsed it again to Julia, who made some suggestions about putting in expression. Betsy ignored them. She went about muttering, "The heroines of Shakespeare were essentially human. . . ."

Tacy sang "Sylvia" for Julia, who gave her some pointers straight from Berlin. Tacy tried to profit by them but she was getting nervous. Her eyes had a hunted look and she swallowed with difficulty.

Tib alone was completely carefree; she had done her chore the night before.

"Nothing to do now but collect my diploma!" she said airily.

"Get out of our sight!" Betsy and Tacy moaned.

There was an early supper at the Rays', so Betsy could start dressing. This was the first appearance of the graduation dress. It was a fine white voile, trimmed with yards of lace and insertion, anklelength, with elbow sleeves.

Her mother, Margaret, and Anna watched while Julia dressed Betsy's hair.

"Too bad to spoil it with a hat," Betsy said. But, of course, she had to. A pale blue picture hat with the sweeping pale blue plume Julia had sent from Paris. Her father held her pale blue opera cape and Anna brought out Joe's red roses, which she had been keeping fresh in the ice box.

Anna watched glumly as Betsy revolved.

"What's the matter, Anna? Don't I look all right?"

"Of course, lovey. You look even punier than the McCloskey girl did. But when Margaret graduates, I'm going to marry Charlie."

"Anna! You wouldn't!" cried all the Rays together.

Betsy put on her long white gloves. She was wearing white slippers, also. They didn't go into a party bag tonight, for Betsy, Tacy, and Tib were riding to the Opera House in a hack! Mr. Thumbler called first for Tacy and Tib, and both of them were sitting inside, wearing picture hats and opera capes and carrying flowers, when the vehicle stopped at the Ray residence.

"We're late," said Tib. "But it doesn't matter. Things can't begin without us because you two are both on the program. I have very important friends."

"I wish they would begin without us. I wish they'd *finish* without us," said Tacy through chattering teeth.

"Stop and think!" Betsy said. "We're graduating! Remember, Tacy, how you cried and went home on your first day of school? If I hadn't grabbed you and pulled you back, you might not be graduating now."

"I wish I wasn't," chattered Tacy.

"And if I hadn't come back from Milwaukee, I wouldn't be with you. I'm certainly glad I came," said Tib.

The hack rolled down the hill to Second Street and

around to the back door of the Opera House. The girls were greeted by a burst of fragrance . . . from bouquets and the blossoming boughs with which the stage was decorated.

As they took off their hats and opera capes, Betsy kept muttering, "The heroines of Shakespeare were essentially human. . . ." She wasn't so nervous as Tacy but she didn't feel exactly calm.

The Class of 1910 was brought to order, seated in ascending rows on the stage. Betsy and Tacy, because of being on the program, sat in the front row, and Miss Bangeter placed Tib there, too, right next to Betsy and Tacy. She said it was because Tib was so small.

Tib looked angelic in a white chiffon dress she had made with her own hands. It looked different from the other girls' dresses; Tib's clothes always did. Tacy's dress was organdy, very white and crisp, below her crown of auburn braids, her fear-struck eyes.

Down in the pit the high school orchestra started to play, "Morning, Noon and Night in Vienna." The music made Betsy's heart shake.

"This is a very important occasion. It's momentous," she kept thinking. But she couldn't seem to realize it, and slowly the curtain rose.

The graduates searched for their families seated in the auditorium. Betsy found her father, a pansy in his buttonhole, looking too cheerful; her mother, in a new hat with roses, looking stern; Julia, in earrings, looking fascinating and foreign; and Margaret a picture of dignity. Anna didn't look glum any more. She was wearing her best hat with a bird on it.

Betsy saw the Kelly family, too, and Mr. Kerr; the Muller family; Joe's uncle and aunt.

She rose with the chorus and began to sing:

> "Hark! Hark! the lark,
> At heaven's gate sings
> And Phoebus 'gins arise. . . ."

The joyful music filled the auditorium . . . and her breast.

But her nervousness increased as the program ran on. While Hazel, who preceded her, delivered her oration with the poise of a star debater, Betsy kept saying under her breath, "The heroines of Shakespeare were essentially human. . . ." She couldn't remember what came after that. She hadn't the faintest idea.

When her turn came, she stepped to the front as if in a dream. The lights swam and the faces beyond the footlights blurred.

"The heroines of Shakespeare," she began, "were essentially human. . . ."

And when she had said that much she remembered it all. It came pouring out almost too rapidly. She drew a long breath, bowed quickly, and sat down.

She wished she could give some of her glad relief to Tacy, who now took the center of the stage. Tacy looked desperate. She couldn't retreat. She had to go on, so she did.

And, of course, she sang beautifully.

> *"Sylvia, take the lilly, daffodil,*
> *Sylvia, take whate'er the garden grows...."*

At the end an usher came hurrying down the aisle. He handed her a corsage of tiny white roses tied with a big bow and dripping with ribbons. She had already received flowers from her father. She went back to her seat, smiling, and Betsy and Tib leaned over.

"Mr. Kerr?" they asked.

Tacy blushed happily and nodded.

Oration followed oration. "For Pearls We Dive," "The Farmer of the Twentieth Century," "Factory Life for Women." Joe came last with "The Bread Basket of the World."

"As Whitman says, 'The earth never tires.'" That was his beginning, and he told vividly of wheat rolling in a golden torrent from threshing machines, of mill wheels turning, of the middle west feeding the world. He spoke clearly and he didn't forget. But Betsy thought he was as near to being nervous as she had ever seen him. He went at a brisk pace back to his seat.

The President of the school board spoke. His topic was, "After Commencement Day, What?"

"An era in your life is ended," he said, and Betsy, Tacy, and Tib regarded each other with bright mischievous eyes. They would have wiped away mock tears if they hadn't been sitting in the very front row. They all felt silly, they were so relieved to have the oration and the solo over.

But the truth of his statement dawned on Betsy presently.

He took his place behind a table piled high with parchment cylinders tied with white ribbons. He called the names of the graduates in turn, and each one crossed the stage to a burst of applause.

"Irma Biscay." She was dewy-eyed and radiant.

"Dennis Farisy." That was Dennie looking cherubic.

"Dave Hunt." He looked sober as a judge.

"Tacy Kelly." "Alice Morrison." "Tib Muller." "Betsy Ray."

For four years they had been in high school together. Some of them had been together since kindergarten. Now they were being blown in all directions, like the silk from an opened milkweed pod.

What would happen to Winona, returning now to her seat looking chastened, to Hazel, accepting her diploma with a frank smile of pleasure and pride? The President of the school board reached the W's and Joe. Then the curtain went down. It was over.

The girls didn't walk home together. Tacy went with Mr. Kerr. Tib went with Ralph, and Betsy went with Joe. They strolled slowly through a warm night full of fireflies, smelling of the honeysuckle in bloom over Deep Valley porches.

Joe was leaving the next day for North Dakota. He was going to work again on the Wells *Courier News*.

"Can I see you tomorrow?" he asked.

"Of course."

"What shall we do? Go riding?"

"I'll tell you," said Betsy. "I'll take you up on the Hill. Why, you haven't even seen the Secret Lane."

"Tomorrow then," said Joe, "I see the Secret Lane." And he left her on the porch of the Ray house.

Joe Willard had lived in Deep Valley for four years, but he had never been up on the Big Hill. He didn't even know which hill the Big Hill was.

"Lots of them are big," he said. "Agency Hill. Pigeon Hill. Why isn't one of them the Big Hill?"

"Agency Hill! Pigeon Hill!" Betsy repeated scornfully. "Better not let Tacy hear you talking like that. *This* is the Big Hill!"

They had reached the little yellow cottage where Betsy had lived until she was fourteen years old. Across the street stood Tacy's house. Beyond that on Hill Street there weren't any houses. There was a bench where they sometimes took their supper plates. There were the hills, billowy and green, running one into another so that you couldn't quite tell where one ended and another began.

Waving at the Kellys, they climbed the steep road which rose behind Betsy's old house. Betsy showed him the thornapple tree she and Tacy used to play under. She pointed out the place where wild roses used to grow, and roses were in bloom there that moment! Flat, pink, wild roses, with yellow centers, very fragrant. Betsy picked some and put them in her hair.

At the top she showed him the Eckstrom house. There was a ravine behind it.

"We thought the sun came up out of that ravine," she said.

"Who lives in these other houses?" asked Joe, looking around at the pretty modern cottages now perched on the brow of the hill overlooking Deep Valley.

"We don't know. We ignore those houses. They weren't here when we were little," said Betsy, leading him on.

"This is the Secret Lane," she said, and they went down a path bordered with beech trees, which cast such heavy shadows that the grass was sparse beneath them. No flowers grew there but the chilly waxy Ghost Flowers.

"Our club used to meet here," Betsy told him. "It was the T.C.K.C. Club. You never could guess what that stands for."

Joe wasn't listening too attentively. He looked harder than he listened . . . looked at Betsy. Now he said, "I love the way the color rushes up in your face when you talk."

They came out on the crest of the hill overlooking Little Syria and the slough and Page Park and the river. They sat down in the grass, and Joe picked a strand and started to chew it. Betsy took off the big straw hat covered with poppies and put her arms around her knees.

They looked down the grassy slope, full of yellow bells and daisies, over the valley at the changing shadows cast by the drifting glistening clouds.

Joe began to recite a poem they had learned in junior English.

> "And what is so rare as a day in June?
> Then, if ever, come perfect days;
> Then Heaven tries earth if it be in tune,
> And over it softly her warm ear lays."

Betsy took it up:

> "Whether we look, or whether we listen,
> We hear life murmur, or see it glisten. . . ."

She broke off. "I'm happy!" she announced.

"So am I," said Joe.

There was a pause.

"That was a pretty serious talk last night, that 'After Commencement Day, What?'" Betsy said.

"Did you think so?" Joe asked.

"Yes. The older I get the more mixed up life seems. When you're little, it's all so plain. It's all laid out like a game ready to play. You think you know exactly how it's going to go. But things happen. . . ."

"For instance?"

"Well, there's Carney. She went with Larry the first two years in high school. Now he's gone to California and she can't fall in love with anyone else until she sees him again. And how is she going to manage to do that?"

"Well, she isn't through Vassar yet," said Joe.

"And there's Cab. He thought as much as any of us that he would go through high school, but he didn't, and he never will now. He won't be an engineer at all."

"He will be if he wants to enough," Joe replied.

"And there's Tony! On the stage! I always thought Tib was the one who would go on the stage."

"Maybe she will."

"And Tacy and I were going to go around the world. We were going to go to the top of the Himalayas, and up the Amazon. We were going to live in

Paris and have French maids. We were going to do all sorts of things, and now that Mr. Kerr has appeared! He says he's going to marry Tacy, and you know how he made Papa stock knitwear!"

Joe laughed. "I don't think he's selling Tacy a bill of goods. I think Tacy likes him."

"Yes," Betsy said. "I'm afraid she does."

"What about you?" Joe asked, looking up at her as he lay in the grass.

"Well, I was always sure I was going to be an author. I'm sure of it still. But I ought to begin selling my stories. I've been sending them out for almost a year now, and I don't even get a letter back. Just a printed slip that says they thank me for thinking of them. Do you write stories and send them out?"

"I write them, but I haven't started sending them out. I'm afraid they aren't good enough."

"I'm sure they are," Betsy cried. "I can't imagine you writing anything which wasn't perfectly wonderful."

Joe looked at her. "I think it's perfectly wonderful that you think so," he said slowly. "I never had anybody to have confidence in me until I met you."

"You never needed anybody. You had confidence in yourself."

"But it's a wonderful feeling, Betsy, having you like me."

"I liked you the first time I saw you in Butternut Center," said Betsy quickly, and then she stopped, color rushing up into her face.

"There it goes," said Joe.

"I can't help it. I shouldn't have said that."

"Why not?"

"It sounds . . . bold," said Betsy, at which Joe laughed and sat up abruptly. He kept on looking at her.

"You're coming to the U, aren't you, Betsy?" he asked.

"Yes, I am. A writer needs a lot of education. Besides, I want to learn a way to earn my living. You can't start living on your stories when your stories don't sell."

"I'm glad you're going to be there," Joe said. "Because I am. I'm going to be working at the *Tribune*, you know. I'd like to finish at Harvard, if I can."

"Harvard!" Betsy breathed in admiration.

"But first of all," said Joe, "I'm going to go through the U."

Then he kissed her. Betsy didn't believe in letting boys kiss you. She thought it was silly to be letting first this boy and then that one kiss you, when it didn't mean a thing. But it was wonderful when Joe Willard kissed her. And it did mean a thing.

"Remember what that fellow said last night?"

asked Joe. "'After Commencement Day, What?'"

"Of course," said Betsy. "That's what we've been talking about."

"I've got the answer," Joe said. "After Commencement Day, Betsy." He smiled and looked enormously pleased with himself. "How does that sound?"

Betsy didn't answer.

"It sounds just right to me," Joe said. "It has the right ring. Sort of a permanent ring."

Betsy smiled, and her fingers lay in his, but she spoke firmly.

"Never mind how it sounds," she said. "You've just graduated from high school. You have college ahead of you. You can't go talking about permanent rings."

Joe's expression changed to gravity.

"I know why you say that," he said. "You understand, I think, that I've always had a Plan for my life. In order to carry it out, I had to rule out girls, and I didn't mind. Even last fall, although I liked you a lot, I wouldn't let you come into my Plan.

"But I've been doing a lot of thinking, Betsy. That Plan has been twisted about to let you in. You're in it, now, that's all. I wouldn't like it without you. I wouldn't give a darn for my old Plan if you couldn't be in it."

They looked into each other's eyes and Betsy felt tears in her own.

Joe kissed her again. He took the wild rose, drooping now from the heat, out of her hair, and put it in his wallet and put the wallet in his pocket.

Betsy jumped up. She shook out the skirts of the plaid gingham dress that she had worn because it was Joe's favorite. She picked up the brown straw hat covered with red poppies.

"We must be going," she said. "Your train leaves this afternoon. Remember?"

"I hope you're going to write me lots of letters," said Joe. "The kind you wrote last year, sealed with green sealing wax and smelling sweet."

"Of course I will."

Hand in hand they went back through the Secret Lane, to the steep road that led down to Hill Street.

But there, at the top of the hill, Joe stopped. They paused and looked out over the town—the red turret of the high school, the leafy streets, the rooftops, the river, the shining rails that would take him away.

"After Commencement Day, the World!" Joe said. "With Betsy."

Maud Hart Lovelace and Her World

(Adapted from *The Betsy-Tacy Companion: A Biography of Maud Hart Lovelace* by Sharla Scannell Whalen)

Maud Palmer Hart circa 1906
Collection of Sharla Scannell Whalen

MAUD HART LOVELACE was born on April 25, 1892, in Mankato, Minnesota. Shortly after Maud's high school graduation in 1910, the Hart family left Mankato and settled in Minneapolis, where Maud attended the University of Minnesota. In 1917 she married Delos W. Lovelace, a newspaper reporter who later became a popular writer of short stories. The Lovelaces' daughter, Merian, was born in 1931.

Maud would tell her daughter bedtime stories about her childhood in Minnesota, and it was these stories that gave her the idea of writing the Betsy-Tacy books. She did not intend to write an entire series when *Betsy-Tacy*, the first book, was published in 1940, but readers asked for more stories. So Maud took Betsy through high school and beyond college to the "great world" and marriage.

The final book in the series, *Betsy's Wedding*, was published in 1955.

The Betsy-Tacy books are based very closely upon Maud's own life. "I could make it all up, but in these Betsy-Tacy stories, I love to work from real incidents," Maud wrote. This is especially true of the four high school books. We know a lot about her life during this period because Maud kept diaries (one for each high school year, just like Betsy) as well as a scrapbook during high school. As she wrote to a cousin in 1964: "In writing the high school books my diaries were extremely helpful. The family life, customs, jokes, traditions are all true and the general pattern of the years is also accurate."

Almost every character in the high school books, even the most minor, can be matched to an actual person living in Mankato in the early years of the twentieth century. (See page 317 for a list of characters and their real-life counterparts.) But there are exceptions. As Maud wrote: "A small and amusing complication is that while some of the characters are absolutely based on one person—for example Tacy, Tib, Cab, Carney—others were merely suggested by some person and some characters are combinations of two real persons." For example, the character Winona Root is based on two people. In *Betsy and Tacy Go Downtown* and *Winona's Pony Cart,* Maud's childhood friend Beulah Hunt was the model for Winona. The Winona Root we encounter in the high school books, however, was based on Maud's high school friend Mary Eleanor Johnson, known as "El."

Another exception is the character Joe Willard, who is based on Maud's husband, Delos Wheeler Lovelace. In real life, Delos did not attend Mankato High School with Maud. He was two years Maud's junior, and the two didn't meet until after high school. But as Maud said, "Delos came into my life much later than Joe Willard came into Betsy's, and yet he is Joe Willard to the life." This is because Maud asked her husband to give her a description of his boyhood. She then gave his history to Joe.

Maud eventually donated her high school scrapbook and many photographs to the Blue Earth County Historical Society in Mankato, where they still reside today. But she destroyed her diaries sometime after she had finished writing the Betsy-Tacy books, in the late 1950s. We can't be sure why, but we do know that, as Maud confessed once in an interview, they "were full of boys, boys, boys." She may not have felt comfortable about bequeathing them to posterity!

Maud Hart Lovelace died on March 11, 1980. But her legacy lives on in the beloved series she created and in her legions of fans, many of whom are members of the Betsy-Tacy Society and the Maud Hart Lovelace Society. For more information, write to:

The Betsy-Tacy Society
c/o BECHS
415 Cherry Street
Mankato, MN 56001

The Maud Hart Lovelace Society
Fifty 94th Circle NW, # 201
Minneapolis, MN 55448

About Betsy and Joe

MAUD'S SENIOR YEAR in high school, fictionalized in *Betsy and Joe*, took place from September 1909 to June 1910. It was a time of great change for Maud, just as it is for her alter ego, Betsy, and it began with two of her best friends leaving Mankato.

At the beginning of the book, we learn that Betsy's sister Julia has departed Deep Valley for "the Great World" at last, to spend the summer traveling in Europe before settling down in Berlin to study opera. Readers will not be surprised to learn that Maud's older sister, Kathleen, also took part in a European tour. The June 30, 1909, issue of the *Mankato Free Press* reported: "Miss Kathleen Hart, daughter of Mr. and Mrs. T. W. Hart of this city, left this morning for Boston, Mass., from which city she will sail on Saturday for Europe. She will join a party going to Europe under the guidance of Rev. Willisford of this city. Miss Hart will make a three months' tour of that country [sic] and then go to Berlin, Germany, where she will receive instructions in vocal music for a year."

Reading and re-reading Kathleen's letters was a big part of the Harts' home life during this period, just as

*Maud is reading aloud from one of Kathleen's letters
while her parents, little sister, Helen, and
grandmother listen.*

it was for the Rays. And almost every time Betsy
quotes passages from Julia's letters in the story, Maud
is really quoting from Kathleen's. Kathleen was eventually offered a position at the Hamburg Opera, but,
like Julia, she returned to America, having decided to
pursue her career at home.

Maud's good friend Marion Willard (Carney) also
left Mankato in 1909. But unlike Carney, Marion first
spent a year at Carleton College in Northfield, Minnesota, before being admitted to Vassar the following

year as a freshman. It was probably simpler for fictional purposes to send Carney to Vassar in the fall of 1909, without the one-year detour to Carleton. Readers can follow Carney's story in *Carney's House Party*, one of the three Deep Valley books, which is set during the summer between her sophomore and junior years at Vassar and tells what happens when Larry Humphreys finally comes back into her life.

In 1909, the Harts pasted a series of photos into a book as a Christmas gift for homesick Kathleen in Berlin. This photo shows Stella Hart weeping as the mailman walks away. The inscription reads, "No mail from Kathleen."

And as in the Betsy-Tacy books, Maud based much of the story on real-life events, down to the smallest detail. While writing the book, Maud wrote to Marion: "I'll send you a copy of *Betsy and Joe* as soon as I can get my hands on one, or a set of galleys. For in that book Carney goes off to college, Vassar, in the clothes you described for me. Since I used them for fall of 1909 . . . you'll have to tell me about some more clothes."

Maud's friend Marion Willard (Carney) is shown here in her graduation photo.

Maud is wearing the necklace of Venetian beads from Kathleen in her graduation photo.

This cartoon of Maud pasted in her high school yearbook is labeled, "Miss M. R. P. Hart in her senior year, her hair as curly as ever, still the object of devotion of all the H.S. boys."

In spite of these losses, Maud still managed to have a fun senior year. She and Midge Gerlach (Tib) were cast for a part in a show called *Up and Down Broadway*. Maud had a small part, but Midge did a dance number. The newspaper review of the show said Midge was "a bewitching little personage in her part, and her dancing brought forth a round of applause, which was well deserved." However, neither Bick Kenney (Tacy) nor Mike Parker (Tony) took part in the show as their fictional counterparts did. Mike Parker left high school well before the end of the year, but he didn't go off to Broadway like Tony does. We don't know if Mike rivaled someone for Maud's affections during her senior year, though we do know it couldn't have been Delos (Joe), because they had not yet met.

This is the year that Betsy finally beats Joe and wins the essay contest. In reality, Maud's rivals in the essay contests, far from being Delos or any other boy, seem to have been other girls. Maud lost to fellow Crowd member Ruth Williams (Alice Morrison) in her junior year, and to a girl named Alice Alworth in her senior year. We don't know if Maud competed in her freshman or sophomore years because, contrary to the description of the yearly contest in the books, contestants were not selected from each high school class—they tended to be mostly seniors.

Maud graduated from high school on June 3, 1910. Just like Betsy, Maud gave an oration entitled "The Heroines of Shakespeare." Bick Kenney (Tacy) sang a solo. The president of the school board spoke. And the chapter of Maud's school days in Mankato came to a close, leaving her looking forward to "the Great World."

Fictional Characters and Their Real-Life Counterparts

Betsy Ray	Maud Palmer Hart
Julia Ray	Kathleen Palmer Hart
Margaret Ray	Helen Palmer Hart
Bob Ray	Thomas Walden Hart
Jule Ray	Stella Palmer Hart
Tacy Kelly	Frances Vivian Kenney
Tib Muller	Marjorie Gerlach
Harry Kerr	Charles Eugene Kirch
Tony Markham	Clarence Lindon (Mike) Parker
Carney Sibley	Marion Willard
Tom Slade	Thomas Warren Fox
(Aunt) Ruth Willard	Josephine Wheeler Lovelace
Joe Willard	Delos Wheeler Lovelace